Night Tastings

Part One: The Ingress

Bervi Adams

Night Tastings
Part One: The Ingress

First Edition: 2021

ISBN: 9781524316600
ISBN eBook: 9781524316068

© of the text:
   Bervi Adams

© Layout, design and production of this edition: 2021 EBL Books

To Nancy, the first person to ever read the original and very, very rough draft of Night Tastings. I was so nervous for anyone to read my renderings, I told her to lie to me regarding her take on my efforts. Months later, she told me she found herself at times thinking about Nikolai and Tatianya. No higher praise can a reader shower upon an author. To know your story has stayed with someone long after the last page has been read, is the ultimate, the pinnacle, the compliment of all compliments. I thank you from the bottom of my heart for this gift. I love you and don't know where I would be without your constant guiding hands.

To Dianne, a cousin first, a friend and confidant second and by choice. I thank you from the bottom of my heart for your support. You were also one of the first to read Night Tastings. Your unbridled enthusiasm and encouragement to pursue this path meant more to me than you could have known at the time. Having your footprints on this path with mine were a beacon in the dark as I summoned the courage to take a chance. I know Thomas is thanking you and Joseph is so proud of you. I love you to the moon and back.

And finally, and by no means the least, to Harold, my rock, I thank you beyond any measure of gratitude. You were the one to push me to pursue this dream. You enabled me to fly high while keeping me grounded to do the hard work it takes to complete this book, the first in a trilogy I doubted would ever come to fruition. Your faith in me, your support means everything. I remember pouring my heart out about my yearnings to see my writings become more than saved documents on my laptop. You said very little, I doubted you had really listened, and I was hurt. But then you started encouraging me to pursue my writing, helping me find ways to be heard, finding a way for me to navigate the world of publishing that had stumped me for so long. And I knew you had heard every word. I knew then you would always have my back. I love you; I hope you always know just how very much.

Table of Contents

Prologue

Isaiah, the Beginning of the Alliance

New Orleans, 1993

Memories of a first snow's quietude caressed his mind. It lulled him. And Nikolai accepted this momentary respite. The winter's cold possessed a serenity he craved, even now. He remembered. Watching from the hills, just above the horizon. Alexi's childhood home. The soaring windows dancing with the fire of a fading sunset. Slowly obscured, made even more beautiful by each and every snowflake's whimsical careless caress.

Thick tranquility whitewashed their vast Russian landscape, bathing his own childhood home with its ice blue brilliance. The precious few hours of winter daylight forced this stoic, unrelenting Russian world to slow. Early sunsets and long winter evenings still had the power to quicken his pulse. He closed his eyes, unaware of how his hands were reaching out for her. He longed to suffocate her with his love, his expectations, even his gentle criticisms. But most of all, he wished he had the power to smother her. Not with malice or the physicality of a man so much larger than his trusting fragile woman, but with a love that knew no bounds. Foolishly, it was this very protection that he, and no one else, had let slip away. He sighed. The bayou would never cast a magic that spoke to him like those fiercely quiet Russian winters had. He wiped away the sweat that had begun to sting his eyes. The bayou's humidity did nothing to lighten his mood. It never had. It never would. Nonetheless, he was grateful for the refuge it had always laid willingly at his feet.

Nikolai opened his eyes, forcing the past to take its place. The bayou glistened with its barely perceptible sexual vibe, so familiar after all these years. This undercurrent was like a slap across his face. Like a lover who would bring you to the brink and then sneer at your unrequited longing. Taunting. He glowered, as reality intruded on his fantasy of a cherished long ago and what he had thrown away. His fear that she was no longer his, really his, was getting the best of him. He turned his anger outward, mindful but not really caring of the consequences to those less powerful than he. And that unrelenting taunting. It just wouldn't go away.

Somewhere on the other side of the dilapidated structure, another man was succumbing, mired in his own self-pity. Wallowing in a very different regret, but with the same loathing of a past gone wrong.

Nikolai, cut me a break. Really man, cut me a God... Damn..... break.

Ulysses winced. His silent rant dissolved as he stared down at the blood dripping from his fingertips. Sudden pain forced Ulysses to relax the grip he had placed upon the rotting verandah's banister. Jagged splinters were wedged deeply within his nail beds. Slowly, he extricated each shard of ancient wood, glistening with his essence. Concentrating on his task, he savored the momentary escape from his much bigger worries.

God damn vampire, leave me alone.

Another silent rant.

He waited for any sign of intrusion into his mind.

Nothing. Hmm.....

Ulysses shook his head, muttering to himself, "Watch your step."

I can't.

The thought throbbed with defeat.

And just a little bit of drama, for good measure.

Again, he tried to caution himself.

*"He will **READ** you."*

I don't care.

Reality oozed with a hint of truth.

"Oh yes, you do....."

Ulysses turned his eyes heavenward, flicking the last blood-soaked splinter across the verandah. He hissed into the inky bayou, stilled by his unwelcome intrusion, "Murdering bane of my existence! I wish you had never found Isaiah. I wish someone could find a way to kill you. You don't deserve her love or my loyalty..... You are the cause of Alexi's loneliness. You are the reason your son never suckled at his mother's breast, aching for her sweet release. God knows how much I hate you."

The spineless accusations fluttered into the stillness. Useless bravado found unwanted crazy laughter bubbling from somewhere deep within his fractured soul. Ulysses was appalled by his unexpected outburst. He had not meant for his thoughts to take flight. He had been helpless to halt their meaningless journey. He jumped as thunder crackled overhead. It was getting closer. His crazy laughter turned to sobs. Tatianya's grief was suddenly too much to witness or just ignore.

Why does this stir me so? What is different this year? Is it just that hurricane in the gulf? Or is it something else?
Get a grip, NOW.

Ulysses' thoughts wound their way back to his beautiful, miserable mistress.

In years past, Ulysses had coolly shied away from Tatianya's pain. This reaction was not so much from cowardice as from vexation. He had done nothing to cause this suffering. He resented having to deal with its aftermath. But pleading azure eyes surrounded by cascades of silken curls in disarray made his mind go places that were taboo. He had no real designs on his master's mate, but her grieving held the key to any man's virility. Her seductive femininity, so fragile, so alluring, cried out for someone to make it all go away. It made her even more gorgeous, downright intoxicating. He dreaded Mardi Gras in a way only a few could understand.

Just how has Alexi resisted all these years?
Mind your own business.
And snap out of It, you moron.

Bitterly, Ulysses struggled to quell his rising anger. And desire. He bristled. He knew Nikolai could **READ** each and every word, spoken or not. It made no difference. His thoughts had never truly been his own.

Go ahead, you son of a bitch, do your worst. I just don't give a shit today.

And there it was. Once again, Ulysses gripped the rotting banister as Nikolai probed, seeping into every crevice of his mind. He braced for the blinding, unrelenting agony that accompanied each **Reading.**

He fought the rising hysteria but allowed a wicked smile. He smirked at the paradox with which he lived.

"Ah Nikolai, how is it that you crave the stain of blood upon your hands each night but abhor the taint of profanity upon your lips? How do you ever reconcile your need for propriety with your lust for human blood, their souls of no consequence to you? Please, do explain. Your humble servant is in desperate need of enlightenment. You must agree; your Old-World code of honor seems so out of place after all those stolen lives. I don't know about you my lord, but I can't help feeling your demand for decorum seems just a tad absurd."

He shook his head and mumbled into the slowly rising wind, "Wow, I am really losing it. Ulera is going to have my head." Nikolai's aristocratic Russian upbringing, his impeccable manners simply could not allow for swearing. But somehow, the basic instinct to cling to life had forced Nikolai to find a way to live with murder.

Ulysses knew he would again pay dearly but just couldn't resist.

"Asshole."

The familiar pain descended right on cue. As he fell to his knees, he screamed into the hushed bayou, "It was worth it, you decorous murdering second-rate royal!"

Birds twittered nervously in the overhang, but his final stab at bluster went unanswered. Satisfied with his small victory, Ulysses' mind returned to Nikolai's only reason for existing. He ignored the pounding that reverberated in his skull.

Anywhere else, Tatianya managed to keep her sadness quietly tucked away. But not here. He wondered to himself, *why was she so driven? Was there no better way for her to honor her dead? And why did this year feel so sinister?* He knew it wasn't just the early spring hurricane.

Hurricanes came and went in the swamps of Louisiana, but this one was different. The timing was all wrong. It was way too early. The energy surging forward carried an intensity Ulysses didn't recognize. Even the humidity seemed alive, vibrant with a secret loathing. Rounding a corner on the verandah, he studied the Spanish moss suspended in the overhang. It eerily swayed ever so gently in the thickening stillness.

Ulysses turned his back on the shadowy mangroves, the rising waters lapping at their roots. He thought of the resident vampires of New Orleans. Somewhere, out in the listless bayou, they too were watching Tatianya's sordid exercise, mesmerized.

Why does she do this to herself?

Ulysses turned condemned eyes heavenward. He shook a fist and again, threw caution to the wind. He shouted out his challenge, "If only you could save me, Jesus! Are you even out there? God, I hate you almost as much as I hate Nikolai!" His eyes darted around the shadowy bayou, ashamed. The time for honesty had slipped away a long time ago.

This is so messed up.

Ulysses tried to calm himself and peered around the rotting mansion that should have been claimed by the kudzo long before his time. He wished the Union soldiers had burned it to the ground when they had had their chance. It was maddening. In silent protest, he kicked a loose wooden floorboard into the swirling muddy waters, watching it disappear. It baffled Ulysses that his master would willingly resign himself to this scenario year after year. Nikolai actually seemed to find a measure of solace among the bayou's filth and decay.

Why? Nothing could change their past. Perhaps a form of penance?

Ulysses sighed, surveying his dismal surroundings. He couldn't wait to escape the bayou, blot out the ugliness these pilgrimages couldn't help but resurrect. "Crazy old vampire," he muttered, picking away at the veranda's peeling paint. He thought of the lavish old home in the French Quarter that Nikolai had meticulously restored but never used. "What a waste," Ulysses mumbled to the alligator circling a nearby mangrove. He watched it lunge at what could very well be its last meal.

Ulysses trudged into the mansion's darkened interior, seeking his own reason for living. Like he did each Mardi Gras, he petulantly groused to Ulera, "What good does this do Tatianya, Nikolai, even Alexi? All this wallowing in the past. Dredging up ancient history year after year is so useless, so stupid....It won't bring him back. Damn, I hate it here."

He broke off a piece of glass from a shattered windowpane, careful not to draw any more blood while he waited for the scorching pain to return. It didn't. A reprieve. His mystically gifted wife was so much better at accepting their path. She cautioned him to watch his thoughts, let alone put a voice to his resistance. Or his swearing. Her soft brown eyes were often rimmed with a panic he failed to see.

Ulysses was a simple man. Not stupid, but simple. Everything to him was black and white. He had never totally grasped this very grey world his forefather Isaiah had accepted so long ago.

Right here in this very spot, in 1857, Isaiah had knowingly hurled himself and his descendants into a convoluted relationship that had no end. Ulysses was told he looked nothing like Isaiah, who had been tall, thin, and regal, a West African prince who had been dethroned by the flourishing slave trade. Destined for Charleston, South Carolina, another early spring hurricane had forced the slave traders to reroute. Fate had conspired to bring Isaiah and his insatiable bride, Kawanaa, to New Orleans.

Ulysses knew he favored his mother's family. Stocky, strong, built for hard laborious work. Although college-educated, he had quickly reclaimed his place working side by side among the crew that tended to Nikolai's precious Napa Valley vineyard. Ulysses couldn't understand why Nikolai cared so much about education. Dutifully, he had gone to college and managed to pass. But it was clear to both of them that Ulysses would never relish discussing current affairs or foreign politics the way Nikolai loved to do. He simply had no interest.

Ulera shook a graceful ebony finger at her spouse, "Ulysses, I don't have time for this. Make yourself useful. And be careful, something is different this year. I can feel it. Something is very wrong. Please don't make matters worse, if you can help yourself. Go." Ulysses shuffled outside to watch the shifting waters and sulk. He was steeling himself to convince Nikolai that Ulera was right, something was wrong. And she wasn't just referring to the advancing hurricane.

Ulysses envied the Mardi Gras revelers, blissfully unaware that a very different world was lurking just beyond their drunken perimeters. As he got older, the past was becoming more of a noose around his neck. He could swear the sweltering humidity was like an executioner's hand, tightening that noose a little more each time they came. He longed for the creature comforts and safety of their vineyard. He felt Ulera slipping her arms around his muscular mid-section. She breathed deeply of his musk, "Ulysses, relax. Soon we will be home. Soon you will feel the vineyard's soil between your hands. But heed my warning, you can't change the past. Theirs. Or ours. Try a little harder to accept what is." She snuggled in a little closer, seductively nipping at his neck, "For my sake?"

Ulera was his lifeline in this world he didn't understand. She was so beautiful; he couldn't figure out what she saw in a man so prone to doubts and regret. Her large brown eyes could coax him to do just about anything. He loved the sleekness of her skin as she writhed beneath him in their moonlit nights. He assumed her own mysterious gifts had paved the way for her to love him so. He was just grateful that a simple man such as himself had found this treasure. "Ulysses, don't sell yourself short. It will be your downfall. Close your eyes and think of home." Obediently, Ulysses blotted out the bayou. He could almost believe he was standing in their vineyard. She felt the tension in his shoulders yielding under her feathery caress.

Ulysses loved Napa. Their lush, gently rolling vineyard sang with the aroma of wine hanging in the air at every turn. Those serenely undulating rows of grapes held no trace of the devastation they knew was ever poised to sabotage. Each spring, the sight of tiny vivid green leaves sprouting from the gnarled grey vines always made his heart take flight. He craved the feeling of the dry dusty dirt crumbling between his hands in the midsummer heat. He savored the wind rustling thru the valley. The delicious mist sailing in from the San Francisco Bay seemed to soothe all their battered souls. He loved to watch the fog bank rolling in, blanketing everything in its path as it shifted and swirled.

Ulera smiled, feeling her husband relax. "That's right my love. Home is always with you."

Ulysses adored being perched high above that Northern California valley floor. Their eagle's eye view had kept them safe, so far. Their private way of existing and co-existing had remained obscured for the most part, until now. He cherished the façade of security the ancient stone walls surrounding their little sanctuary evoked. This fortress that Nikolai had surrounded them with kept the mildly curious at bay. Nightly forays deep into the vineyard provided fleeting assurance that their borders were secure. The cave system rambling beneath their vineyard provided further false assurance of protection. But Ulysses knew, just as Isaiah had known so long ago, nothing would ever truly shield them and their ugly secrets from those that held the knowledge. It was a burden that Nikolai shouldered and carried with him day in and day out, year in and year out, and now century after unending century. There was no choice.

Nikolai, you brought this on yourself. Ulysses fought to keep the hopelessness at bay.

He turned to face Ulera and cradled her face in his hands. He searched her eyes for their ethereal quality. It was like a drug to him. "I love Napa, the vineyard, but you are my home." Ulera opened herself to her husband's yearnings. She received the kiss he wished could lead to more. Just as quickly, she withdrew. She extricated herself, "Behave. Go. You are needed elsewhere." She sauntered off, smirking. She had felt his hardness begging for her acceptance.

Ulysses rounded a corner on the verandah that encircled the entire first floor of the once-stately plantation's manor house. He stared for a moment, transfixed by the sight of his master tending to his grieving wife. He was mesmerized by the beauty of the demons his forefather Isaiah had forever chained him to. It amazed him how their kindness could survive unscathed alongside the boundless cruelty he had seen unleashed far too many times.

Hesitantly, he approached the languid figures regally lazing on the dilapidated mansion's once majestic verandah. It had seen so much, maybe too much. But today, the only vision was of

Tatianya's golden curls dancing brightly in the gathering breezes. Their carefree buoyancy belied her heaviness of heart.

God that woman is beautiful.

Nervously, Ulysses rubbed the small scar on his wrist out of habit.

Almost a whisper, he managed a tentative plea, "Nikolai, it's coming. We should go while there still is time." Ulysses watched as Nikolai cautiously brushed a wayward tendril away from Tatianya's large blue eyes, glittering with tears, ignoring his halting words. He saw Alexi tense out of the corner of his eye. It was in moments like this that no man, not even Alexi, was immune. The trio was unmoved by his paltry attempt. He could see they were being pulled to stay and witness the fury, participate in some unknown manner. Timidly, he waited for his master's gaze to turn his way.

Ulysses allowed a tattered smile. So like these demons he had come to love and hate, the bayou would be under siege in just a few hours. He scanned the Spanish moss hanging like a canopy over the swamp. Soon, daylight would be obliterated. The massive monster churning in the gulf was finally turning its eye north. Each hour it edged a little closer. The mangroves were already beginning to creak and moan in protest to the coming assault. The stinking, murky waters surged, all but strangling any thoughts of escape. The once-proud plantation's allee had already been claimed.

Ulysses eyed the water lapping at the wide stairs leading up to where he stood. Swirling breezes were beginning to descend. He imagined the centuries-old canopy of Spanish moss being ripped from its moorings, flailing wildly in the coming chaos. Creatures of the swamp from all walks of life, both natural and unnatural, were bracing for its unwelcome arrival.

Ulysses turned a sad eye back to Tatianya. For all the pain and destruction she herself had unfurled over the years, she still retained a quality of innocence, fragility. It beckoned protection, ridiculous as this was. She cast her spell wherever she went; her grief making those fathomless blue eyes swell with something only a mother could both understand and fear. Ulysses respected, even reluctantly supported the grieving that perpetuated these annual pilgrimages. He glared at Nikolai, not caring that his petty defiance was testing his master's patience. The early spring hurricane was getting to them all. Under his breath, Ulysses muttered, "jackass," and waited for the blinding pain to rise.

Valiantly, Ulysses pushed aside the drumming in his head. It was nothing in comparison to Tatianya's grief. He wiped away a useless tear.

No one ever really gets over losing a child. Standing before the tiny grave, these yearly pilgrimages always brought Tatianya dangerously close to madness, the deep scar etched upon her life never more apparent. But with maternal devotion, she came year after year. In the quiet serenity among the graves, Tatianya's own tranquility remained just out of reach. Her demonic essence did its best to rob her of the peace death bestows upon a mother's tattered soul. For well over a hundred years now, she had been compelled to come and grieve. She would stand by her infant son's grave in the crumbling, ancient cemetery. Lovingly, she would finger the time-worn lettering. Over and over, she would wind and unwind that same blue sash around her delicate fingers, causing Nikolai to cringe with shame. She would wail in agony, sending her grief sailing towards a heaven that had rebuked her soul.

In agitated desperation, Nikolai would pace the cemetery's narrow alley. He agonized if this would be the year for Tatianya to finally slip thru his fingers. The otherwise confident aristocrat knew there was no one else to blame. Sacrilegiously, his oldest friend lazed against another granite monolith. "Alexi....." Both knew there were no words.

Most times Alexi merely shrugged his shoulders. If it became necessary, he would reluctantly shove off his perch to cradle Nikolai in his embrace. "You must gain control. You know countless immortals are watching for a chance to take you down." He would kiss Nikolai's tear-streaked face. His embrace would be just a little too endearing. His kiss would brim with intensity. He would then cruelly shove Nikolai aside, admonishing, "You look weak."

Alexi would longingly eye Tatianya. "Even after everything you have inflicted, your wife is still by your side. Go. Be a husband. Or would you prefer another man step in?" Alexi's sharp tongue would clear Nikolai's mind. The two friends would exchange the whisper of a smile that spoke of loyalty from another time. Ulysses was forced to look away. This brotherhood was far too complicated for his simple view of life.

Both Nikolai and Alexi knew there was nothing anyone could do. Nikolai knew he alone was the architect of Tatianya's eternal devastation. His hand would hover just above the necropolis that cradled his infant son. Ulysses would watch year after year thinking to himself, "touch it, you crazy Russian son of a bitch, just once, touch it!" Then those dark, fire-filled eyes would turn their gaze upon Ulysses. Their hate would pierce the night, bringing Ulysses back to his senses. His short-lived bravado would crumble under the weight of this gaze. Ulysses' own reality would suffocate the fury that burrowed deep within his soul. He was helpless to rail against the destiny Isaiah had accepted so long ago, forever chaining himself and now his descendants to Nikolai's unyielding immortal grasp.

Alexi would intervene, "Nikolai, stop, none of this is Ulysses' doing."

It was the same scenario year after year. Alexi understood them both. He was more worldly than Ulysses but enjoyed a simpler view of life than Nikolai. He was sophisticated enough and cultured enough to fulfill everything Nikolai would ever need in a true friend. He could debate far into the night with Nikolai. He understood Nikolai's complicated humor. And yet he found immeasurable peace in the solitude of tending to the vineyard. It was an oddity to Nikolai that his aristocratic friend would sweat and toil as a commoner. Alexi's soft blond waves and clear grey eyes stood out among the Mexican and African families that coaxed the beautiful chardonnay, merlot, cabernet, and even a small lot of charbono grapes to produce those elegant rich flavors year after year. Alexi's relaxed manner was of one who had known privilege. But he was strong and tall and craved the satisfaction of a day's hard work. The other men pitied his need to soothe his soul like any mere mortal. They knew his immortal powers did nothing to dim his loneliness.

Ulysses shook his head to clear his thoughts. Again, he took a chance, intruding on Nikolai's dour mood, this time with more authority. "Nikolai, we should go while there still is time." Ulysses understood his concern was unwelcome. He knew his demonic master would survive the coming onslaught, but it would spell disaster for his own family.

Waiting for Nikolai's response, Ulysses found the twisted path fate had thrust upon his forefather Isaiah beckoning. He thought of the letter Nikolai had written to Tatianya's father, the duke, confessing to his selfish, fateful misstep. This letter had been destroyed the night it had been written. But each generation ensured the next had it committed to memory. It helped to remember how far they had come, how things could have ended up so much worse.

Ulysses knew this was dangerous, but found himself powerless to halt the obsessive thoughts. Isaiah seemed to haunt him most when surrounded by the bayou's gloom. He could see today would be no different. Foolishly he hoped Nikolai would not **read** him, see this forbidden path, the poignant letter's confession coursing through his mind. Unable to dismiss these thoughts, Ulysses gave in, allowing his mind to walk among his long-dead ancestors. Looking for solace, he missed Nikolai quietly whispering, "Go. Take the jet. Alexi will also be staying behind." Ulysses missed the careless waving of that dismissive aristocratic hand. He missed the warning in those dark piercing eyes. Nikolai shook his head in disgust. Ulysses would never measure up to Isaiah. For a moment it made Nikolai regret insisting Isaiah die a mortal death.

It was easy to understand why Isaiah had so readily entered into this alliance with Nikolai. In 1857, a slave accused of 3 murders in the Deep South accepted any protection afforded him. Isaiah's path had intertwined with Nikolai's out of necessity. The acceptance of both his protection and servitude was passed down from generation to generation. It was mired in a closely guarded history, housed only in the bloodlines that surged with heightened abilities, deadly knowledge, and shame. No written proof could ever be discovered. Giving the world confirmation of their hideous deceits would do no good. All their hands were stained by the unending river of stolen souls. It was simply wiser to perpetuate the aura of eccentricity that surrounded their genteel Napa Valley vineyard.

Lightning sizzled overhead, causing Ulysses to shield his eyes. Looking down, he fixated on his scar. Anyone seeing the compact, almost surgical imperfection, would never guess just how deep it ran or what it signified. He surmised Isaiah's scar must have looked no different. He knew the bondage; the subsequent enlightenment Isaiah had accepted had forever chained himself and then his descendants to this fearsome being. It was hard to find fault with Isaiah. But he had laid a heavy burden upon them all. Ulysses found himself wondering if Isaiah knew how his descendants' lives had unfolded, that their chance for any freedom had remained forever just beyond their fingertips. Ulysses smiled wistfully. He knew his life in many ways was better than most. Nikolai's vast wealth and generosity never failed to provide. Even though it came at an unimaginable price, none of them would ever want. But he couldn't help lamenting how ironic it was that Isaiah had been reduced to trading one type of slavery for another.

In 1857, just after Mardi Gras, Tatianya had discovered Isaiah wandering this very swamp, his mind clouded by fear, grief, hunger. Isaiah had narrowly escaped from a neighboring plantation that had also once bordered these sluggish tidal waters. Brutally snatched from their idyllic life on the African savannah, Isaiah's striking wife Kawanaa had caused a stir standing in shackles on the docks of New Orleans. One man, in particular, could not tear his eyes away from the gentle fall of her breasts, the voluptuous curve of her hips visible beneath her threadbare tattered clothing. He wasted little time claiming Isaiah's woman for his own. The once-proud prince found himself powerless to prevent these unwanted advances.

Night after night, Kawanaa endured depravities that a fragile, reluctant wife had been incapable of satisfying. A southern belle graced with a gentle soul, her sheltered upbringing and natural shyness had left Elizabeth ill-prepared for a loveless life overshadowed by sexual demands she didn't understand. Despite the relief Elizabeth could not deny she felt as her husband turned his nightly attentions elsewhere, she also felt ashamed. She berated herself that she had brought this on, failing to fulfill her duties as a proper wife. It stung deeply that she was unable to satisfy her husband the way this stranger in her bed did night after night. This ultimate affront overwhelmed her delicate psyche. Those around her surmised any remaining ties to reality had been severed.

As it became apparent that her husband was only becoming more obsessed with Kawanaa, Elizabeth sunk deeper and deeper into her abyss. Having been replaced in her own bedroom, she would sink against the door each night listening to her husband's ecstasy. Unable to bear anymore, she would eventually wander the darkened halls. Without fail, Isaiah would stand in the moonlight, praying for the desecrations to end. Elizabeth came to dread the sight of Isaiah's silent vigil. His tear-streaked face only served to mock her failure, as if she alone was the cause of all this pain.

One evening, as the floor above her head creaked with the rhythm of her husband's exploits, Elizabeth found herself clutching a knife to her heaving chest. She was oblivious to the sharp blade slicing through her fingers, the blood running down her arms. Silently, she climbed the stairs, knowing freedom was finally within her reach. No longer afraid, she swung wide the bed chamber's door. Her gaze lingered on each exquisite detail of what should have been her haven. She hesitated just a moment before she allowed her eyes to descend upon the sight of her handsome husband cupping the breast of that beautifully exotic, brown-skinned stranger.

Giddy with her newfound courage, Elizabeth flew across the room. Laughing maniacally, she viciously slit her husband's throat. She then turned her attention to Kawanaa and her laughter abruptly turned to silence. It was widely believed that in the farthest reaches of her soul, Elizabeth had known Kawanaa was not a willing party to this perversity. But in her twisted, tortured mind, Kawanaa had stolen her husband. Kawanaa's large brown eyes searched Elizabeth's, blazing with insanity, and knew her life was over. Elizabeth allowed herself a moment to savor her victory before plunging the knife within her broken heart.

News of the murder-suicide had spread like wildfire through the bayous and city of New Orleans. Isaiah had become the perfect scapegoat, his innocence of no concern to Elizabeth's shame-riddled family. With nowhere to hide, Isaiah ran into the swamp, evading the snarling dogs snapping at his heels and the bullets whizzing past his head. As he propelled himself deeper into the swamp, his captors and their dogs pulled up short on the fringes of the darkness. The sounds of their pursuit faded into the stillness. Isaiah cursed their ineptitude at halting his footsteps. Or his misery.

Isaiah wandered the swamp for hours, crushed by an overwhelming loss. His mind could not release the gruesome image of his Kawanaa's slender, eviscerated neck.

Overcome by his grief, Isaiah had been unaware of the elegantly attired, delicate creature perched among the mangroves. He failed to notice just how enraptured she had become with his human essence, beautifully pulsating with the lifeforce she could not help but crave.

As Isaiah slowly became aware of his surroundings, he found himself standing knee-deep in the murky waters of the swamp. The sun had all but disappeared below the horizon. Long shadows filled the silence. He forced his eyes to adjust, impatiently wiping away his tears. He fixated upon an erratic movement just below the muddy surface, careening in his direction. As an alligator surfaced, jaws gaping in anticipation, Isaiah made no move to evade. Overwhelming exhaustion crushed any thoughts of attempting another escape. He quietly made his peace, believing this world had nothing left to offer. He simply closed his eyes and thought of Kawanaa.

He braced for a decimation that never came.

A horrendous attack ensued with unearthly screeching, but Isaiah was not in the fray. He tore his eyes wide, recoiling in shock. A fragile-looking beauty was in a frenzy, ripping to shreds an animal that should have been her own demise. Her golden curls were flying, glittering in the fading light. The woman's beautiful clothing was now soaked with the alligator's blood. Torn between fascination and horror, Isaiah found himself perversely drawn to this enchantress, spellbound as she feasted on the animal's blood. He searched her eyes for a sign of humanity but they were wild and unfocused.

Tatianya had mystified Isaiah. Simultaneously, she exuded the stench of death and the aroma of recent birth. He had never seen such large blue eyes. Her long golden tresses gently outlined the inviting curve of her rounded hips. Wispy tendrils surrounded those eyes. Even tainted by the alligator's blood, he could see she was breathtaking. He was appalled as he found himself staring at her barely concealed heaving breasts. Aroused by curiosity and his recent neglect, he was ashamed by his desire to caress those creamy white treasures he knew were aching to release a mother's milk.

He watched, captivated, as she flung the now limp carcass into the farthest reaches of the swamp. She then turned to face him. She bestowed the smile that had robbed many men, young and old, of their freedom. Just as Tatianya began her graceful advance, now lusting after his devastating essence, Isaiah caught a blur of movement out of the corner of his eye. He heard a masculine voice with an unfamiliar accent murmur, "Tatianya, please, not this one." Hot wet breath on his neck made him shriek in horror.

It was then that Isaiah first met Nikolai. In the growing shadows of the gathering dusk, Isaiah had faced the remnants of a man looming over him. Like a voyeur, Isaiah witnessed

Nikolai wistfully gazing at his beautiful companion. Even as she stood there anointed in mud and blood, it was obvious she was his everything. By comparison, she barely acknowledged his existence. He gently, tenderly reached out to wipe away the faint trickle of blood staining her delicate chin. She stiffened and recoiled at this caress. Icily she sneered, "Yes, Nikolai, deprive me once again."

Isaiah was stunned to see a silent tear escape from Nikolai, fingers running thru his lustrous black waves in frustration. Dark piercing eyes did nothing to hide his longing for this woman. Her retort only seemed to heighten his desire. But he struggled to accept her rejection.

Isaiah could see this man was used to being in command. Isaiah was tall, yet this man towered over him. His aura was of power and there was strength in his physique. Isaiah was curious what had precipitated this docile acceptance of such harsh words. He wondered what had become of the newly birthed child.

Isaiah was awed by this devotion, so freely given and yet so easily rebuffed. In that instant, Isaiah knew this demon still possessed a shred of decency. Silently, an alliance was born out of their failures. Neither man, human nor demonic, had been able to protect the women they adored. Isaiah realized at that moment he would rebuild his life with this creature.

He watched in fascination as Nikolai produced a thorn from a rose and deftly pierced his own wrist, allowing a trickle of blood to stain the murky waters. Curiously, Isaiah felt little fear. He found himself offering his wrist. Nikolai's grasp was strong, masterful, compelling. He was intrigued by the inferno emanating from this touch.

Nikolai quietly warned, doing his best to dim the fever in his caress. "If you accept my offer, there will be consequences and expectations. There will be no turning back, for you or your descendants." Isaiah merely nodded, shocked at Nikolai's nearly perfect command of his African dialect.

As Nikolai drew blood with the thorn, **Searing** Isaiah's wrist with what should have been excruciating pain, branding him, beckoning him into servitude; Isaiah felt nothing but relief. Standing in the shadow of this demonic creature who was also attempting to right his own universe, Isaiah understood. For a brief moment, as the blood-soaked thorn pierced his skin, mixing his blood with Nikolai's, Isaiah caught a glimpse of this creature's soul. He was seduced by the decency that had miraculously survived.....

Shit

A shadow fell, blocking what little moonlight remained, catapulting Ulysses out of the past. He felt that familiar, blinding pain and knew Nikolai had **Read** his thoughts. So consumed with self-pity, Ulysses had missed Nikolai's arched eyebrow as he prepared to scan Ulysses' mind. He had missed the slight dismissive flick of Nikolai's aristocratic wrist. He had missed his cue to flee the coming onslaught as his mind had sunk deeper and deeper into thoughts of the past, of Isaiah, and the beginning of this unholy alliance. He had missed Nikolai's eyes flashing with anger as thoughts of Isaiah forced memories Nikolai had no time for today.

Ulysses flinched as he found Nikolai towering over him, eyes black with anger. Seething, Nikolai managed to whisper, "I told you to go." He had **Read** Ulysses, been confronted with the letter he had been forced to write the duke. The pain was as fresh today as it had been in 1857. He was beyond incensed, livid with Ulysses for reliving his past, his darkest hours. He felt betrayed by Ulysses, resurrecting the bitter memory of Tatianya's rejection. "How dare you. I should rid myself of you. But you are the least of my concerns today. Thank the hurricane you fear for your life. Go before I change my mind."

Ulysses cursed his careless reverie. The events that had intertwined his ancestors' path with that of this powerful, malevolent, and yet at times benevolent vampire dissipated into the uneasy silence. He bowed his head in subservience. He backed away from the demon who was trying his best not to lash out at a reality of his own creation.

As Ulysses disappeared into the dilapidated mansion's lightless interior, he missed the tears welling in his master's eyes.

The thought of that letter........

Chapter One: Nikolai

Moscow, 1856

Life in Moscow had been good to Nikolai Rozumovsky. His privileged birth in 19th century Russia had secured a privileged life. The family's lineage was not close enough to the czar to bring unwanted expectations, but the perks of palace life were theirs for the asking.

Despite having the best of everything, life had cruelly conspired to make Nikolai something less than a man, a true man. On the surface he had it all; looks, wealth, intelligence, privilege, breeding, it was all there. But none of this had been enough to turn that key. His father could not deny that the elusive quality that sets a man apart had never truly taken hold in his only son. On those rare occasions when Nikolai allowed his father to search his eyes, peer into his soul, Daniil Rozumovsky could not deny that his son was adrift. And it was killing him.

Nikolai's father relentlessly sought the counsel of his wife, "Xenia, how did I fail him?" He hated being at odds with his only son.

"Maybe he just needs time Daniil." They both knew this was a lie.

"Time is the one thing I am running out of! It is time my son fulfills his duties and provides me with an heir!" he would retort.

Xenia would become surly. "Time and patience are both escaping you. And your civility I must add." Daniil's rumination had taken on an irritating quality. "Foolish man, Nikolai has never taken a chance on love because no one has ever been worth the gamble. There is nothing you can do to force his hand."

Nikolai was so like her. Lustrous dark waves that glistened in the moonlight, piercing eyes that tore through his resolve. They were both so direct, so volatile. Daniil's mellow gentility was no match to their high-spirited manipulations. It was difficult feeling like an outsider in his own home when they banded together. It was futile to berate this mother's son. But the elder Rozumovsky was right; Nikolai could not seem to find his way.

Daniil's wife would soften, sensing his defeat. "My handsome guardian, love will not be rushed. You have little choice but to be patient." Xenia brushed her full lush lips across his furrowed brow. "Pray your son will be as fortunate as you."

Alluring caresses stirred a desire for his vixen. Xenia accepted his advances. "Fear not my love, you display your dominance when I crave it most. How is it that you fail to see restraint is your most potent weapon?" She had coaxed a truce, but a new approach would need to be conceived.

Nikolai's father proposed he be educated abroad and use his boundless energy and intellect to further the family fortune. Daniil sensed change was in the air. He feared their way of life would one day come to a fragile crossroads. Subtle signs were everywhere if one chose to see them. Maybe not in his lifetime or even Nikolai's, but he felt the Russian feudal system would one day give way. He wanted his family to be prepared. He was driven to do what he could to provide and protect, even if it meant reaching out from the grave. He secretly hoped this time away from Russia would somehow settle Nikolai's restlessness; help him find his way, and just maybe, a wife.

Reluctantly, Nikolai agreed. Despite his initial reticence, he found himself enjoying the stimulation of academia. He threw himself into his studies, just as Daniil had envisioned. He came back a changed man. His time away from Russia had served him well. He was more aware of the world and had developed a keen understanding of international business. Nikolai agreed with his father that their descendants would one day have to deal with a much different Russia. But that quality Nikolai's father longed to see shining in his son's eyes continued to remain elusive.

Nikolai's initial business ventures were shockingly successful and drawing uneasy attention.

It was considered vulgar for an aristocrat to toil. His father became concerned that the ruling family would not approve, not understand. The badgering resumed.

Nikolai was more than encouraged by Daniil to take a wife from a highly respected family, more closely connected to the czar than they. But Nikolai had other ideas. The last thing he had on his mind was finding a wife. His father was quick to point out that although several of his friends by now were married, nothing had really changed for them. The elder Rozumovsky's pestering became obsessive, "I need an heir, a legitimate heir. This means you need a wife and an heir, preferably a son, one that will listen to reason. For God sake's Nikolai, you are 30 years old!"

Paternal pressure coupled with paternal respect capitulated Nikolai's resolve and he finally relented. Word spread quickly that the handsome Nikolai was now searching for a wife. Many young ladies were enthralled with Nikolai and had set their caps for him. He made half-hearted attempts at courting but soon grew weary of weak endeavors to ensnare him. He retreated from the process, exasperating everyone with his maddening reluctance. There was a tedium to the process and Nikolai found himself suffocating with the agony of overbearing expectation. He desperately wanted to find a wife, marry her and get back to his life. But something in his heart beyond his control was preventing him from simply, blindly, marrying just anyone.

At his father's insistence, Nikolai had agreed to attend yet another ball at the home of a duke near St. Petersburg. "Find a beautiful aristocrat! If she is pretty enough you will forget about the rest. It is time."

Dutifully, Nikolai attended the ball but found no one caught his eye. He was frustrated and had lost interest in requesting dances or forcing small talk. Miserably, he dreaded going home.

Nikolai decided to slip out a side door and get some air. The pristine grounds sparkled in the late spring moonlight. He had left the ballroom with a crystal snifter of brandy in hand. Lazily he meandered up and down the rows of neatly trimmed hedges, swirling and sipping the brandy as he wandered further and further from the ball. He found himself drawn into a flower garden at the far end of the estate and was surrounded by the dizzying aroma of roses beginning to bloom. The magnificent palace was grand but in an understated manner. Nikolai found himself feeling strangely at home.

In a far corner of the garden was a gazebo partially hidden by cascading roses. A settee inside the gazebo beckoned. As he approached, he saw an unescorted woman. At first, he thought she was a courtesan, waiting to meet a lover who had been unable to break away from a clinging wife. Nikolai envisioned a tryst in the beautiful rose garden with the mysterious woman. He ran his fingers thru his lustrous dark waves. He felt his pulse quicken with anticipation.

But as Nikolai drew near, delighting in this unexpected tryst, he heard the woman sobbing. So distraught, she was completely unaware of his presence. Upon hearing her anguish, Nikolai forgot his initial inclination for physicality. He felt it his duty to discover the cause of her distress. He would need to deliver her back to the palace. How had she gotten so far from the palace alone in the first place?

As Nikolai entered the gazebo, he realized she was little more than a child. She was wearing a sweetly demure party dress. Her hair was done up with flowers surrounding a dazzling cascade of blond curls. In her hand was the end of the pale blue sash that encircled her tiny waist. She was rolling and unrolling the end of it around her delicate fingers.

She looked like an angel. Her beauty, her innocence made him gasp. She looked up with a start. The tears running down her alabaster skin only made her large blue eyes look like fathomless pools of water. These tears were like a current, pulling Nikolai under, drowning him with their caresses. Nikolai had to steady himself with the railing of the gazebo. No woman had ever affected him so and here was this gentle lamb effortlessly bringing him to his knees.

The silence was broken between them as she sniffed and sighed. Nikolai was unable to speak. He knew he should not be alone with her; it would ruin her reputation. But they were far from the palace. He felt secure the gazebo would allow shelter long enough to discern the cause of her distress.

Finally, Nikolai was composed enough to speak, "My dear child, why are you so unhappy? You look beautiful."

Without thinking, he swept her tears away with as gentle a touch as he could manage. As his hand caressed her cheek, he realized that she was devoid of paint. She had yet to be introduced to society. Just how old was she?

As he touched her cheek, an electric shock tore thru his body, searing him with her magic. Again, he needed to steady himself. But there she sat, totally unaware of the effect she was having on him. She finally took a large breath and began to speak in a whisper, "I so wanted to dance tonight. But papa won't permit it."

She shot Nikolai an impudent look before once again lowering her gaze, "And I am not a child, I am almost 16."

Nikolai smiled broadly. It was good her head was bent. He had no desire to further bruise her already hurt pride. But Nikolai found himself completely incapable of keeping a ridiculous smile from spreading across his face. He felt like the world had just pulled the rug out from under his feet. This little angel was resonating with something deep within his soul. And it felt glorious.

Nikolai tilted her fragile chin to look up at him. He knew he was treading on forbidden territory. But he was so entranced, he no longer cared. She was definitely still a child, but very much on the cusp of womanhood. He gallantly bowed and offered his hand. She looked puzzled.

"You wish to dance and your wish is my command."

She smiled a smile that blinded him and he knew he was lost to this fragile flower.

The angel giggled and stood, responding with the curtsey of an aristocratic child. Her dress was a pale blue which only made the blue in her eyes glisten like oceans, sweeping him away. He didn't care. In fact, he rather enjoyed this odd sensation of being out of control.

The music from the palace could be very faintly heard wafting across the manicured gardens. It was a waltz. Slowly they began to dance and Tatianya melted into Nikolai's embrace. Innocence kept her from realizing she should maintain a proper distance between them. Nikolai hoped he wouldn't crush her. He found himself never wanting to let her go. Her juvenile gown hid the womanly figure she already possessed. As they danced together, he became acutely aware of her swelling bosom, the fullness of her hips. She would grow into a woman that would make any man drop to his knee. He found himself relieved she seemed unaware of the powers she had at her disposal.

Nikolai realized he didn't even know her name. After their dance was over, they sat on the settee. Her head was again bowed in sorrow. "Little angel, may I inquire, what is your name?"

Softly she replied, "Tatianya Yusopova".

With a start, Nikolai realized she was the youngest daughter of his host for this grand ball. Duke Grigorii Yusopov was extremely protective of his three daughters. Rumor had it that the duke was especially irrational when it came to Tatianya, the youngest and most cherished.

"Why are you out here unescorted? You know this is not proper. Your papa will be furious."

She bowed her head even more. Nikolai, unable to control his need to swim in those big blue eyes, dropped to his knee and peered into her downturned face.

"I wanted so much to attend this ball. Papa had said yes, but at the last minute he changed his mind."

Tatianya defiantly stuck out her chin, asserting her disdain, "And I ran away."

Nikolai found himself smiling indulgently. She had run away to her backyard. Gently, gently he held her chin, another mistake. "Tatianya, I know why your father changed his mind."

Her eyes grew even larger and another electric shock scorched his mind, blotting out all reason. "You do?"

He smiled tenderly. "Yes. It is that you are so very beautiful tonight. Take pity on your poor papa. He is not ready for you to be so grown up."

At that, she brightened, "Poor papa, I am going to be leaving him soon. He will miss me so."

Her sweet reply brought Nikolai's world crashing down around him. Was she promised to someone? If this was so, why had she not been presented to society? He hesitated, not sure he wanted to know the answer. With the hint of a quiver, Nikolai managed to whisper, "Tatianya, are you going somewhere?" He was dreading her response.

Before Tatianya could reply, her disheveled governess came rushing into the gazebo. It was clear who had had a tryst. She began to admonish Nikolai, but he cut her off. "How dare you leave Tatianya alone, defenseless in the dark, crying her heart out?" The governess recoiled. She knew she would be in far more trouble than this handsome stranger if the duke became aware of her dalliance.

Nikolai escorted the pair back to the palace. He winked at Tatianya who didn't understand his intent. Nikolai approached the duke and explained the cause of Tatianya's tear-streaked face. All eyes had watched the trio enter from the garden. The duke had been alarmed by Tatianya's disappearance. When the duke realized he had caused his youngest such anguish, he fell silent. The music faded away. The air filled with tension as the duke struggled with the fact that suddenly Tatianya had the wants and needs of a woman he could no longer ignore.

Nikolai sensed the duke's dilemma. He bowed deeply to the duke, requesting the honor of dancing with Tatianya. An audible gasp erupted from the crowd. The shock was palpable. Nikolai half expected the duke to have him shot.

Shyly, Tatianya peered from around Nikolai and her governess. "Please Papa, just one dance?"

The duke sighed. His shoulders sagged as he shot Nikolai a look. "You realize this is just one dance, nothing more."

Again, Nikolai bowed deeply, but this time to Tatianya, requesting the honor of a dance. She knew all eyes were on her. She no longer looked like the small waif in the garden. She looked regal and the dress now appeared far too childish to contain her sensuous body. This angel was driving Nikolai mad. With lustful gazes caressing his prize, every eligible bachelor in the room confirmed they were under her spell as well.

Nikolai's spirits were renewed. He knew the duke would never have allowed this dance if Tatianya was betrothed. The music resumed, a waltz. He escorted her to the middle of the ballroom and again bowed deeply. He would do his best to make her remember this dance, this night, him.

Tenderly, he took her in his arms as his friends looked on in amazement. They could not believe what they were witnessing. If Nikolai hadn't been so concerned with etching a memory on Tatianya's delicate mind, he would have seen the irony of the situation. Cold, aloof, oft times cruel Nikolai wanted this newfound treasure to love him as much as he knew he loved her.

As Tatianya took the stranger's hand, she realized she didn't even know his name. Her hero. No one had ever stood up to her father for her before and been successful. She looked at him with adoring eyes, as if he were a god. Nikolai saw this and his heart took flight. She leaned into him again, but this time Nikolai held her at a distance. She looked hurt and puzzled. Nikolai nodded toward the circle of onlookers and said, "Your papa." She smiled and accepted his lead.

"What is your name, kind sir?" Her sweet breath made him ache to smother her in kisses. Towering over her petite figure, Nikolai caught the duke's stern look. As the two men's eyes met, the duke could see this stranger was in love with his Tatianya. He became frantic. He prayed Tatianya was still too young to accept or understand the plans Nikolai was obviously devising. Nikolai twirled Tatianya and as she laughed, the duke relaxed. Despite his misgivings, he momentarily allowed himself to enjoy those infectious giggles.

"Nikolai Rozumovsky", he replied as he nuzzled her soft blond curls.

She sighed and whispered, "Thank you, Nikki." Big blue eyes ensnared him with their love and trust, so freely given to a man who only hours earlier had been a stranger. It shocked him to realize he could be her everything, that he wanted to be her everything. He barely noticed that the music was fading away.

The waltz had ended much too soon. Nikolai's eyes pleaded with the duke to allow another dance. The duke hesitated. Just as he was about to deny Nikolai's request, the duchess lovingly slipped her hand into her husband's. She was tired of the chokehold he could not help exerting over Tatianya when it came to men. She squeezed his hand.

"My love, look how happy your Tatianya is. What is the harm?" The duke was powerless to fight both wife and daughter. With a curt nod from the duke, the musicians struck up another waltz.

Tatianya had never danced with a man before. This was nothing like the timid awkward movements of the boys in her dance classes.

Nikolai's embrace became more certain and as he held her closer, she could feel his masculinity rippling through the well-tailored suit. His black hair was just long enough to brush the collar of his evening coat. It shimmered in the candlelight as they whirled around the ballroom. He was much taller and held her in a way no boy would have known how. It felt exciting. Even a little bit dangerous. But somehow Tatianya felt safe in this stranger's arms. She succumbed to the protectiveness of his embrace. She knew he did not want to share her with anyone. She laughed at the look on his face when she called him Nikki. Tatianya could see no one called him that but he didn't seem to mind.

Eventually, there was a tap on Nikolai's shoulder. Jealously, he spun around to confront the intruder. He was shocked to see the duke standing there, anxious to retrieve his youngest. Nikolai cursed his quick response. It was obvious he had gone too far and displeased the duke. Nikolai fought to regain his footing and smiled down at his treasure. Her happiness melted the tension between her father and her suitor. She felt alive in a way she hadn't even known existed until tonight. She smiled sweetly, unaware she had them both eating out of the palm of her tiny hand. Reluctantly, Nikolai handed Tatianya over to her father. He retreated to the fringes of the circle where all eyes were now watching the duke and his daughter.

For the remainder of the evening, Nikolai's eyes were glued to the tiny blue-eyed goddess. His friends stood close by, completely aghast at what they were witnessing. No one tried to reason with him. He wouldn't have heard a word. He was utterly, totally lost in her magic.

Eventually, the duke signaled for the governess to take Tatianya to her chambers. She was looking happy but tired. The excitement had taken its toll. She left the ballroom and began to ascend the grand central staircase.

So enraptured, Nikolai was oblivious to the spectacle he was creating, straining his neck to maintain eye contact with her diminutive movements. Just before disappearing from sight, Tatianya stopped to scan the crowd below. When her eyes met his, she locked onto his face. She bestowed a radiant smile meant only for him. It made everything right in his world. He sagged against his closest friend Alexi who finally whispered his concern, "Nikolai what is going on? Have you lost your mind? She is only a child. Where can this possibly go? If you hurt her, the duke will surely have you killed. I fear you are contemplating a dangerous path, my friend."

Nikolai looked at his friends with a dazed expression. He sighed, "I have finally found her." He smiled a lovesick, loopy smile. He looked ridiculous.

They had never seen him in such a state. They whisked him back to their suite in the palace. There, in privacy behind closed doors, they would try to make sense of what had just happened. He had just turned 30. Tatianya was not yet 16. True, many men did take younger wives, but not the youngest daughter of Grand Duke Grigorii Yusopov.

By the time they reached their chambers, Nikolai was regaining much of his composure. He knew he would have many questions to answer tonight and even more tomorrow. Nikolai was certain the duke would not let him depart without discussing his unmistakable intentions.

Nikolai had recovered enough that he was able to deflect a good portion of his friends' concerns.

A loopy smile still very evident, he began, "I will not deny that I have fallen for this angel. It is beyond obvious that I have fallen hard. It is futile that I beg you to keep my good fortune to yourselves."

The normally composed Alexi was pacing the room. He threw his crystal champagne flute against the palace wall. He dove straight into the decanter of vodka. He tore at his evening coat, downing most of the decanter's contents without stopping. He then smashed that empty vessel against the wall as well. Alexi practically shouted, gesturing scornfully, "Dammit Nikolai! Half of St. Petersburg society witnessed you acting like a schoolboy! Your father wants an heir, not a scandal! What is the matter with you?"

Nikolai just smiled. "Alexi, calm down. In reality, you know this is a relief. I have found my wife. Be happy for me. "

Nikolai's other friends had settled Alexi in a chaise by the window where he glumly peered into the starlit night. "I am, Nikolai. You know I want this for you. By why her? Such a pity. Tatianya isn't old enough to accept a courtship. Always the hard way with you. I guess this should have been anticipated." He got up and staggered over to Nikolai. "You make me drink too much." He laughed uncontrollably, devilishly taunting, "Small wonder why my Olga hates you so."

Nikolai's drunken friends eventually went to bed when they saw he was resolute in his decision to pursue a life with Tatianya. They could not believe it had taken a virginal, inexperienced adolescent to get him on his knee. The look on his face as he had danced with Tatianya told them there was no going back. He had stood by each one of them in their times of need. It was now time to return that favor. God knew he was going to need their help.

Nikolai had expected a summons from the duke the next morning, not in the middle of the night. Standing in front of the duke's closed study door, he steeled himself to be his most persuasive. He gripped the ornate knob. He convinced himself that he was opening the door to his future.

But as he entered the duke's study, he found the duke and duchess quarreling. They continued to argue even after he had been announced. Nikolai had not counted on the duchess being an ally. He waited for them to acknowledge his presence. He dejectedly looked around the duke's study, trying to gauge this man who had clearly become his enemy. He had never imagined wanting so desperately to curry someone's favor. The study's vast library told Nikolai that the duke was a man of intelligence. Nikolai would have enjoyed long complicated debates over a rare vintage with this man. It saddened him that the duke had a blind spot when it came to his daughter. Nikolai pushed these thoughts of what his future could have been aside. It was clear his intended's father wanted no parts of him. He squared his shoulders. This would be an uphill battle against a man who wouldn't go down easy.

The duchess kept one eye on Nikolai as he took in his surroundings. She felt this newcomer could be everything she had ever wanted in a suitor for Tatianya. But the duke's ridiculous stubbornness was blinding him to this opportunity. Duchess Irina Yusopova had grown very weary of the duke's overprotectiveness. She was secretly delighted to see that the duke was no longer in control of Tatianya's destiny. She had known this day would come and had tried to reason with him. But the Duke had turned a deaf ear, obstinately donning rose-tinted glasses. And now here stood his worst nightmare, a tall, handsome, wealthy Russian of good stock who, in the blink of an eye, had slammed the door on Tatianya's childhood. It was little comfort to the duke that this man was head over heels in love with Tatianya. Not knowing what else to do, Nikolai stood his ground, resolutely waiting to persuade the duke of his good intentions. The duchess was thrilled at the prospect of this match, while the duke was heartbroken. He hadn't known his time with Tatianya would be so short.

At last, the duke turned on Nikolai and bellowed "Get out!"

Nikolai fell back against the door. The duchess advanced toward Nikolai and caught him by the arm. A conspirative smile danced across a ravishing mouth lit by the passion of her anger, "You and I have work to do."

The duchess turned to face her husband, eyes flashing with conviction, signaling that this fight was far from over. She advanced towards her husband, a slight sneer invading her luscious mouth. "My love, no curiosity regarding what Tatianya's suitor has to say for himself? After all, he is an invited guest in our home. Or have ALL your manners abandoned you?"

The duchess abruptly turned to gently smooth the lapels of Nikolai's jacket, causing her husband to cringe with each caress, "Irina, don't."

She smiled at Nikolai, "Go, plead your case. Make my duke see you are worthy to join his household."

Nikolai responded that he had not anticipated what had transpired. "Your lordship, please believe that until our chance meeting in the garden, I only knew of Tatianya by name. I swear I had never dreamt of loving her. For years my father has begged me to marry. Until tonight, I did not know what was preventing me from accepting a betrothal. But now I do. I know in my heart; I was meant to wait for Tatianya. I know I am much older. But I will adore her until my dying day. I will guard her, care for her; protect her like I know you have done so well. I will make it my reason for living, every day, to ensure nothing but happiness and love will ever embrace her. I beg for the chance to win her hand and earn your trust."

He tried to reassure the duke that he would be good to Tatianya if the duke would allow a courtship. But the duke was resolute. "So, you think you are the first to be so presumptuous? Must I remind you that you are in my home speaking to me about my daughter who you barely know? She is a child, MY child. She will be presented to society when I deem it is time. I see no place for you in her future. And as for winning my trust, that will never come to pass. If you are as intelligent as you appear to be, do the gentlemanly thing and withdraw your request to court a child that is not of age."

The duke held his ground that Tatianya would not be presented to society for several months. He continued that his wish was for her to find someone closer to her age and more importantly, closer to home.

The Duchess Irina Yusopova smirked at her duke, "Ah my love, so now you have taken up lying in addition to vulgar displays of anger! Be honest with our handsome guest. The truth is that no one will ever be good enough for Tatianya! More than half of the ruling houses in Europe have tried in vain to secure a contract between their prince and our Tatianya.'

The duchess thumped her husband on the head. Nikolai was appalled at her brazen sarcasm, "This obstinate buffoon has rejected each offer. Other Russian nobles' inquiries have met with this same resistance." The duchess retreated to her gilded secretary, managing to look simultaneously regal and sensuous.

The duke glared at Nikolai, avoiding the duchess' steely gaze, "Nikolai, you and your entourage will be leaving in the morning, before breakfast. You are fortunate I do not insist you remove your party tonight."

Nikolai pushed his luck, "Your lordship, may I be permitted to properly say goodbye before my departure?"

His request was met with cold aloofness, "I think you know the answer. We are done here. Did you really think your pathetic plea would do less than magnify my anger? Impudent fool...." He waved Nikolai off. The duchess was incensed. She stalked out of the duke's study and disappeared into the gardens. But the air still sizzled with Irina's fury.

For hours, Nikolai wandered the halls of the palace, seeing nothing but his bleak future. Toward morning, he happened upon a portrait of Tatianya. He studied her sweet expression. "That smile must belong to me. How else can I go on?"

At daybreak, Nikolai woke his friends. They made their preparations in silence. They could see he was a broken man. He was disheveled and unshaven. His few words were tinged with defeat. They were shocked by this sudden change and kept their thoughts to themselves. As they departed the palace, the duke smugly watched their every move. He would ensure they took their leave without further incident.

Tatianya had expected this reaction from her father. Her mother had awoken her and confirmed her suspicions. Tatianya knew she could not disobey her father, but he had yet to formally forbid her from speaking to Nikolai. Very quietly she made her way down a side staircase and waited patiently for her chance.

Nikolai had requested his horse be saddled. He would ride alone, for now, needing to sort his thoughts and feelings. He mounted his horse and was about to depart when he heard footsteps. The duke was blindsided as Tatianya appeared at Nikolai's side. Nikolai was stunned to see his intended. He could no longer contain his agony and let the tears spill over. It was now Tatianya's turn to be the strong one. In her hand, she held a small bouquet made from the roses near the gazebo. She had tied them with the blue sash from her party dress. She smiled brightly at him, pretending not to see her father. Nikolai no longer cared what the duke thought. He would have at least one kiss from this angel. He jumped down from his horse and swept her into his embrace. He accepted the bouquet as she gently wiped his tears. "Nikki, we will fix this, just you wait and see."

Nikolai was astonished by her maturity. Determination surged from the depths of his shattered heart. He was now certain that she felt something, anything for him. He avoided the duke's heated stare. He held her tighter and again Tatianya melted into his embrace. Nikolai had expected to kiss Tatianya but instead, he found himself on bended knee. He took her tiny hand in his, kissed it, and then held it to his heart. "This now and forevermore belongs to you. As long as it takes, whatever it takes, I will be back for you. I will wait as long as your father commands. And then nothing will ever come between us. I pray this is what your heart desires."

Tatianya took Nikolai's quivering chin into her delicate hands. Her large blue eyes were electric, reaching deep within his soul. Once again, Nikolai found himself drowning in those sapphire pools that he could scarcely believe were looking back at him with love. Awkwardly, she leaned into him, bestowing a virginal kiss.

The assembly that had gathered to watch the growing spectacle was swept away by her brazen action. It happened so swiftly that Nikolai could not help but return the kiss. He wanted so badly to devour her beguiling mouth. But he knew this had been her first kiss. He restrained himself, accepting her gentle gift. He knew he had been her first. He vowed to be her last. She gazed into him, thru him, making him ache to be a man bound only to one. He ached to unleash the man he had never dreamt was trapped within his depths. Unknowingly, this child had finally turned that elusive key. She kissed away his tears, drinking in his saltiness, inviting his essence to reside deep within her soul.

This tender gesture only made him want her more, made him vow to be worthy of her love.

"Come back for me Nikki. My soul cries out for you. I feel so secure in your embrace. I know I am young but I am certain this is where I belong." Just for a moment, the corners of her mouth unknowingly swept into a seductive curve. She leaned into him and whispered, "Be the one to rescue me from my father's misguided clutches."

Nikolai saw echoes of the duchess in his young intended and it was glorious to behold. Too overcome, Nikolai held her gaze until reason was once again within his reach. He fought the allure of her inviting mouth, fought the urge to devour her, consequences be damned. He resisted his desire to feast, not wanting to mar the magic of the moment. Instead, he whispered, "Wait for me, my angel. I beg of you, wait for me. I will wait a lifetime for you. I already have."

Nikolai had no choice but to tear himself away.

With renewed conviction, he remounted his horse. Turning for home, he caught the approving eye of the duchess, his ally, imploring him to follow his chosen path.

Chapter Two: Tatianya

Grigorii Yusopov understood Nikolai's predicament far better than anyone. History was simply repeating itself. His own courtship with the duchess had also been tempestuous. The duke and duchess had been forced to conspire to overcome the endless objections of her overbearing father. The duchess was right for empathizing with this handsome stranger; Nikolai was simply a younger version of her own hero. The duke cursed himself for having over-reacted to Nikolai's sudden appearance.

That evening, after witnessing the duke's shameful treatment of Nikolai, the duchess had stunned her husband by withdrawing to her chambers, alone. "You have no place here. Sound familiar?" She slowly closed the door between them, shutting him out of her intoxicating world.

Her indigo eyes were alive with the fire of their unfinished battle. It made the duke ache with a longing he was not accustomed to enduring.

Never in all their years of marriage had his Irina once turned a cold shoulder to Grigorii's advances. Never once had a desire been rebuked. The duke was frightened that he may have lost his true reason for living. But pride and stubbornness overruled; unwittingly painting him into a very tight corner. Grigorii was at a loss as to how to make things right without losing face.

In the end, the duke held fast to his decision. The duchess grew tired of attempting to intervene and withdrew from her husband entirely. The duke had never seen the duchess so determined. They were at a stalemate for weeks.

Meanwhile, Tatianya had also been very defiant, at first. But when she learned that her father repeatedly refused to receive Nikolai and then Nikolai's father, she became withdrawn. When it was divulged that Nikolai's gifts and his attempts to see her were rebuked time and again, she became inconsolable. She refused to attend palace functions for fear of seeing Nikolai with a new love interest. Stricken with love that could not be publicly professed, Tatianya lost her youthful zest for life. She slipped into a stuporous existence. Her once spirited and happy self dissolved into a memory, somberly clinging to one magical night. Gone was that radiant smile. Her endearing giggles had dissipated into a deafening silence.

In an effort to restore peace, the duke proposed that Tatianya be introduced to society earlier than he had intended. He had hoped to wait until she was 16. The duchess was thrilled at this change of heart. She graciously accepted the duke's peace offering and once again dominated the landscape of her husband's fantasies. Night after night Grigorii found Irina's chamber doors unlocked, her smile inviting, her eyes shining with desire as he took her in his arms. Her lithe body clung to him, eager to accept his advances, be they nurturing or domineering in nature. Carefully, she led her husband to believe all was right again in his world. So sweetly did she submit to any and all of his desires, the duke was completely unaware he was no longer in control of the situation. The duchess knew her husband well enough to know just where those chinks in his armor lay.

Unaware of her mother's scheming, Tatianya remained engulfed in despair. Nikolai had stopped trying to reason with the duke. Tatianya could only surmise that he had grown tired of waiting for her father to relent. She tortured herself that a more sophisticated woman had caught his eye. She couldn't really blame him. But his embrace had felt so right. She found it hard to believe he had given up on their love. It took every ounce of the duchess' self-control not to divulge her plans to her lovesick daughter.

Secretly, Tatianya's mother had been in contact with Nikolai's father. Both Nikolai and Tatianya were suffering. Nikolai had become reclusive, throwing himself headlong into his businesses. He took his meals alone in his chambers, rarely receiving even his closest friends. Sadly, he had stopped journeying to the palace. He simply could not bring himself to be refused by the duke one more time. Countless pleas had been cruelly met with the same rebuff. He had hoped to catch a glimpse of his sweet blue-eyed cherub but had not been so lucky. If only he had known how she was wasting away.

About a month before Tatianya's ball, the duchess made a journey to Moscow on the pretense of visiting an old friend. She requested to be received by Nikolai and his father. This request was met with hope and enthusiasm by Nikolai's father, but Nikolai was uneasy with fanning the flames of his unrequited love.

Nikolai reluctantly agreed to meet with the duchess. She was shocked when she saw the transformation in his appearance. He looked gaunt and so much older. His eyes were filled with defeat. For a moment the duchess questioned her plans. But this separation had also taken its toll on her daughter.

The duchess came right to the point. She informed Nikolai that Tatianya would be presented to society in one month's time. Nikolai jumped to his feet at this unexpected news. He began to pace, much of his old spark returning. His eyes flashed angrily. He practically shouted at the duchess, "Why are you telling me this? Why are you torturing me so?" He stumbled blindly towards the door, fearing what he might hear next. The duchess bolted out of her chair, knocking over the tea service in her haste. She reached

Nikolai just as he was making his escape. She whirled him around crying out, "Stupid fool, do you think I am so cruel as to pour salt into a wound? Do you think I don't have more important things to do aside from causing you pain? No, I am here to help as best I can. True, I cannot force the duke to issue you an invitation." Large blue eyes so similar to his beloved's held his gaze, piercing thru his misery. The duchess smiled with just a hint of mischief, "But you can."

Nikolai was stunned at the speed and strength of the duchess' actions. These truly belonged to a mother worried about a child. Nikolai knew the duchess had done as much as she dared. She had taken great risks going against the duke by coming to see him, lying to the duke. Nikolai knew the rest was up to him. The flash in his eyes told his father and the duchess the old Nikolai was back. He would resume his journeys to the palace. And this time he would not take no for an answer. He resolved to wear the duke down.

Hastily Nikolai prepared to implore the duke for an invitation to Tatianya's ball. Even if he was commanded to keep his distance, it would be a comfort to be in her presence. Alexi, his oldest and dearest friend, played devil's advocate, "What will you do when you see her dancing with her many admirers? How will this make you feel? More importantly, can you keep from causing another scene?"

Nikolai ignored Alexi's inquisition. The only thing he knew for certain was that he had to be there. Maybe his presence would be enough if their eyes could meet, she would remember. She would know. It would be a start. Something. Anything. He had to try.

Nikolai's father knew that distance was needed between Nikolai's folly and their family's reputation. But he couldn't risk allowing Nikolai to face the duke alone. Gratefully, he accepted

Alexi's offer to accompany Nikolai to the palace. Alexi would be the voice of reason, and God forbid, a witness if things went terribly wrong. Knowing his son's rebellious nature and the duke's reputation, anything was possible.

Nikolai rode in silence for most of the journey. He needed to escape Alexi's well-intentioned but completely irritating lectures. As the palace came into view, Nikolai could feel Tatianya's presence, sense her, smell her. It was thrilling to know his everything was just beyond those palace walls. He allowed a brief indulgence, permitting those sensual fantasies he had denied for weeks to surface. It was beyond intoxicating. He struggled to calm his mind as best he could, intending to be as gentlemanly as possible. But as the palace door swung open, Nikolai strode past the unsuspecting doorman without so much as giving his name. Wildly pacing the expansive grand hall, Nikolai demanded an audience with the duke. Alexi strode thru the open doorway and flanked Nikolai, silently signaling a united front against a proposed enemy.

Nikolai's raucous entrance and Alexi's subsequent arrival had caused quite a disturbance in the normally peaceful palace. The main hall was now alive with curiosity. Doors up and down the long expanse were opening one by one to gasps as shock settled over the growing crowd. Finally, the duke emerged from his study on the upper level. He became incensed upon seeing Nikolai and Alexi standing amidst the gathered assembly. He flung the documents he was holding, causing them to rain down into the hall. He screamed "Get out! You have no place here!"

But this time, Nikolai did not respectfully recoil as he had weeks earlier. He was no longer afraid. The duke had miscalculated, grossly underestimating his opponent. It was now the duke, in his own home, who was on the defensive. Nikolai had succeeded in gaining the advantage, hurling a stubborn father into unfamiliar territory.

The duke was at a loss, blindsided once again by Nikolai's appearance. Voiceless accusations flew as the two men stood face to face, barely separated by inches, neither backing down.

It was Alexi who broke the tension. "Nikolai has come to ask a favor. Please, Nikolai. Proceed as the gentleman I know you to be."

Nikolai awkwardly attempted to plead his case. It wasn't going as planned. He had anticipated speaking privately with the duke in a civilized manner. But the duke and Nikolai had simply picked up where they had left off weeks earlier. As the duke was triumphantly preparing to once again rid himself of Nikolai, a door upstairs creaked open.

All eyes turned to see a waiflike figure at the railing. Nikolai gasped at the sight. Tatianya was a shadow of her already diminutive self. She was haggard from weeks of self-deprecation. Her eyes no longer gleamed with the promise of a future just waiting to be discovered. She was emaciated, her legs barely held her as she gripped the banister for support. Gone were the womanly curves that had been blossoming. Her hollowed cheeks only intensified the blue of her eyes. Unfathomable depths of pain and despair were etched across that once innocent expression.

As their eyes locked, both Nikolai and Tatianya let a silent tear escape, each realizing neither had given up on their forbidden love. Blinded by stubbornness, the duke failed to accept what was transpiring and turned to Nikolai. With a grand gesture toward his youngest daughter, he said "See what you have done, you are the cause of all this nonsense." Nikolai was lost in Tatianya's gaze and couldn't respond. But Alexi knew he was witnessing his friend silently recommitting himself to his future. Never having experienced the rapture of love at first sight, this moment was almost too much for Alexi to bear. But it was Alexi who turned to the duke and very quietly murmured, "No, you sir, are the cause." The duke was taken aback. He motioned to the governess to remove Tatianya as he made to continue this encounter in private.

Neither Nikolai nor Tatianya were willing to be separated again so soon. As he walked to the foot of the stairs, Tatianya evaded her governess. With unsteady steps, she began to descend the stairs. She did not realize just how weak she had become and midway down, she collapsed. Nikolai and Alexi raced to break her fall. Nikolai scooped her into his arms, fearing the worst. But as Tatianya's rail-thin arms encircled Nikolai's neck, the entire household swooned, releasing the tension that had hung in the air for weeks. Her fingers dove into Nikolai's cascading locks, pulling his face close to hers. As their eyes met, she smiled, the first time in weeks.

"I thought you had given up on me." Nikolai was unable to speak. His voice was choked by emotion. He merely shook his head as his tears cascaded onto her lips. She pulled him closer and opened her mouth to receive his tears, his lips, his tongue. She had never kissed a man before Nikolai, had no knowledge of what transpired behind closed doors at night. But everything with Nikolai was instinctual. She parted her lips and kissed him unabashedly. She wanted him to know she was his. She prayed he still desired her.

Nikolai responded with a desire he had no strength, no wish to restrain. He knew it was not the right place or time but he was out of options. He cast decorum aside, returning her kiss with a hunger that had been denied too long. Ferociously, he devoured her. Despite her weakened state, Tatianya responded and Nikolai's kiss became more urgent. He felt Alexi's grip cautioning him and he came to his senses. Tatianya became alarmed at his sudden reserve. He tenderly stroked the curve of her cheek. He smiled, "We will have plenty of time. You yourself told me that we will fix this. And we will. I will make your father accept us." Tatianya relaxed inside the warm embrace of her hero's arms. She felt alive and peaceful. Although she tried to fight it, the sleep that had eluded her for weeks now descended with a heaviness she could not stave off, try as she may. She gave Nikolai a dreamy smile. He leaned in, but not to deliver the kiss of a lover driven wild by separation. Gently now, he kissed her eyelids into submission of their much-needed rest. With one last stolen kiss, Tatianya gave into the needs of her healing body. She drifted off to sleep; confident Nikolai would be there when she awoke.

All those present had gathered by the staircase, mesmerized by the unfolding scene. After recovering enough to take command, the duchess made her way to where Tatianya lie ensconced in Nikolai's loving embrace. The duchess directed the governess and a footman to take Tatianya to her chambers, but Nikolai would not hear of anyone wrenching her from his arms. He gently lifted Tatianya from the stairs and strode past the governess. He motioned for the duchess to show him to Tatianya's suite. He simply could not relinquish his connection with her while she was so fragile. This quiet but authoritative gesture surprised the duchess. Like a child, she silently obeyed. Nikolai carefully ascended the stairs with his precious cargo, Alexi following closely behind. As they entered Tatianya's bed chambers, the duchess blocked the governess from entering, locking the door behind Alexi. She was unsure how the afternoon would unfold and did not want to be disturbed. She needed this time to observe Nikolai and Tatianya together, away from prying eyes. She would have preferred to exclude Alexi but saw he had no intention of leaving Nikolai's side. Graciously, she acquiesced. She cautiously welcomed this unknown but obviously important presence in

Nikolai's life. Perhaps she could draw information from Alexi. Prove the duke correct for having his suspicions, or confirm that the duke was simply a foolish father pathetically standing in the way of love and the march of time.

As all eyes had been bewitched by the scene unfolding on the stairs, no one had seen the duke collapse. He was visibly shaken. The situation was clearly out of control. He was now truly at a loss as to how to proceed. For the first time in his life, he was uncertain as to what his next move should be. And he was afraid.

Alone and afraid, he sought the solace of the gardens to clear his mind. He struggled to formulate a plan. This man, this Nikolai, while not a bad man, was twice Tatianya's age. The duke worried that Nikolai would not be patient with Tatianya as she matured. He worried that Tatianya would grow tired of Nikolai. The duke realized that he had no rational objections to Nikolai other than his age. He smiled to himself. Nikolai truly was a younger version of himself. Memories flooded the duke's mind of his courtship with the duchess, who was many years his junior. Why was he being so cruel? The fact that he had caused so much pain shook him to his core. Nikolai had yet to truly provoke such wicked responses. On his way to the gardens, the duke passed a large ornate mirror. He paused to examine his visage. He was a good-looking man and had become more distinguished with age. But the hardened look that starred back at him was that of a stranger. Try as he may, his kinder side simply could not surface. Nikolai had turned his whole world upside down. The duke had lost his footing for the first time in his life.

He wondered if this was how his own beloved's father had felt. He was ashamed that he was not able to accept the inevitable as graciously as his father-in-law had managed. While the duchess' father had protested their love and had placed stumbling blocks along their path, the duke was at a loss to remember any true, overt unkindness or loss of temper. He had always been received as a gentleman by a gentleman. He shook his head. What must his wife and daughters think of him? He cringed, staring at the monster in the mirror. What was it about Nikolai that was causing so much dread? Why did this man cause him to fear the future so? Why was he the only one who could see the black clouds gathering?

As the duke made his way to the gardens, the duchess led Nikolai to Tatianya's chambers. She instructed Nikolai to lay Tatianya on her ornately feminine bed. But Nikolai was not ready to be parted from his angel. She had nestled against his chest and the magic of having her so close had given him renewed confidence. He quietly instructed Alexi to throw open the balcony doors. It was now late into summer. The unusually warm day and fresh air felt good after the tension of the past hour. Nikolai settled himself on a settee and allowed Tatianya to continue sleeping curled up in his arms.

The duchess was becoming concerned by this sudden turn of events. She also felt control was slipping away. She stumbled over her words, searching for a way to restore a measure of order. "Nikolai, you have made your point. You have the duke on the defensive, questioning his motives. You have done enough for today. I must now think of Tatianya's reputation...."

As the duchess began to protest that perhaps Nikolai was carrying this too far, she stopped. Alexi was motioning for the duchess to observe the pair. One of Tatianya's delicate fingers had found its way to a buttonhole on Nikolai's finely tailored riding jacket. This finger was threaded through the hole, clutching the jacket tightly to her chest. The fingers of her other hand were now worked inside the jacket's silken lining. When Alexi drew back the jacket, the duchess smiled. Nikolai had kept the small bouquet Tatianya had given him weeks ago. She was fiercely clutching this bouquet and the faded blue ribbon she had used to bind the roses. Alexi bade the duchess to retreat from the balcony in an effort to buy Nikolai a little more time.

The duchess began to follow Alexi to the sitting area of Tatianya's chambers. But as she turned, she felt someone watching from the gardens. The duchess scanned the elegantly sculptured expanse of topiary, hedges, and mazes, squinting into the sun. She was startled to see the duke standing alone. He looked much older than his years and he wore a look of defeat. The duchess made no move. She knew she was way out of line having this unwelcome man holding Tatianya in his arms, in her bedroom no less. They stood for a moment, neither one bending. The duke finally relented and offered a weak smile. He raised his hand, managing a small wave. The duchess relaxed and returned the smile. The duke's gaze then settled on Nikolai and Tatianya and his countenance visibly shifted. The duchess retreated with Alexi, choosing not to meet the duke's gaze again.

Alexi had started a fire in the hearth. The sun would be setting soon in the vast Russian sky. He wanted the room warm and welcoming for Tatianya when she and Nikolai retreated from the harsh night air. The duchess accepted Alexi's invitation to relax by the hearth.

The duchess mentally prepared her line of questioning for Alexi. She could see Alexi was far less prone to outbursts than Nikolai. They were a good foil for each other. At length, Alexi broke her reverie.

"Yes, Nikolai and I do complement each other's ways. I have known him all my life. My first memories are of us playing as children. Our fathers had different plans for us when it came to our futures. My father has directed my life and to a large degree, I have allowed this. Nikolai always was far more passionate and his father was wise to recognize that no one could ever truly tame his wild streak." Alexi paused and smiled wickedly, "At least until now."

The duchess laughed and nodded in agreement. "He does seem so smitten with her. But I worry. Do you think this could last? They barely know each other. She is so much younger and has led a much more sheltered life."

It was now Alexi's turn to smile, "So you have done some investigating of my dearest friend?"

The duchess' cheeks colored faintly, "Well if I am to go against my husband, it would need to be for a very, very good cause. I know you must think the duke horrid. If I were you, I would also be so inclined. My poor husband has expended ridiculous amounts of energy attempting to control Tatianya's exposure to men. I think he feels that when his youngest is gone, I will see him as nothing but an old man. But he is the love of my life. I am shocked that my beloved doesn't see the irony in this situation. It so very closely resembles our own tentative beginning. Grigorii had to overcome my own father's objections, but I have no recollection of my father ever behaving so rudely. This has been such a disappointment to me. Alexi, you need to understand that I am taking great chances. I just hope they are worth my risk."

Alexi nodded that he understood. He proceeded to tell the duchess that while he and Nikolai were the closest of friends, more like brothers, their lives had taken very different paths. But as his demons surfaced, his voice faltered. His vacant stare unnerved the duchess who was now too far invested to do anything but wait. She studied the beautiful grey eyes that were suddenly awash with remorse.

Alexi's marriage had been arranged and while Nikolai would never have agreed to this, Alexi consented to court his intended. Olga turned out to be very beautiful, possessing a sweet, calm nature that Alexi found enchanting. Shortly after marrying,

Olga became pregnant and bore a daughter. The pregnancy had been difficult, not something Alexi had envisioned. Nonetheless, sweet obedient Olga knew she was expected to produce an heir and was eager to try again for a son. But Alexi had been repulsed by the pain and suffering the first pregnancy had caused. The responsibility of a wife and daughter became oppressive and Alexi found it easier to retreat from family life. He resumed carousing with Nikolai and their friends, leaving Olga alone with their tiny infant daughter.

One night after a very late interlude, Alexi came home to find Olga softly singing to their daughter. A drunken Alexi stumbled into the nursery. Gruffly he confronted Olga, "Why are you tending to the child? We have servants to do this. Why do you let them sleep?"

Olga turned to him. A single tear had stained her cheek. She sighed, tentatively stroking his face. She swallowed her pride as the scent of another woman pervaded her world. "Alexi, my love, I know I disappoint you that I am not more exciting or vivacious. But I do love you with all my heart. This precious baby is the only part of you I am permitted to love. Every night finds me by her cradle."

Olga's honesty set Alexi back on his heels. In his drunken stupor, he sank to the floor. Olga sat close by and placed their baby in his arms. "Hold her, you never hold her. I never hear you say her name or ask after her. Anastasia needs to know her father."

That night, as Olga fought to save her happiness, she found a way to reach her husband in a way no other woman had or ever would. So calm, Olga's tranquility had hidden her strength from all, especially Alexi. That night, Alexi found himself back in Olga's arms. She prayed for a son, hoping to secure her place in Alexi's heart, but no child came for several months.

Olga was growing discouraged but Alexi was in no hurry for another child just yet. He continued to enjoy his social life away from home while slowly accepting his roles of father and husband. While Olga knew he was not always faithful, she could see he was growing tired of his old habits. Patiently, she waited for the day he would realize just how much he loved her and their daughter.

When Nikolai had come home from university, they had gone into business together. While Nikolai took care of most of the details, from time to time, Alexi went along, mostly for the social side of things. One such journey took them away for several weeks and Alexi found himself restless to get home. For the first time in his life, he missed Olga's caresses and Anastasia's naughty ways. Alexi was uneasy as his letters were strangely going unanswered. When he arrived home, he was shocked to learn that Olga had been pregnant before he left. She had forbidden anyone from telling him as she had suffered so with the first pregnancy. She didn't want him to see her that way again. They had come so far. He cursed his selfish ways. How could he have been so blind?

Olga's second labor was no easier than her first. She slipped in and out of consciousness for hours, as the child was unable to make his way into the world. The doctor prepared Alexi for the worst. As Alexi knelt by the bed, weeping and lamenting his lack of concern, Olga seemed to reach deep inside herself for strength. She opened her eyes and held his gaze. She had never seen Alexi weep for her or show such concern. It was what she had so desperately craved. She began to labor with all her might.

Alexi was spellbound by Olga's strength. Every previous notion of Olga being reticent was dispelled. Here was a woman on the brink of death, giving her all to save his child. Toward daybreak, Alexi heard the cries of his newborn child, a son. He was humbled as he watched Olga taking their newborn son to her breast, refusing to allow the wet nurse to nurture his child. He sank to a chair and savored the sight of mother and son bonding as the babe hungrily suckled. As Olga's eyes met Alexi's over the head of their son, they shone with love. It was the night that Alexi found himself utterly ensnared by Olga's charms. He happily abandoned his wild nights, thankful that this beautiful creature was able to love a man so full of flaws.

The duchess sat in silence, waiting. She could see Alexi was struggling with his own demons. He finally leaned forward, looking the duchess directly in the eye. "I need to make you see the true Nikolai. Once he sets his mind, it never waivers. It has been this way his whole life, none more so than with his feelings for your daughter. Tatianya will be the center of his universe. She will always be his everything. I suspect she already is."

Alexi roused himself from the comfort of the fire. He approached the balcony and bade Nikolai come in from the evening air which now possessed a chill. Reluctantly, Nikolai carefully rose from the settee. He now had no choice but to wrench himself away from his sleeping goddess.

As the duchess, Alexi and Nikolai retreated from her bedside, Tatianya stirred and beckoned. She had so much she wanted to say. The sleep that had eluded her for weeks would not allow her mind to clear. Nikolai softly kissed her words away. He understood what she wanted to say, all of it. Again, a tear slowly slipped from his eye, landing on her cheek. She implored Nikolai to reason with her father. "Please Nikki, please. Make Papa understand. I can't go through this again. I won't survive without knowing I will always have your love."

As Nikolai bent forward so that only Tatianya would hear his words, he vowed to make her father accept their love. "Shhh, my darling. You have my word. I will make your father accept that what we have is forever. Trust that I will prevail." For a moment, she willed her eyes to open. She held his gaze one last time. Again, the healing sleep descended over her now peaceful face.

When Nikolai was certain that Tatianya was peacefully sleeping, Alexi was able to steer him into the hall where they came face to face with the duke. The sight of the duke jolted both Alexi and Nikolai. They were unaware that the duke had been sitting for hours outside of Tatianya's bed chamber. Very quietly the duke asked if his youngest was unharmed. Nikolai was only able to nod but Alexi stated that she had been sleeping peacefully and would most likely do so through the night. The duke nodded and invited Nikolai and Alexi to join him and the duchess for a late supper. He insisted that they stay for the night. Warily, Nikolai accepted.

As Nikolai and Alexi prepared for supper, Alexi cautioned Nikolai not to push the duke. But Nikolai began pacing in their suite. He felt he had lost so much time. After holding Tatianya as she slept, he was finding it difficult to wait any longer to ask for her hand. Alexi turned to his friend in amazement. He shook Nikolai by the shoulders. "Think Nikolai, think! You have made great strides, don't press the duke. You will ruin everything. Don't be a fool!" Deep down Nikolai knew Alexi was right and while he did not want to wait, he relented. He agreed to only request an invitation to Tatianya's ball. Alexi said a silent prayer that Nikolai would allow reason to rule.

Meanwhile, the duchess was having much the same conversation with the duke. She described the afternoon to the duke and pleaded with him to see the wisdom in allowing this romance some room to breathe. She reasoned that perhaps by allowing Nikolai to spend time with Tatianya they would see that there was not much future for them. "By keeping the fruit of their future from them, my love, you are only making them desire it that much more." The duke couldn't argue with this line of reasoning. The duke intended to allow Nikolai to attend the ball but would make him work for this honor. The duchess silently prayed that this blossoming love would be allowed to grow. The afternoon's events had convinced her of Nikolai's good intentions. She was now more than ever determined to provide whatever support she could.

The duchess and Alexi steered the supper's initial conversations into neutral territory. Their meaningless banter allowed the duke and Nikolai time to ease into the discussion they all knew was coming. Nikolai made the first move. He again reassured the duke that his intentions were honorable. He stated he was completely aware of the need to move slowly given Tatianya's age and inexperience with love. He convinced the duke that he was smitten with her sweetness. He vowed to do anything within his power to protect her and allow her to grow at her own pace. The duke wished he could just let himself trust in this young man, pleading so eloquently for a chance to prove himself. He had never been so at odds with his duchess and his daughter. He became impatient with his inability to trust in this future. But the doubts continued to loom over this unlikely coupling. He struggled not to revert to his anger and throw Nikolai out.

The duke finally spoke and his words stung Nikolai. "Nikolai, I admire your determination, your conviction. You make it all but impossible not to see the logic in allowing you to court my Tatianya. Unfortunately for you, I continue to have my doubts and I must trust my instincts. You have failed, at least for now, to convince me that no other would be a more suitable match." The duke stated he believed Nikolai's intentions were honorable but it was his daughter's needs that were his concern. Nikolai would be permitted to attend the ball provided he made no efforts to monopolize Tatianya's time. He continued that Tatianya would be instructed to accept the attentions of any suitable suitor that she found remotely pleasing.

Nikolai was outraged. Alexi spoke up and pointed out that great strides had been made. Nikolai ultimately accepted the duke's terms but not before pointedly remarking that Tatianya's feelings were aligned with his. The duke fought hard to restrain himself as he also pointedly remarked that Nikolai was pinning his future on the capricious feelings of a child. Both the duchess and Alexi saw that it was best to end the supper at this juncture. Nikolai resigned himself to the duke's terms but not before he secured the duke's word that he would be permitted to spend the coming morning with Tatianya.

The duke could see that fate was conspiring against him. Morosely, he eyed the man who was aching to transform his child into a woman. The duchess whispered into her husband's ear. "My love, doesn't our handsome guest remind you of someone?" She slowly let her finger trace his finely chiseled chin. She seductively made love to him with her eyes. The duke sighed and smiled. He relented and agreed to Nikolai's request. The two men bid their host and hostess a hasty good night. The duchess continued to woo her wounded lover as they left. She would indulge the duke his every whim, whatever it would take to smooth the road for Tatianya. She would do whatever was in her power to placate her own hero's wounded ego. She knew how hard these past few weeks had been on her aging duke. She found herself falling more in love with him the more he struggled to understand a child whose world no longer revolved around him. Nikolai and Alexi were shocked into silence by the duchess' blatant display of arousal and desire. Both men understood she was clearly in Nikolai's corner. They silently left the duchess to work her magic.

When Alexi and Nikolai returned to their suite, Alexi smirked and remarked that if Tatianya was anything like her mother Nikolai was a lucky man. Nikolai shot Alexi a shaky smile but agreed. It had been shocking to witness the older couple engaging in what amounted to foreplay. Alexi cautioned Nikolai not to push any further during their remaining time. The two friends spent the early morning hours discussing their journey's outcome. Alexi encouraged Nikolai to be grateful that he had accomplished what he had come to do, "Patience my friend, patience."

The following morning Alexi and Nikolai found themselves being received in the morning room by the rest of Tatianya's family. Nikolai sipped his tea with an exterior facade that belied the raging storm within. Tatianya's sisters had arrived during the night. The two brothers-in-law were discreetly sizing up Nikolai. What was going on in that handsome aristocratic head? What had Nikolai seen in their little sister-in-law that they had never even remotely seen? Here was a worldly, educated man near to their age making a fool of himself over their little Tatianya. They were gradually coming to realize what Alexi already knew. They were witnessing love at first sight. They too envied Nikolai even though he currently felt miserable. They knew that if he succeeded in winning over the duke, he ultimately would be greatly rewarded. Like Alexi, Tatianya's brothers-in-law had accepted arranged marriages and like Alexi, they had grown to love and cherish their wives. But it was nothing like this torrent of passion so palpable when Nikolai was in the room.

After what seemed like a lifetime, Tatianya entered the morning room and sat between her parents. She looked lovingly and openly only at Nikolai; unaware of the fury she was unleashing. An electric shock once again ruthlessly scorched Nikolai's entire being; mercilessly igniting a desire he had no way to quell. All else in the room seemed to fade away. The sight of Tatianya's lovelight shining only for him gave him the courage to fight for what he knew he had to possess.

After several attempts at gaining Nikolai's attention, the duke spoke. He was coming to accept that he was waging a losing battle. He was losing interest in prolonging the inevitable. He stated that after breakfast, Tatianya and Nikolai would be permitted to stroll the gardens under the watchful eye of her governess. Nikolai was stunned that the duke was not intending to join them. Alexi was given the option to join the stroll or remain with the family. He quickly accepted the company of the duke's sons-in-law.

As the sun rose to kiss the sky, Nikolai smiled down at his intended. He wondered if she knew this was the beginning of their courtship. The governess dallied a small distance behind. As they ventured further into the gardens, Nikolai knew he could convince the governess to find amusement elsewhere in the tall hedges, even if for only a short time. Nikolai knew he would not see Tatianya again before her ball. He was determined to make the most of this stolen interlude the duke had foolishly afforded him.

With the palace lost from sight, Nikolai bargained with the governess to allow them some hard-fought privacy. He had angered her the previous day, but now....

"So, it seems I have another ally in my battle? What is it that you know now that you did not know yesterday, as you joined your lordship in his scorn of my presence? I will tell you that you will never need to fear for Tatianya's safety when she comes under my care. I will guard her as you have done. I will watch her slumber, watch for the rise of her chest, the curve of a small smile as she endures only dreams of all that is good. Can I persuade you to traverse a different path through these hedges, if only for a short time? I beg you to grant me this small reprieve."

The governess was swept away by Nikolai's light flirtation. She found herself incapable of refusing his poetic plea, Tatianya's soulful eyes searching for her vow of silence. She could do nothing but acquiesce, seeing how happy and alive Tatianya was today compared to those previous weeks of affliction. She gave Tatianya a light kiss on her cheek and Nikolai a wicked little smile.

When finally alone, Nikolai fought valiantly with his longing to crush Tatianya right then and there in his embrace. She was still very fragile although today she looked considerably better. Instead, he steered her toward the gazebo where they had first met. Tatianya tentatively took his hand in hers. He was shocked at just how diminutive she truly was. As they sat in the gazebo, safe from prying eyes, Nikolai searched those large blue eyes. Once again, he was being pulled under, drowning in their depths. He found himself weeping, not exactly what he had been planning. But Tatianya understood. Presently she spoke. " Nikki, don't. You see our wishes are coming true. Papa came to me this morning and told me you will be attending my ball. But he also instructed me to dance with others and that I need to be open to many suitors."

This statement invaded the muddle of emotions swallowing Nikolai's ability to think. He looked at her with his piercing dark eyes and grabbed her shoulders much rougher than he had intended. He did not want to frighten her, but it was he who was now frightened. The look of panic in his eyes both amused and aroused her. She leaned forward and whispered, "Do you think you are in danger of losing me?"

Nikolai was shocked to see that Tatianya was mocking him, if only slightly. She leaned into him and again he felt their electricity. She sighed, "Oh Nikki, there is only you. There will only ever be you." She then pulled him closer. When their lips were barely touching, she sighed. The sweetness of her breath drove reason beyond his grasp. He found himself falling ever deeper into her abyss. He spanned the space between them and once again allowed himself to devour her lips. But this time there were no prying eyes, no Alexi to stop him. He feasted as a man who had been denied far too long. He knew he should slow down but couldn't. He feasted on her lips, her face, her neck. She was his and she freely gave in to his demands. He knew that she had never been with another in this fashion. He could see her responses to him were instinctual. Her uninhibited passion brought him dangerously close to losing all control.

Nikolai's rational side suddenly surfaced. He abruptly pulled back. Tatianya was breathing raggedly. The look of love was now mingled with one of confusion. He had gone too far. He cursed his selfish exploration.

"I am so sorry my love. Please forgive me. I fear control is slipping thru my fingers. I need to know; do you feel the same? Please put my soul at rest. Let me know what I am to do with this love I have for you. I lay myself, all that I have and ever will have at your feet. I beg to be your humble servant. I intend to ask for your hand after your ball. You must be gentle if your desire is not as mine. I pray I never hear those words."

Nikolai found himself on bended knee. He was wracked with sobs, finding it hard to breathe much less speak. He feared he looked weak and foolish as his intended just stared at him with those big blue eyes. In his misery, Nikolai failed to see these eyes were now fixated on him, alive, dancing with the fire of desire his urgent kisses had ignited. Her thoughts were in disarray, wondering how he could possibly doubt that he would always be her everything. Her inexperience kept her from realizing just how rare and fragile a love like this truly was.

After a moment, Tatianya's tiny hands caressed Nikolai's much larger ones. She gently kissed them and placed them over her pounding heart. "Do you remember when you did this to me? I am now telling you that my heart belongs to you. True, I will have to accept the attentions of many suitors at my ball. But you have to believe me, Nikki, I am only doing this for my papa. We need to please him. His concern is understandable. But you are my first, my last, my only. Please prepare to speak to Papa after the ball. No one else could ever make me feel as I do now. I don't ever want to be without you."

Before Nikolai could respond, Tatianya placed a golden curl tied with that same blue sash in the palm of his hand. Silently she closed his fingers around it. She looked up at him and smiled. "Now you will always have a part of me with you."

Nikolai then remembered the locket he had brought in the event he would be permitted to present her with a gift. He proceeded to extract the exquisitely carved porcelain box.

"Open it, my love." Tatianya carefully opened the box. She gasped as she saw the heart-shaped locket that was set with diamonds and sapphires. Nikolai took the locket and placed it around her neck. "The diamonds represent my love for you. The sapphires remind me of your blue eyes. I pray they will always shine for only me."

Before Nikolai could once again fan the flames of their desire, Tatianya's governess made her presence known. She had watched their tender exchange. She had held her tongue while this man had ravished Tatianya with his fervent kisses. She had seen enough to know that the duke would not be victorious this time.

She too understood that love could make one turn away from all that was familiar. Despite her slowly dissolving reluctance to accept this courtship, she understood. She herself had once been loved beyond all reason. But fate had not seen fit for it to culminate. She smiled wistfully remembering her own torrents of passion. She sadly smoothed the drab green dress over barren full hips that were past their youthful prime. She was grateful that this sweet girl would never know the pangs of loneliness, be reduced to accepting fleeting snatches of hurried loving among the hedges. She was comforted that Tatianya would never suffer professions of adoration devoid of substance. She wiped away the tears she rarely allowed and focused on today. She was unaware of the tiny victory smile trailing across her face.

Tatianya's governess falsely donned a mask of consternation, signaling it was time to return to the palace. She would live vicariously, remembering what could have been.

Chapter Three: Tatianya's Ball

Instead of chattering excitedly about the details of her ball, all Tatianya talked about, incessantly, was Nikolai. To most young girls, this event was a milestone, a signal to society that she was now a woman. It was maddening to the duke that Nikolai had stolen this moment from her, from him.

"Irina, my love, how can you not find anger in your heart toward this thief? He has ruined everything we have worked so hard to nurture."

"Grigorii, you have forced a hand and brought this on yourself. Nikolai has found a home in Tatianya's heart. Why is this so hard to accept? Do you honestly believe she would ever look at another man the way she looks at Nikolai?" Her words caused that darkness to return.

"Irina, my Irishka, is it so wrong of me to place objection when I have my doubts?"

Irina flashed a mocking smile at her duke, "Only when you have just causation for these fears. Just what has Nikolai done that is so heinous, aside from capturing your daughter's heart? I only see an irrational man stubbornly clinging to a foolish notion. Time is marching on, with or without your consent. Can't you see they are in love?"

The duke looked darkly into the glass of brandy Irina had placed in his shaking hand, "No. I find myself praying for a way to end this nonsense with Nikolai." It pained him to see the sadness in Irina's eyes. He set the brandy down. "I wish I could find a way to see what you do. But all I see is heartache for our baby."

Although Grigorii had nothing to base his fears upon, the duke could not shake the feeling that no good would ever come from a union between his daughter and Nikolai. Despite the duchess' belief that fate had brought these two together, the duke still wanted Tatianya to attend balls and enjoy being pursued. He just couldn't get beyond having been blindsided by the appearance of Nikolai. He doggedly believed that he could still somehow rid his household of Nikolai and the frenzy his appearances seemed to cause. It didn't help that after the last visit, Tatianya was more than ever devoted to Nikolai. She refused to remove the locket he had given to her without the duke's consent. Even worse, the duchess now had both sisters and their husbands imploring the duke to give Nikolai a chance. The duke often found himself sitting in the gazebo where Nikolai had cast his spell, wondering, "What do they see that I don't?" He couldn't shake the gloom, knowing it was possible that he saw what they couldn't.

As the day for the ball drew near, Alexi and Olga also received an invitation. Although it was very late in coming, Alexi convinced Olga that they should attend. Given Nikolai's history with the duke, he felt obligated to be at his friend's side. He was concerned that while Nikolai's intentions and feelings only seemed to be gaining momentum, he was not sure if Tatianya's situation had changed. He had seen many young girls fall in and out of love without warning. He was afraid of how Nikolai would react if he found himself cast aside.

Olga had to admit she couldn't deny a curiosity about this little vixen who had conquered their wild Nikolai. Olga mused, "Alexi, my love, this Tatianya must be something of a force herself, although, at fifteen, I doubt she understands the true potential of her powers," Olga smiled to herself, watching her husband squirm at the thought. She teased her husband, "Your Nikolai is in over his head." She soothed his worried brow, feeling guilty for her momentary devilment, "Shhh, everything will be alright. Knowing Nikolai as I do, he would have wanted this no other way."

The duchess had failed to convince the duke to provide Nikolai with chambers within the palace. The duke was now also demanding that Nikolai arrive late. He hoped to instill disappointment in Tatianya that Nikolai thought so little of her as to miss her grand entrance, her shining moment. Nikolai agreed to all of the duke's demands but had little intention of complying with any of them. He had no intention of missing one moment. He had no intention of missing the opportunity to survey the reactions to her entrance. He needed to know who his competition would be if it came down to that. He prayed night and day that his young intended still felt the same. He obsessed that her feelings had been a whim, flattery that an older gentleman could be so completely ensnared in her charms. Nikolai beleaguered Alexi with his incessant ruminations, "Did you see the way she looked at me? She must love me. You must tell me if you think I will be victorious. How I wish I knew what she was thinking, who she was with this very moment." Almost hourly, Alexi had to reassure his friend, pointing out the obvious.

During the weeks following Nikolai's visit, Tatianya had been thriving. She now looked vibrant and healthy. Her mother knew it was the tender kiss of love caressing her daughter. The duchess was thrilled. She knew the ball would be a fun evening for Tatianya, but it would not hold the same intrigue that it had for her elder daughters.

Tatianya had selected a very feminine gown for the occasion. It was a far cry from the one she had worn the evening Nikolai came into her life. Despite the duke's attempts to select a more demure gown, the duchess had allowed and even encouraged a very seductive fitting. The gown was sky blue which made Tatianya's eyes come alive with fire. The dress was made of many fine layers of chiffon that floated as she moved and twirled.

The bodice was tightly fitted to show off her tiny waist. The bodice also allowed Tatianya to proudly display her now ample breasts. Her tiny waist was to be encircled with a sash the color of midnight. The sash was a nod to the sapphires in Nikolai's locket. The duchess hoped Nikolai would be astute enough to pick up on this and feel encouraged. She prayed he was still as intent as he had been. She knew that Tatianya would have no trouble making a good match with another, but it would never hold this same heat. The duchess knew Tatianya would always pine for Nikolai if his fire had dwindled to embers. The very low cut of the dress would surely make clear to Nikolai that Tatianya was a woman and that if he had changed his mind, she would soon be in the arms of another.

On the morning of her ball, Tatianya giddily pranced around the empty grand hall. She weaved in and out of the staff fretting over each and every detail. She watched the careful arrangement of the champagne flutes that would soon be in the hands of her guests. She ooohed over her cake as the kitchen staff struggled to settle it on the heavily laden sweets table. Slyly, she stuck a finger in the buttercream icing of her cake. "Tatianya!" chided her exasperated governess. Her infectious giggles and big blue eyes softened the reprimand as a delicate finger danced across the icing again, insisting that her governess also take a sample, "Isn't it gooood?"

Tatianya's father watched from the balcony as his daughter delighted in the preparations for her ball. He naively indulged the fantasy that Tatianya was finally ecstatic about the possibility of many suitors. In reality, she couldn't wait to see Nikolai's eyes when he first gazed upon her in her gown. She dreamed of their first dance, of his eyes ablaze for her. She longed to feel his possessive hands once again pulling her into his magic, masterfully encircling her waist, desperate that it be known her place was by his side.

Hours later, as the carriages began arriving, Tatianya's sweet romantic notions came crashing down around her alabaster shoulders. Watching the never-ending parade of arriving guests from a parapet high above the courtyard, Tatianya was beside herself when she saw Alexi and Olga step out of their carriage, but Nikolai was nowhere to be found. Her eyes trailed after their carriage, willing him to emerge. Unbeknownst to her, Nikolai had slipped in a side entrance to avoid a scene in the receiving line. She had not known of the constraints her father had placed on Nikolai. The duke smiled triumphantly when he saw Alexi and Olga arrive without Nikolai. Alexi also smiled triumphantly, knowing Nikolai was already somewhere deep inside the palace. As Alexi studied the duke, he knew this man was fighting a losing battle, despite having all of the advantages. Alexi smugly whispered to Olga, "So this is what the face of a fool looks like." She quietly admonished her husband to behave, "Alexi where are your manners? This man is our host." He kissed the curve of his wife's neck, "I will try to not disappoint you, my love." The glint in his eye let Olga know his promise had nothing to do with the duke.

Tatianya was on the verge of tears as her mother escorted her to the duke for her presentation, "Tatianya! Hold your head up high! This is your shining moment. Have a little faith. You are jumping to conclusions."

But inside, the duchess' heart was breaking, her mind drenched with doubt and confusion. Where was Nikolai? Surely

Alexi would not have come without him. She began to fear that Alexi had come bearing bad news.

As they made their way into the ball for the presentation, relief washed over the duchess. She had spied Nikolai casually standing among Tatianya's guests. He smiled wickedly at her, raising his glass of champagne. She desperately wanted Tatianya to see him before she was announced. She knew his were the only pair of admiring eyes that mattered. But she resisted the temptation to whisper in her daughter's ear, fearing the duke would overhear.

As Tatianya was announced and began to descend the grand staircase, her eyes searched the crowd below for the only one that mattered. A smile was dutifully plastered to her face but her eyes were filled with tears. She surveyed the gathering and initially did not see her love. As she continued her descent, her heart began to sink. Nikolai saw her pain.

His piercing eyes valiantly tried to reach her. She scanned the crowd for the origin of this heated gaze.

And then she saw him.

The electricity flew between them with increased intensity. Her smile took on new life and finally shone thru in her eyes. Nikolai returned her smile with a small bow. Her radiant smile alighting on his face encouraged him that her commitment had not wavered. It was all he could do to refrain from sweeping her away.

He dreaded the coming hours. He knew another's touch could change all this, destroy his world. He miserably looked about the room filled with other males lusting, longing to place their hands upon his universe. He had never felt so vulnerable. It was going to be a long night.

Tatianya now knew all was right in her world. Although she would have to accept the attentions of many tonight, the only one that mattered was there. She would eventually be united with him and her hope was to end the evening in his arms. She hoped he understood. She fingered his locket. A seductive smile fluttered across her face, blue eyes gently bestowing their innocent embrace. He fought the tears welling at the thought of losing her to another. He knew no one could ever love her like he did, like he would for all eternity.

Nikolai successfully eluded the duke long enough who seemed satisfied when he finally spotted Nikolai mulling among the guests. He was placated that Nikolai did not rush to Tatianya's side and monopolize her time. The duke was pleased that Nikolai seemed to be playing by his rules. It shocked Alexi that Nikolai was behaving so well. It shocked Alexi that the duke could be so blind to this charade.

Outwardly, Nikolai was the picture of calm and civility. But inside, a relentless storm tormented. He had known from his first dance with Tatianya that she was blossoming with a figure that would drive any man to distraction. From the reactions he was encountering, any number were already planning on courting Tatianya. Most would gladly be on bended knee by the evening's end. Coupled with this knowledge, he was reeling from the vision of her in that very seductive gown. It was a far cry from her childish blue party dress. Both Nikolai and the duke were cursing this dress, having to restrain themselves from throwing a cape over her shoulders. Nikolai laughed to himself, isn't this a change? He looked miserable, eyes following the blond curls whirling around the ballroom, dance after dance in yet another competitor's arms. It was killing him to watch her bestow that smile he wanted only to shine for him.

Olga found herself pitying Nikolai. She had never seen this side of him. It was as if she had never truly known him before tonight. She sidled up to Nikolai and offered him a glass of champagne, "Nikolai, she is lovely, do you think you still have a chance? You have waited long enough. Go and request a dance before it is too late." Glumly, Nikolai searched her eyes for encouragement. This vulnerability caused a lump to fill Olga's throat. Without thinking she brushed a dark wave out of Nikolai's eyes. "Go claim what is rightfully yours." Just for a moment, the doubt turned to resolve. He drank the champagne to steady his nerves. He made his way toward the beautiful blond curls in the center of a crowd of admirers.

Alexi had watched Olga's tender exchange with his oldest friend, her biggest nemesis. He had never thought he would see a time when Olga would feel anything but contempt for Nikolai. He encircled her waist as they both held their breath watching Tatianya's face. "What you just did for Nikolai was beautiful. How can I ever repay you?" He planted a gentle kiss. Not wanting to ruin the mood, he continued playfully, "Or should I now worry that he has you under his spell as well?" Olga gazed up at Alexi, pleased that he would feign a shred of jealousy over where her affections lie.

When Nikolai approached, Tatianya did little to hide her pleasure. This gave his agonized heart a lift. Several men scowled and turned to see who was lighting up her beautiful face.

Nikolai ignored them all. He had waited long enough. He felt that if any were to have made a move, made an impression to displace him in her heart, there would have been time enough. His place now seemed secure. He acted like a man in control. Her other suitors reluctantly surmised the same.

Nikolai bowed to Tatianya as the music started once again. But an equally handsome younger man strode forward and also bowed. This was not to be Nikolai's dance it seemed. He hastily secured several dances. He did the gentlemanly thing and withdrew. Nikolai sensed this younger man had had his eye on Tatianya far longer than he and would not give up so easily. As he whirled Tatianya around the dance floor, he whispered in her ear and she laughed gaily. He nuzzled the golden crown of curls. Their easy familiarity caught Nikolai off guard. He vainly tried to keep eye contact with the couple as they danced further into the ballroom. This man was no fool. He deftly maneuvered Tatianya away from Nikolai. His eyes met Nikolai's briefly as he drew her in close. It took the last of Nikolai's restraint not to stride out onto the dance floor and challenge this threat.

Casually, the duchess took her place next to Nikolai. This did wonders to deflate his growing rage as she had hoped. "Who is he? Should I be concerned?" Nikolai pleaded with the duchess to allay his fears. The duchess smiled. Before Nikolai's arrival, this younger man would have made a good match for Tatianya. The duchess replied, "Your competition out there is making a last attempt to regain his place. Sergei had made it known to the duke some months ago that he was intending to court Tatianya. She has known him all her life. True, he holds a place in her heart, but poor Sergei is just now realizing that his place is that of a friend and nothing more. You should pity him. Let this play out, Nikolai. Let Sergei have his dance. You, it seems, will have her for the rest of your life. Did you not notice the color of her sash and how it resembles the sapphires in your locket? That was for you, Nikolai. You have been with her all evening, thru every dance." With that, the duchess drifted on to another group so as not to draw more attention to Nikolai.

Nikolai agonized until it was finally his turn to hold Tatianya in his arms. As he approached to claim his dance, his eyes devoured her from head to toe. She looked radiant. Her newly unleashed sexuality beckoned to him. He was stunned at how effortlessly she could beguile. As he took her in his arms, he was grateful for the slow pace of the waltz. It was finally his turn to nuzzle those golden curls. It enraged him that so many others had had the same opportunity tonight before him, the scent of their heat and longing lingering. He vowed with a renewed vengeance that this would be the last night any would even remotely consider they had a chance. She sensed his anxiety. It was true; she had enjoyed all the attention tonight, a little more than she had anticipated. Tatianya now understood her father just a little bit better. But all that paled when she saw how sad it was making Nikolai and how silently he had endured this evening. It made her love him all the more. As they danced, she smiled up at Nikolai, giving him the courage he needed. "Tatianya, my little angel, has anyone caught your eye tonight?" Again, she smiled up at him. Just for a moment, she caressed his cheek and stroked away a frown. "Oh yes, Nikki, someone very wonderful is here tonight."

For a moment Nikolai thought he would faint. All of the color drained from his face. He struggled to stay on his feet and keep moving to the music. He was crestfallen, his plan had failed. "Are you happy with this man? If you are, then I am happy for you. As I said weeks ago, I would never stand in your way." He could no longer meet her gaze. His embrace became stiff. For a moment Tatianya gazed up at him, watching as her hero thought his world was crumbling. She was humbled that this confident worldly man could be so easily crushed by her few words. She was overwhelmed by the depths of his love and vulnerability. Tatianya stood on tiptoe to kiss his cheek, causing a stir in the crowd. Nikolai was now the only one who did not realize she was in love with him. She gently touched his chin and made him look at her, really look at her. "Oh Nikki, can't you see, you are my one and only? I could only endure tonight because you were here. When I didn't see you arrive with Alexi and Olga, I wanted to die. You Nikki, you are the one who has caught my eye. Please don't ever be this sad again, I couldn't bear it."

Tatianya's gentle affirmation tore thru Nikolai's misery. She felt his passion ignite, the heat of his need seeping deep within her soul. It was as if the sky had been ripped wide with fireworks. Just as she had envisioned this moment, his eyes blazed with passion and desire for her, only her.

Nikolai fingered the locket hanging about her neck. The locket sat just above her rounded bare breasts. The restraint he had been exercising all evening suddenly evaporated. Brazenly, he let his fingers drift ever so slightly, softly caressing the upper edges of her breast. Tatianya could not contain a soft moan. Nikolai had hoped to elicit such a response. He needed to know she needed him as much as he needed her. He was caught off guard by the intense reaction this stirred within himself. It was almost beyond difficult to contain his desire, but he knew he must. Reluctantly, Nikolai commanded his fingers retreat from her beckoning bosom that was now rising to meet his caress. He leaned in to cover his hand and when he pulled away his hand was gently tracing the outline of her face. No one had seen his hand one last time brush against her breast, lingering, caressing, before tracing a path to her face.

Tatianya was clearly now ablaze with desire. He was relieved to see he could arouse such need in her. He had never felt so compelled to please a lover. He was burning with madness to please her in every way. He needed to see her smile, hear that infectious laugh. But at this very moment, more than anything, he wanted to see her in the throes of ecstasy, hear her moaning as she clung to him, calling out his name as they came together. He knew he had to regain his composure or they would not be able to keep up this façade. The evening had gone so well, he couldn't risk spoiling everything. But he was dangerously close to losing all control.

Tatianya's tender age left her incapable of realizing any of this. And so, he softly whispered "We need to be careful my love. I couldn't resist. I will speak to your father tomorrow if that is what you wish."

Tatianya could hardly see straight, so great was the longing he had stirred within her soul. A violent unfamiliar storm was raging deep within. She wanted him to sweep her into his arms, carry her deep into the gardens, to the gazebo where they had first met. She imagined him loving her, dominating her in the moonlight, the dizzying smell of roses surrounding this magic. Blinded by passion, she could barely nod. Nikolai held her as close as he dared. He had caught Sergei staring at them. He prayed Sergei had not witnessed their passion rising. He couldn't risk any more. When the dance ended, Nikolai delivered Tatianya to her mother. The duchess at first looked concerned, but quickly caught on and offered up a small knowing smile. "Have you had one too many dances my dear little one?" The duke appeared out of nowhere, Sergei at his side. He was concerned that Tatianya had become overwrought with the evening. The duke was impressed that Nikolai would be more concerned with her welfare than his need to hold her in his arms. Maybe he had been wrong about Nikolai. He impatiently waved Sergei aside. Nikolai felt relieved that they had gone undetected.

Tatianya was seated as the doors were flung open to give her some air. Nikolai began to back away but Tatianya caught hold of his hand. Too overwhelmed to speak, her eyes implored the duke that Nikolai be permitted to sit with her while she regained her composure. Much to Sergei's disappointment, the duke quickly agreed, motioning for Nikolai to take his place by Tatianya's side. At that moment, Sergei realized he had lost his chance with Tatianya. He had surrendered his advantage. He too had been blindsided by Nikolai's appearance. He knew there was nothing more he could do. Any could see her heart had been won.

With a head hung low, Sergei cast one last glimpse at Tatianya. He closed the book on a life he had naively assumed was just about to crest the horizon. She smiled back at him, completely unaware of his turmoil. The casual smile she cast his way paled in comparison to the gaze she bestowed upon Nikolai. It made him feel foolish. It made Sergei realize he had never had a chance. This stranger had stolen the future he had been carefully nurturing for years. It ripped at the very fabric of his soul, leaving him vulnerable to a now unknown fate. Unable to witness any more of Tatianya's shameless passion for Nikolai, Sergei turned and headed for the darkened gardens.

As he stumbled through the hedges, he let a wail escape into the loneliness. He cursed Nikolai's very existence, begging for a way to make this man pay. His plea for vengeance took flight upon the subtle evening breeze.

Chapter Four:
The Proposal

Nikolai remained with Tatianya as long as he could following the close of her ball. It had been a huge success. Tatianya had graciously accepted the attentions of many potential suitors, but even the duke could see she had been bored and only going thru the motions for his sake. He was glad he had tried. He was now strangely anxious to make peace with the idea of Nikolai joining his growing family. Willfully, Grigorii ignored the growing panic that something was terribly amiss.

Back in his bed chambers, Nikolai paced as he swirled a snifter of brandy. He was going over and over what he would say to the duke. Alexi and Olga were exhausted but felt guilty abandoning him in this state. Alexi finally broke Nikolai's ranting, "Nikolai, enough!" He smiled with feigned exasperation, stroking away the deep furrow marring Nikolai's striking features. "I am sure by now the duke has thoroughly investigated you and knows you are more than capable of supporting Tatianya even without her substantial dowry. But let's be honest, the duke is worried about your wild past. What you need to do is assure him that those days are over, really over. Make him see the love you hold for his daughter. Make him trust in you." Nikolai slumped against his oldest friend and surrendered the snifter of brandy he had barely touched. He was suddenly very tired.

Nikolai knew Alexi was right. Good clear-minded Alexi could always cut thru to the heart of the matter. Nikolai would humble himself in front of the duke and allay any fears. He would not relent until he had secured a marriage contract, had officially placed his ring on Tatianya's finger. He wanted a wedding date as soon as possible. He no longer wanted the affections of just any woman but he was a virile man. By choice, he was doing without for the first time in his life. He found himself craving what Alexi went home to night after night. He finally understood how one woman could bring a man to his knees, making him happy, content in the process. He wasn't sure how long he could hold out. But he was adamant about one thing. Tatianya was a virgin and would remain so until their wedding night. Dancing with her tonight during the ball had made it very clear that he would have trouble restraining himself much longer. The only solution in his frazzled mind was to set a wedding date as soon as the duke would allow.

The next morning Nikolai sent word to the duke requesting an audience. He was shocked when he quickly received word back that the duke would receive him that afternoon. The response also carried an invitation for Nikolai, Alexi, and Olga to join the duke and his family for a luncheon.

This gathering ended up being torture for Nikolai. He so desperately wanted to discuss his and Tatianya's future with the duke. But the duke was in a festive mood and would not be rushed through the soiree. The duke then proposed a hunting expedition. Nikolai agreed but looked as if he would explode. The duchess chided the duke who smiled at Nikolai for the first time. Nikolai returned the smile amid his confusion. The duke stated that perhaps he and Nikolai should first attend to business. The hunting could wait. Nikolai was grateful for this turn of events. Just before leaving the room with the duke, Nikolai turned and found Tatianya's gaze upon him. She blew him a kiss. It gave him all the courage he needed.

The duke led Nikolai thru the grand palace, pointing out valuable art and portraits of ancestors long gone. Nikolai knew the duke's royal lineage but respectfully listened as his host named each predecessor; identifying their place in his family's impressive past. Beautifully painted vases, amber carvings, and exotic gifts from foreign dignitaries were nestled in the alcoves lining the expansive hall. Thick Turkish rugs muffled their footsteps as the duke led the way to his private sanctuary. It was apparent only those closest to him roamed here unencumbered. He paused as he watched Nikolai examine a large jade bowl. Its rich hue gleamed against the polished dark woods that soared into the upper reaches of this enclave. The duke studied Nikolai a little closer, remarking, "You have a cultivated eye." Nikolai chanced a smile, allowing his knowledge of the arts to be discovered.

Eventually, they made their way to the study. The duke silently poured each of them a cognac and handed one to Nikolai. "You look like you need one. I know I do." The duchess had instructed him to behave. "First I want to apologize to you. I had no reason to be so cruel when we first became acquainted. But it has helped me get to know you as a man of honor, one that has not wavered in his feelings for my daughter. I see how you two look at each other." The duke looked directly into Nikolai's expectant face, wanting to see his reaction to the coming statement, "It is no secret that you two have great passion for each other."

Nikolai was not ready for an apology from the duke. And he certainly was not ready to hear the duke had witnessed his little display during the ball last night. This completely rattled Nikolai to the core. He could not reply, much less meet a father's knowing gaze. The duke smiled and motioned for Nikolai to sit with him beside the fire. He was satisfied that he had unnerved Nikolai. The duke would now wait patiently while Nikolai collected his thoughts and attempted to persuade him to bestow Tatianya's hand.

Nikolai was horrified he had been discovered stepping over the line with Tatianya. He felt ashamed and unworthy. Momentarily he questioned if he should proceed. But when he looked up miserably at the duke and saw the kindness on his face, Nikolai felt he was no longer at war with the father of his intended. The duke looked sad, resigned, but strangely at peace. Nikolai steeled himself. He would ask for Tatianya's hand.

At first, his plea was tentative. "Your lordship, you must know by now how much I love your daughter...." Nikolai stumbled over his words. His normally commanding influence was nowhere to be found. He gazed around the duke's domain, fighting to regain his easy charm. Nikolai thought to himself," You fool, you are losing what little ground you have gained!" Instead of flourishes of undying love and promises to protect, silence filled the vacuum between a reluctant father and an anguished suitor.

The duke was not impressed and wondered at this sudden lack of conviction. On previous encounters, Nikolai's masterful ways had impressed the duke while also angering him. Nikolai gradually found his voice. He began in earnest to build his case that he would be the perfect match for Tatianya. "Your lordship, my love for Tatianya has taken my heart to a place I never dreamed existed. I never envisioned myself as one hopelessly obsessed with concern for the welfare of another. And yet, here I am, eager to lay down my life if it will shield her from even the faintest whisper of harm. Her happiness, her safety is all I think of night and day. It is true, I have behaved poorly at times in my shameful wild past. But from the moment Tatinyna's eyes illuminated my future, I can pledge without a doubt those days are over."

Nikolai continued to profess his love, his true self shining brightly, blinding the duke, "This all-encompassing need I have to give Tatianya anything her heart will ever desire is a destiny I pray you will see as mine. It would be my honor to ensure no tears will ever fall from those blue oceans by my or any other hand. No one will ever love her as I do. I swear to you, no harm will ever come to her under my care."

Just the mere mention of Tatianya's name made Nikolai's face light up. It touched the duke to see the extent of this devotion. It was what the duke had needed to see. It gave him the courage to place his treasure in another's care. He wanted someone who would fight for Tatianya, be able to defend and protect her at all personal cost. Duke Grigorii Yusopov ignored the fleeting wave of concern elicited by this promise to protect. He chose to squelch the warning simmering in the farthest reaches of his soul.

The duke finally agreed that this would be a good match and Tatianya's hand was given with one reservation. He wanted Nikolai to wait to marry Tatianya until she was 18. Nikolai hung his head and gloomily accepted this contingency, "Yes your lordship."

Already knowing the answer, the duke pointedly inquired, "What is your rush?"

Nikolai was brutally honest with the duke, "Your lordship, I fear my desire for your daughter has placed certain control beyond my grasp. I am ashamed to admit this flaw. I cannot promise I can wait that long to indulge my desire to lie in Tatianya's arms. I have never been in love before. I am now overwhelmed by what I have been denied all these years. I have not been with another since meeting Tatianya." Nikolai lowered his eyes. He quietly told the duke, "I no longer want my hands on anyone but Tatianya. As you saw last night, my ability to be honorable is slipping through my fingers. But you must also understand, she will never doubt my affections or feel betrayed."

Nikolai convinced the duke that he cherished Tatianya's virginity but as the duke had seen, he was having trouble controlling himself. He bemoaned his overwhelming desire. He felt ashamed of this shortcoming but if the duke wanted honesty, there it was.

The duke stood and looked out the window at Tatianya walking arm and arm with Olga, Alexi bringing up the rear. It touched his heart to see them loving Tatianya, drawing her into this new life. The duke smoothed his morning coat and turned to Nikolai. "She is very young despite her newfound womanly needs. She will also fight me on this and I have run out of reasons to keep you two apart. Promise me you will not rush her, not overwhelm her. Let her set the pace of your physicality. If she says no, respect it. If you can promise me this, you may marry on the date of her choosing." The duke then embraced Nikolai and welcomed him to the family. Alexi turned just in time to see this exchange. He smiled but did not draw the women's attention. He knew Nikolai would want to surprise Tatianya with his proposal.

The afternoon hunt was then arranged, but when Alexi mounted up, Nikolai was nowhere to be found. He looked over at the duke in puzzlement but then smiled as understanding dawned. Good thing Nikolai had brought the ring along. Alexi thought it had been presumptuous at the time but now silently admired Nikolai's confidence and courage.

Nikolai found Tatianya standing alone on the verandah watching as the hunting party rode off. She had become alarmed when she didn't see him. She was confused when she saw Alexi in the hunting party looking relaxed and enjoying the company of her father. She was startled when Nikolai came up behind her and encircled her waist with his strong protective arms.

"My love, may I entice you to stroll the gardens with your lovesick admirer?"

Tatianya began to call for her governess but Nikolai smiled wickedly. "This is just for us."

Nikolai had scattered rose petals on the floor of the gazebo. He could think of no better place to propose. As they walked arm in arm, Nikolai delighted in this familiarity. He knew he would cherish every second with Tatianya, no matter what the circumstance. As they approached the gazebo, she saw the floor had been strewn with rose petals. She exclaimed how beautiful but didn't comprehend the meaning. Nikolai was touched by her sweet reaction. He silently vowed to do his best to protect his fragile flower as long as he had breath.

As they climbed the stairs, he led her to the settee which sheltered them from prying eyes once again. When Tatianya beckoned him to join her on the settee, he reached into his pocket for the ring he had purchased for her tiny finger. He knew the stone was too large for her tiny hand but couldn't help himself. He wanted anyone who looked at her to know she was spoken for, that she already was someone's everything.

On bended knee, he gently took her hand in his and kissed each tiny perfect finger. He lovingly gazed into her eyes. It took her a moment to comprehend that her father had given his blessing.

"Tatianya my dear sweet little blue-eyed enchantress, you have bewitched me to the core. Since the day we met it has only been you. It will always only be you. I fell in love with you that first evening, right here in this very gazebo. I will always love and cherish you. I am yours forever. Tatianya, I pray you feel the same. It is my fondest wish that you consent to be my wife."

Unable to speak, Tatianya nodded her consent and watched as the huge diamond slipped perfectly onto her finger. Nikolai was awed as he saw how at home his ring looked, how right everything had turned out. She was now officially his intended. He allowed himself to kiss her. But this kiss was not that of passion. It was one of love and respect and promise. He knew now he could wait for her. He would have waited forever.

Tatianya broke the silence, "When Nikki when?" Nikolai was still reveling in the fact that the duke had agreed and that his ring was finally in its rightful place. He was adjusting to no longer worrying that she would be snatched away from under his watchful gaze. The weight of the world had just been lifted from his shoulders. He was lightheaded from the freedom this commitment was granting to his once wild and restless heart.

As she snuggled against her betrothed, Nikolai proceeded to describe in detail his meeting with her father. Tatianya blushed when he described admitting to her father that he was unsure how much longer he could wait.

Playfully, Tatianya walked her fingers up and down Nikolai's chest, "I think we should listen to my father. Waiting until I am 18 makes sense, don't you agree?"

Her sweetly angelic gaze, her wide-eyed conviction that the duke must be obeyed stopped Nikolai dead in his tracks. But when he saw the devilish glint seeping into her eyes, her lush full lips curving seductively, he knew she felt the same. True to his word, Nikolai gave Tatianya the option of setting the date. She thought only for a moment. She drew his face close to hers, her sweet breath making him dizzy with desire. Barely a whisper, she cooed "One month from today, my handsome hero."

Chapter Five:
The Wedding and
Wedding Night

Simultaneous frowns rained down upon their youngest as the duke and duchess heard Tatianya's wish to marry Nikolai within one month's time. She had no idea of the details that would need attention to pull off an event of this magnitude. Not to mention the speculation.

But Nikolai did. Sheepishly, he flashed that lovesick loopy smile. It had been worth a try. And the duke *had* said he would let them marry on the date of Tatianya's choosing. Seeing the depth of Nikolai's devotion and desire actually pleased the duke. In the end, a wedding date was set for three months' time.

Wanting to spend every waking moment with his intended, Nikolai took up residence in a nearby villa. He discovered that the palace could be reached by walking over a meadow that was alive with lavender during the summer months. As winter now approached, the meadow was barren and austere, the hushed tranquility holding a beauty all its own. Nikolai found the crisp turn in the air, the solitude, combined with the exertion of these daily treks did wonders to quiet the whispers of foreboding he couldn't seem to shake.

A nagging worry regarding Sergei was growing day by day. It was relentless, constant, casting a pall over his happiness. During the week following the ball, Sergei and his father had made frequent visits to the palace, demanding an explanation as to why the verbal agreement regarding a courtship between Tatianya and Sergei had been cast aside. Patiently but firmly the duke met time and again with Sergei and his father. At first, Nikolai feared that their arguments would reverse the duke's decision. Nikolai had to admit they had a point. A verbal agreement appeared to have been inferred, although Sergei had read far more into this than the duke had ever intended. It also was a source of contention that Nikolai had not officially courted Tatianya. The duke knew his stubbornness had prevented a courtship. He felt he could overlook this issue as he so chose. His house, his daughter, his rules.

The duke's support was a surprising source of comfort, but Nikolai found himself obsessing over Sergei's disappearance into the gardens that night after Tatianya's ball. As the duchess had warned, Tatianya was very loyal to Sergei, even if only as a friend. Sergei had refused to see the lack of sparkle in her eyes whenever her gaze had caressed his face. He was like a brother and would never have been more than that. Nikolai knew that Tatianya's ball had been a difficult humiliating night for Sergei. His finely tuned intuition cautioned him that a malicious force had preyed upon Sergei's vulnerable soul in the darkness, but why? And what did any of this have to do with his own future? He was forced to ignore his growing panic.

Tatianya was an immediate hit with Nikolai's family. His parents doted on her, constantly showering her with outrageously expensive trinkets and family heirlooms. His sisters had immediately taken her into their confidences, delirious that their only brother had chosen such a sweet soul. The duke and duchess were ecstatic that Tatianya's new family was as smitten with her as Nikolai. The duke felt more and more like a fool. How could he not have seen what a good man Nikolai was? He also did his best to banish that shroud of doubt.

Tatianya's and Nikolai's sisters were fast becoming inseparable. Tatianya had asked all of them and Olga to be attendants. They were ensconced for hours fretting over the smallest of wedding details. All the nieces and nephews in addition to Alexi's two children were also to take part. Tatianya could not have done anything dearer in Alexi's eyes than to include his shy wife in her celebration. It warmed his heart to see Olga smiling and laughing, excited about Nikolai's wedding. He felt everything was falling into place. The bliss of ignorance.

Both Nikolai and the duke lay down the law that Tatianya's wedding dress was to be exceedingly more discreet than her ball gown had been. The duchess smiled wickedly at Nikolai, readily agreeing. She was satisfied that the seductive detailing of the ball gown had done its duty. Nikolai made it known he had no desire for his wedding guests to be leering at the future mother of his children. He demanded a more innocent cut to the dress. He spoke in private with the duchess that he wanted the bodice to be very fitted as to dispel any lingering suspicions that the wedding had been planned in haste due to indiscretion. True to his word he was doing all within his power to protect Tatianya's innocence and reputation. The duchess grew more and more to love Nikolai. He was turning out to be exactly everything she could have wished for in a match for Tatianya. He almost seemed too good to be true.

Nikolai to all outward appearances was a very happy groom to be. But he was a virile man and that lingering sense of malice did nothing but heighten his need to possess his future. He found each time he and Tatianya managed to be alone, his self-control was failing him more and more. His kisses and embraces were becoming more urgent. He could no longer command his hands and mouth not to roam and explore in ways that were not appropriate for an unwed couple. Tatianya in her innocence was a willing party to these encounters, trusting in his judgment; certain this was acceptable behavior for a betrothed couple. So great was her trust in him, she had no idea how close he was to losing all control. It was only when she looked up at him with those trusting loving eyes that he could somehow muster a shred of composure. He desperately wanted to marry her as a virgin. He desperately wanted her first time to be perfect, not some out of control stolen moment, performed in hast and then laced with shame. No, he would wait, even as it was killing him.

On the long walks home after one of these stolen moments, Nikolai consoled himself that his restraint would be well rewarded. Tatianya appeared to be very much like her mother as Alexi had once teased. It was amazing to him that her responses to his advances were met with such abandon, with such instinctive knowledge. True, she had much to learn but from what he had been able to discern, she was a tigress just waiting to be unleashed. Coupled with those big innocent blue eyes, he knew he would never be able to touch another, much less love another. He was becoming more and more thankful that he was so much older. He knew he would not last a single day if she were to precede him in death.

As the wedding day drew near, Nikolai wanted to be certain that Sergei would not somehow spoil Tatianya's day. He spoke with the duke for the first time regarding this fear he had been harboring. The duke confessed he too had misgivings. He declined to admit that his misgivings were as much about Nikolai as they were about Sergei. It was decided that they would pay a visit to Sergei's residence.

As the two men made their excuses for the cause of their mysterious outing, Tatianya placed her tiny hand in Nikolai's. He could sense she was frightened. For the first time he confided the concern that Sergei could possibly cause a scene. She sat wide eyed in disbelief. She had been oblivious to Sergei's unrequited love.

"Would you have wanted the opportunity for his courtship?" Nikolai quietly asked, convinced his world was coming apart. He cursed his misstep in being so honest. But Tatianya quickly allayed his fears. It made her heart break to see him look so lost and uncertain.

"No, Nikki no! You are everything to me. I had no idea that Sergei felt any more for me than friendship. I never meant to encourage him or give him false hope."

It was now Nikolai's turn to console. "Angel, unprofessed affection cannot be accepted or rejected. We need assurance that he is coming to terms with the reality of the situation."

Tatianya nodded and leaned into him for a sensuous kiss. Just that quickly, Sergei was a distant thought in that curly blond head. She had no intention of wasting this opportunity for one of their magical trysts. It made Nikolai laugh to himself just how quickly Sergei had faded from her mind. He felt a twinge of remorse for Sergei. A twinge of panic for himself surfaced like an unwanted premonition. He hoped she would never be so dismissive of his affections.

Nikolai was unable to respond as he would have liked. "My love, your father is waiting. Tomorrow night will be ours." She sighed as she released the chokehold she had on his riding jacket. He bent and gently kissed the hand that wore his ring. He fought the urge to rip the pale peach satin gown from those alabaster shoulders.

Nikolai and the duke had been correct in their concerns regarding Sergei. He had become despondent, stirring unwanted reactions in Nikolai. He felt a kinship with the younger man. He knew he would have sunk to this depth of despair, probably worse, if he had not succeeded in winning Tatianya's hand.

The conversation was not as productive as Nikolai would have liked. Days of grieving for a lost love were drowning in what appeared to be reckless intoxication. Sergei's father revealed his son had taken to living in the shadows, refusing to meet the light of day, only consenting to short infrequent dialogue at odd hours of the night. Dining with the family was a thing of the past. It was like Sergei had died but continued to walk among the living.

Nikolai was able to get thru somewhat to Sergei. He encouraged Sergei to move on. He gently relayed to Sergei he had given Tatianya the opportunity to reverse their engagement, paving the way for a courtship with Sergei. It hurt to see the momentary flicker of hope that quickly receded into the safety of a surmised drunken haze.

Although there was no easy way to tell Sergei Tatianya had declined this offer, it seemed to be what he had needed to hear. Sergei let out a long sigh. He stated he knew he had been acting liking a child, pining for a lost love that had never been his to lose. He was ashamed of his sullen behavior. Nikolai understood Sergei more than he let on. Sergei stated he was not sure he could bear to attend the wedding. Nikolai merely nodded, resisting the urge to question Sergei about that night in the gardens.

Sergei and his father ended this encounter with a new respect for Nikolai. The duke silently wondered again at Nikolai's uncanny ability to time and again win over any foe. He cursed the gloom that refused to allow his instincts to really bless this union.

The anxiously awaited day had finally arrived. The duke and duchess were saddened that tonight their baby would no longer be under their care. Tonight, she would be a married woman on her way to a new life. Nikolai had planned an extensive honeymoon in Europe. They had received many invitations from royal households all over Europe. Friends from Nikolai's days at university had also rolled out the red carpet. Nikolai fully intended to accept any and all invitations. He wanted there to be no doubt he was the man in her life.

As evening shadows fell and candlelight filled the cathedral, Nikolai and his groomsmen took their places at the altar. Nikolai surveyed the assembled guests in search of Sergei. He made eye contact with Sergei's father who shook his head no. Nikolai felt a wave of concern but pushed it aside. This was their special moment in time and he refused to let anything or anyone ruin it. He wanted only Tatianya on his mind.

As the bridesmaids were preparing to make their way down the aisle, Sergei staggered into the cathedral. All eyes turned and gasped as they saw him approach the vestibule where Tatianya waited for her walk down the aisle. Nikolai bolted from the altar, Alexi at his side. He was furious. He couldn't believe Sergei was causing a scene. The bridesmaids blocked Nikolai from entering the waiting chamber, something about bad luck for him to see Tatianya. He thought this was a ridiculous wives' tale but their mounting panic made him relent. He anxiously watched them usher Alexi in and close the door.

Sergei had merely come to apologize. He didn't want Tatianya to walk down the aisle without her knowing that he was sorry for being irrational and childish. As Sergei left the room he came face to face with Nikolai. His breath held an odd odor Nikolai could not place. His eyes were bloodshot from lack of sleep and God knew what else. Tears stained his face. He shook his head and held up his hands to Nikolai, stating it had been difficult to see Tatianya in a wedding dress she was wearing for another man. Something was not quite right with Sergei. Nikolai sensed something far worse than lost love was stirring Sergei's soul. Nikolai had no choice but to push this ominous premonition aside. He watched as Sergei staggered out into the winter cold.

As the wedding march began to stream into the cathedral, all eyes turned to watch the bridal party making its way down the aisle. Tatianya had selected attendant dresses in various shades of blues and purples. Each bridesmaid looked beautiful and each admiring husband shone with pride as their wives took their places at the altar. After a moment's delay, Nikolai saw the duke and then Tatianya turn the corner. He watched with growing anticipation as they readied Tatianya's wedding gown for her walk down the aisle toward him, toward their future.

Even from the back of the cathedral, he could see the dress was everything he had hoped. The bodice was tightly fitted, immediately dispelling any thoughts of indiscretion. The gown was heavy with pearls and lace. Her face was covered by the veil. Blond curls cascaded around her shoulders. The effect was more of innocence and promise than sophistication. Nikolai was entranced as she regally made her way down the aisle. When the duke and Tatianya reached the altar, Nikolai stepped down to meet the pair. A teary-eyed duke slowly lifted the veil and carefully arranged it over Tatianya's shoulders. He gently placed Tatianya's tiny hand in Nikolai's much larger protective hand. It was then that Nikolai looked directly into Tatianya's eyes. They were shining brighter than ever. They were brimming with tears of happiness. She looked more beautiful every time he saw her but this; it was almost more than he could bear.

Time stood still. He devoured the moment. He wanted to savor every last detail. He was now able to see the rest of the dress. She had encircled her tiny waist with the same blue ribbon from the ball. The bodice was strapless but demure. His locket hung about her neck. Nikolai was thankful that the vision of his bride on her wedding day would be of innocence and purity. He was lost in her.

Nikolai eventually heard Alexi clearing his throat. He quickly came to his senses and carefully helped Tatianya take her place beside him at the altar. He caught a glimpse of Alexi smirking at his lovesick surrender to the moment. He didn't care. This was his wedding and he wasn't rushing it for anything. All the waiting for the days to pass now slowed and went out of focus. He barely remembered saying his vows.

Tatianya also was lost in the sight of the tall handsome protective man who had just been pronounced her husband. As he passionately kissed her and she responded, she too did not wish to rush anything. She wanted to savor each and every moment. Turning to face their gathered family and friends for the first time as husband and wife, their love was obvious. The darkly swarthy Nikolai towered over his diminutive, innocent bride. They struck a chord with the multitude. He would protect her with a vengeance. She would adore him with all her heart. She had captured the heart of this once wild, hard living man. He was gladly giving up that old life. He was ready. So unlikely was their match and yet all could see now that Nikolai had needed to wait for Tatianya. There had never been anyone else for either of them, their love was pure.

Their first dance as husband and wife was much the same as their first in the gazebo. Tatianya melted into Nikolai and he did nothing to stop her. He no longer required anyone's approval. The duke and duchess were proudly watching their dance. They appeared to be happy that the newly married couple was happy. It was all that mattered. Presently the duke and duchess made their way out to the dance floor and soon other couples joined in. The rest of the evening passed with much dancing and toasting. Champagne and cavier as far as the eye could see.

Sergei had been absent for most of the reception. When he finally did appear, it was obvious something was horribly wrong.

Alexi intercepted Sergei just outside the grand hall where the wedding festivities were still in full swing. The long shadows cast by the candlelight initially hid the disarray exuding from Sergei's countenance. Stepping closer, Alexi saw that Sergei's evening coat was splattered with blood. He was disheveled and one of his sleeves was ripped. His wrist was encircled by something Alexi had never seen. He surmised Sergei had somehow severely burned himself in a drunken stupor. It was encircled with a deep angry looking gash that would undoubtedly leave a nasty scar. It spoke of struggle. A desperate, other worldly life or death struggle. And yet there was a sinister quality to the way he now commanded attention, the curious tilt of his head as he fixated on Nikolai's bride.

"Sergei, what has happened....?"

He cut Alexi off mid-sentence, "Stay away, I am warning you. Step not one foot closer."

Sergei's appearance was shocking and obviously of no concern to him. He showed little interest in anything but satisfying his lust for another man's bride. Eyes so very black with desire, fixated on his prize. He leered at Tatianya who mercifully had her back to him.

Alexi met Sergei's steely gaze with one of his own.

"Now I am warning you, step not one foot closer. Do not mar this evening....."

Again, Sergei cut Alexi off mid-sentence, sneering, stepping ever closer with a malice Alexi had never witnessed. "Do you really think you are a match for me?" The smell of blood, of death were laced with the taint of desire. An eternity ticked slowly by, neither making a move to further ignite an already volatile situation.

Coming face to face with Alexi, Sergei found his desire to possess evaporating. Seeing Tatianya just inside the ballroom, Nikolai tenderly coaxing a wayward curl back into place, deflated his desire. His need to escape overcame. Scornfully he hissed, "This is far from over." Sergei vanished once again into the shadows, leaving an uneasy trace of foreboding in his wake.

Nikolai was seething. He had witnessed the brief but intense exchange between Alexi and Sergei. He knew what Sergei was thinking, wishing he had laid claim to Tatianya's bed. He fought to stay calm. Nothing would ruin this day for his angel. Sergei's desire for his bride made Nikolai suddenly anxious to shut out the world and love her the way she deserved to be loved. He was no longer interested in prolonging the wedding festivities. He signaled to the duke it was time for them to say their farewell.

Arm and arm they ascended the grand staircase. Nikolai's gaze sought out Alexi. As their eyes met, Alexi raised his champagne flute in a silent toast to the battles waged and victories won on these stairs. They knew how very different things had been for Nikolai in this very room not so long ago. It was where he had managed to stun the ruling class of Russia with his undisguised longing. It was where Tatianya had collapsed after weeks of despondency. And now these stairs were leading Nikolai to his heaven on earth. They chose to ignore the obvious question of what had happened to Sergei. Ugliness had no place in this candlelit evening.

Approaching the door to their wedding suite, Nikolai scooped Tatianya into his arms as she gaily laughed, blissfully enthralled with her handsome powerful husband. Now in the quiet shadows of the darkened hallway, alone, he kissed her with a roughness that sent shivers down her spine. She knew her sheltered life was over. Wherever Nikolai went and whatever he did, it was always at a fever pitch. In her innocence, it never occurred to her to question what it was about her that rocked him to his core, causing him to pursue her with the same unrelenting abandon contained in this kiss. He continued to kiss her, making her weak with longing.

He kicked open the bedchamber door. He slammed it shut, overwhelming desire making it impossible to wait any longer to possess his bride. He didn't care anymore what anyone thought. She was his. He would lock out the rest of the world as he claimed her, finally.

Tatianya's governess jumped with a start as they came crashing into the room. Nikolai fought to regain his composure, cursing her presence. What the hell was she doing here? He gently set Tatianya down and the governess began to help her undress. Nikolai poured them all some champagne. He forced himself to luxuriate in a chaise by the fire. He became entranced, watching each layer of the wedding dress fall away.

The governess was unnerved by Nikolai's intense scrutiny and suggested he attend to his own toilet. He ignored her suggestion, rousing himself out of the chaise. He tersely bade the governess good night. She was disconcerted and began to protest that she had not completed her evening tasks. Nikolai grasped her gently but firmly by the shoulders and ushered her towards the door. He handed her a second glass of champagne and suggested she go enjoy the remainder of the reception. Nikolai's piercing gaze silenced her protests. He would finish undressing his bride alone.

Tatianya waited patiently for Nikolai to turn her way. At first, he merely stood in front of her. His heated gaze caused that now all too familiar aching desire to swell. Nikolai could smell her passion mounting, coaxing him to love her. But he resisted the urge to force their union. Instead, he allowed his eyes to feast on her partially exposed breasts. At last, he reached out, a tentative caress barely grazing her slightly parted lips. He smiled, thrilled to know only he would ever satisfy this fire he was building.

Slowly he allowed his caress to fall away from those beautiful lips, begging for his kiss. He began to trace a finger along the fall of her breast, allowing his caress to become more demanding.

Tatianya let her head fall back and closed her eyes. Nikolai then traced a finger around her waist as he reached for the back of her dress to finish undoing the intricate fastenings. Slowly he undid each one as he alternately kissed her neck and caressed her breasts, delighting in the feel of her hardening nipples.

When all was free, he let the last of the undergarments slip thru his fingers. In the candlelight he took in her full beauty for the first time. As their eyes met, he saw a touch of fear. He cursed his hunger, forcing himself to recover a remnant of restraint. He needed to go slowly tonight. He hoped he could.

He turned his attention to the negligee the governess had eyed as he had all but pushed her out into the hall. The governess had feared he would overwhelm Tatianya and spoil this moment. But as much as he was on fire, he was no fool. He led her naked vulnerable figure to the bed and picked up the nightgown. Relief flooded Tatianya's face. Although she was on fire, she was petrified of the unknown.

Nikolai gently bent to kiss her face, her neck. For the first time he allowed himself to gently suckle her breast. She moaned much as she had done during their dance at her ball. The negligee fell to the floor. Nikolai hesitated for a moment and then saw she no longer looked as frightened. While still suckling, he allowed a hand to drift and tenderly caress the soft blond hair between her legs. She gasped and he pulled back. Anxiously he scanned her face, "Too much?"

Nikolai slowed his pace. He had forever now to love her and needed to do this right. He picked up the nightgown and silently slipped it into place. Tatianya looked very surprised. "Why did you stop Nikki? Am I doing something wrong?" He sat her down on their wedding bed. He knelt in front of her and laid his head in her lap. She ran her fingers thru his dark waves. "No, my love, you are doing every right. I vowed not to rush this moment.

I know this is your first time and I want it to be perfect for you. I want you to always want me as you do tonight. We will go at your pace, well, as long as I can stand it." His understanding smile and devilish wink made her laugh. He had succeeded in breaking the tension.

Silently he stood and began to take off his wedding suit. He saw her eyes grow large with curiosity. This made him laugh. "I hope you are not disappointed." he teased which made her blush. She threw a pillow in mock exasperation. He was glad to see she was relaxing.

He stopped after removing only his coat and shirt. He gently picked her up and settled her on his lap in front of the fire. He fed her strawberries that had been dipped in chocolate. She sipped champagne, relaxing her enough to allow her natural curiosity to take over. Tentatively she took in his arms and shoulders, muscles bulging from the protective embrace that nestled her to him. She traced a shy finger over his shoulder and down into his dark nest of chest hair. She twirled her fingers into it, the feel and the smell of him being etched into her mind. It made him ache thinking of how she had twirled the blue sash around her finger that first night in the gazebo.

"What are you thinking my love?" She looked up at him with those deep blue pools in awe. "I never saw a man like this before." He laughed, "Well I should hope not!" She looked right into his soul, "I never saw anything so beautiful in my life." She let a single tear escape as he tightened his embrace, resting his head on hers. "It is I who have never seen anything so beautiful. I waited so long for you. I thought I would never find love. Promise me you won't ever leave me. I wouldn't want to live without you, without this."

As the fire danced and crackled in the exquisitely carved marble fireplace, she reached up to wrap her arms around his neck. "Love me Nikki", she murmured. He had waited for her to be ready. She had understood his nurturing, his patience. She was now ready to be a woman, to be a wife.

Nikolai carried Tatianya to her wedding bed, laying her among the pillows. He ran his fingers thru her tresses. He had scattered rose petals earlier in the day on the bed, their scent now reminding them both of the gazebo. He loosened her negligee but did not remove it. Thru the garment he could see her nipples straining for his touch. He gently kissed them thru the gossamer fabric. He slowly slid his hand beneath the gown's hem. He sought out the soft blond hair between her legs that now belonged to him. Despite her yearning for him, he felt a remnant of tension in her young body. He replaced the gown and lovingly caressed her face, wide eyed with anticipation.

Dropping the last of his garments, he came to face her. Standing by their bed, just close enough for her to reach out for him, he waited. Hesitantly, she allowed her gaze to take in his physique. Slowly she let her eyes wander over his broad shoulders. She reached out to caress the hair on his chest. She traced the hair down to his waist. Momentarily she stopped to sip the champagne he handed her. Nikolai then took the glass from her hand which had become unsteady. After looking up into his face she shyly beheld his manhood which was full and ripe for love. She said nothing but slowly allowed her hand to continue its journey. She tentatively allowed herself to trace his generous shaft that was now aching for her to receive him. Her feathery touch caused Nikolai to gasp. He could no longer control himself. He crushed her into the pillows rougher than he intended. He tore the nightgown from her shoulders. He spread her legs, settling himself at the gates of his heaven. And then he stopped.

He slowed his breathing and looked deep into her eyes which were now wild and unfocused from desire. He began to sensuously kiss her lips and breasts. His hands and mouth drifted into the soft hair between her legs. She gasped and Nikolai froze. His eyes sought hers. He saw her gasp was from pleasure and not pain or fear. He settled himself over her and met her eyes. He found they were pleading for his love. Nikolai wanted to drive deep into her core, but still he resisted. He knew once over the edge, control and restraint would be elusive. He needed her to be beyond her desire. This had to be everything he wanted it to be for her.

The months of anticipation and fear of not ever reaching this moment came crashing down around him. Nikolai found he could wait no longer. He possessed Tatianya with a fever and in one swift movement he was deep within, thrusting with abandon. He had planned to go slowly but desire to lay claim proved too strong. Instinctively, Tatianya wrapped her legs around him, inviting him deeper into his heaven. She screamed his name as he continued to move against her, over her, within her. He wondered what she was thinking. He prayed his violent thrusting wouldn't ruin future encounters. But he was no longer in control. And neither was she. She propelled her hips against his until he exploded deep within as she also crested and shuddered.

For a moment neither of them moved. He was still deep within her, wanting to remain there forever. Nikolai was afraid to look at Tatianya for her reaction. She seemed to have been able to accept his loving, but he now cursed his roughness, his abandon.

When their eyes finally met, Tatianya looked frightened, confused. Nikolai immediately withdrew and held her protectively. When he looked down at her again, she looked so small and fragile. Nikolai couldn't take it anymore and finally spoke, "What is wrong my love, did I hurt you?" Tatianya shook her head and very meekly asked "Did I do it right?" Nikolai realized she was unsure of her sexual prowess. He let out a sigh of relief and offered a very shaky smile, "Better than you know. *Everything* you do is right." With that Tatianya looked up at him and slyly smiled. She brought his face close to hers and whispered, "Let's do that again."

Over and over, they soared to new heights, he with the need to release the love that had been pent up for months, she with the need to accept his love. In the small hours of the morning, the excitement overcame her fragile body. She fought to stay awake but was unable. Nikolai was wired from all of the months of worry, of denial, and had no need for sleep. He lay against the pillows, settling her on his chest, her fingers wrapped in his chest hair. Her legs were draped around him, her curls enveloping him in her cocoon. As he cherished the rise and fall of her slumber, heart to beating heart, he kept his vigil, guarding this sweet angel who in such a short time had become the center of his universe.

As night gave way to morning, Tatianya stirred, stretching over her lover with cat like reflexes, purring with satisfaction. Silently she reached out to pull his face to hers. His own desire had stirred long before she had awoken. He was hers for the taking, forever. He laid her back among the pillows and drove deeply, possessing all she had to offer. Although they had loved only hours before, he felt it had been an eternity. He was shocked at his insatiable craving for her, his roughness born out of needing to stake his claim. He silently prayed she would understand this love, so desperate it would break him should she ever turn away. He was grateful that as he scanned her face, her eyes, he could see she understood. This primal instinctive loving he offered answered any doubts she may have had about his past. She knew she was his present, his future. He knew he could unleash his love. He knew it was what she desired. No one would have ever suspected her need rivaled his.

As much as it pained him to leave her wedding bed, Nikolai roused himself to bathe and dress for the coming day. He had hated to wash her scent away. Over the past few months Nikolai had not spent as much time on his businesses as he knew he should, taking advantage of Alexi's offers of support while he had alternated between wallowing in self-pity and waging the battle of his life. Now as he prepared to be away for weeks, he called for Alexi and his father to discuss last minute details and to again review his business plans. Tatianya's governess, anxious to see for herself how her charge had fared last night, tentatively entered the parlor of their chambers, under the guise of needing to help Tatianya dress and bathe for the coming day. Nikolai was impatient with this intrusion. His sweet wife slept peacefully in his bed, exhausted by her journey from child to woman. As his wedding night had released the months of denial and had been perfect for Tatianya, Nikolai was more pliable than usual. Nikolai was moved by the governess' true concern and relented.

Touching a finger to his lips demanding her silence, he allowed her to steal a peek of the sleeping angel. With a raised eyebrow he sarcastically whispered in the governess' ear, "Satisfied that I did not kill her? You may relay that she survived." The governess' face colored as her mission had been so easily discovered. Nikolai merely laughed. He had seen this all before when his sisters had married. It was a harmless curiosity that he would indulge. Soon enough he would be in total control of his wife as they left for Europe. He was more certain than ever he had made the right decision to build Tatianya her own home. He would have forever been subjected to these unwanted intrusions residing within his father's estate. Under his own roof he would lay down the law that suited him and no one else.

While waiting for his father and Alexi, Nikolai pulled a chaise alongside their bed. He wanted to be near her, but knew she was exhausted. He would let her sleep as long as she needed. He wrapped a wayward blonde tendril around a humbled protective finger.

Nikolai heard Alexi's familiar rap upon their door. As he had no wish to disturb her repose, he closed their bedroom door and beckoned Alexi to join him by the fire. Alexi's face was as curious as the governess', but this was one intrusion he would not mind. "Well, you look much happier than you have in months." Alexi began his good-natured kidding. "Tell me, is she as we had suspected? Is she her mother's daughter?" Alexi had always closely guarded Olga's secrets from all but Nikolai. Nikolai could not help but beam. "Her mother's daughter and then some." Alexi let out a low whistle which prompted Nikolai to give him a shove. "Ahh, the lion has been tamed by a lamb", Alexi continued to tease. Nikolai retorted, "Shh, she is still sleeping you imbecile."

The two friends peeked inside to where Tatianya slumbered. Alexi stood by as Nikolai gazed upon his universe. Both friends became silent, grateful that Nikolai had prevailed. "She really is beautiful. I doubt she even knows just how beautiful she is Nikolai.... Hard to believe she fell for you." Nikolai raised an eyebrow, "I could say the same about Olga." Alexi draped an arm over Nikolai's shoulder "Touché, dear friend, touché."

When Nikolai's father joined them, he also stole a quick glance at his young daughter in law. He hugged Nikolai when he saw the peace on her face, the look of care and tenderness on his son. He had all but given up on Nikolai finding a match, let alone love. As always, Nikolai had followed his path. It had been a long road, but he had held out and, in the end, had triumphed. Not wanting to disturb her rest, but needing to keep an eye out, Nikolai positioned himself so that he could steal glances of her while they dealt with the last-minute details. He thanked them both for their help, now and over the past few months. Both Alexi and Nikolai's father were more than happy to have offered their support. So many lives would benefit from him settling down, from him producing an heir.

As they were concluding their business, finalizing the details, Tatianya cried out in terror, "Nikki!" The panic in her voice made all three men jump to their feet. She was sitting against the pillows, only her blond tresses covering her breasts. As their eyes met, with horror on her face, Tatianya pointed to the balcony doors not visible from where Nikolai had been sitting. They had heard nothing. Nikolai had felt she was safe within the confines of her wedding bed. As Nikolai threw open the bedchamber door, they were shocked to see Sergei at the side of the bed barely inches from Tatianya. He was feasting his eyes on the sight of her, laying there among the bedding that had been tangled in the throes of loving. He had somehow scaled the palace walls and gained entry to this sanctuary that had been denied to him. In her innocence, Tatianya had sat up upon discovering Sergei sitting in the chaise watching her sleep. She had forgotten that she was naked from her wedding night of loving. Even now with 4 grown men in her bed chambers, she made no move to modesty. Nikolai went to his bride, pulling the coverlet around her shoulders. When she realized she was still naked, she was horrified and began to sob into his jacket. Sergei had initially frightened her. He had now also succeeded in humiliating her, making her feel like a child just as she had begun reveling in her womanhood.

It was clear something was very wrong with Sergei. Darkness pervaded his countenance. He kept his face to the shadows; a hooded cape obscured his face. He had not been able to accept her refusal of him. He had come with the intention of claiming what he had always thought would be his to dominate. Sergei sneered at Nikolai embracing his bride, "Well, well, it looks like you have done a superb job of breaking her in for me. So thoughtful. Virgins, such a bother don't you think? Come here you little tease. My turn." Alexi viciously punched Sergei, knocking him out. Nikolai stroked Tatianya's face relieved that she had escaped this intrusion unharmed. He watched Alexi and his father drag Sergei's limp body out of sight. Alexi kept Sergei's face shrouded. His brief interlude with Alexi the night before made him cringe, dread looking into that face again, the smell of death still so very evident.

Not wanting to upset the entire household, Nikolai's father quietly summoned the duke. Together they hurried to a far corner of the palace as Nikolai's father detailed Sergei's treachery. When he saw Sergei sprawled on the floor, he became furious. The duchess and Nikolai's mother had sensed the tension and joined their husbands. Alexi assured them Sergei had not had time to force himself where he had never been wanted. They hurried thru the palace, frantic to confirm that Tatianya was unharmed. They knocked on the door of Tatianya's and Nikolai's wedding suite. Nikolai opened the door, anger darkening his face. Nikolai could not help but remember all those times he had come to the palace formally requesting the smallest amount of time with his beloved, bearing gifts that had been rejected. He felt violated that his honest, proper intentions had been denied while this monster had freely reigned.

By now Nikolai had helped Tatianya into a dressing gown but her tears continued to flow. Nikolai was furious that his plans to cradle her in nothing but love and safety had been destroyed, in her wedding bed. He felt a failure as a protector. He had Tatianya possessively tucked within his embrace. His eyes were wild with hate, contemplating vengeance. Tatianya did not fully understand how close she had come to an assault. She could not comprehend that Sergei had meant her harm. But as the anger boiled over in Nikolai and the two mothers were overcome, the realization dawned on her.

She turned to face Nikolai, "I am sorry. Maybe I am too young for you, for marriage." Tatianya was sobbing uncontrollably, bordering on hysteria, holding her face in her hands. Nikolai was now beyond reason. Sergei had not succeeded in violating Tatianya physically, but he had violated them both mentally, her soul now poised to shut him out. Nikolai's mother and the duchess motioned for him to calm down. Her words had been said out of embarrassment.

Nikolai's mother knelt beside her mortified daughter in law. "Sweetheart, you did nothing wrong. Don't let a weak person like Sergei destroy your happiness. Didn't you have a beautiful wedding?" Tatianya nodded, her large blue pools looking deeply into her mother in law's eyes, the older woman now finally understanding the depth of the hold Tatianya had on her son. "Didn't you have a beautiful wedding night with your loving husband?" Again, Tatianya nodded, a small smile fleetingly trailed across her face. "Well, my little love, hold onto that. No one would have reacted any differently. You poor thing. Come and give me a hug. There, there, that is better, no? How about a nice hot bath?"

Nikolai knew his mother had always had a way of handling disasters. He looked up at her now with the love a son has only for his mother. He hadn't needed her help in a long time. She bent down and kissed his dark waves. "We will leave you and Tatianya now to continue your honeymoon preparations. Do not give another thought to anything but your love. Nikolai, we will deal with the problem. Give your mother a smile and maybe another grandchild?" The duchess watched this exchange in silence. It was clear now where Nikolai got his strength.

When Nikolai and Tatianya were alone again, he held her face in his hands. "Did you mean what you said? Do you not feel ready for love, for marriage, for me?' His voice cracked with sadness that she had been robbed of some of her innocence, under his care. "I won't hold you to our marriage if you have changed your mind." His head was in her lap, his gentle hands encircled her hips, his tears staining her dressing gown. Tatianya was running her fingers thru his luxurious mane. Why had she said that? She was overwhelmed, the child in her struggling for what a woman would say. She knew she would never want another; she knew last night had felt so right. But the words would not come and so she sat in silence, running her fingers urgently thru his hair.

Her silence was deafening to him. He forced himself to look up into her pools. As she was making no move to free herself of him, of their marriage, he held onto the smallest hope that she still was his. "Tatianya you have to tell me what you want me to do. I will do anything for you, even if it means leaving you. For God's sake, please speak to me." Try as she may, no words would come. As her thoughts could not speak for her, she knelt down beside him, kissing his face. Gone was the confidence she had gained last night. Once more she was the small figure standing by his horse, sweetly bestowing the small bouquet bound by her blue sash. Their first kiss had been tentative, innocent. Now again she was unsure. But she had to try to reach him, let him see her heart.

Nikolai saw she was throwing him a lifeline. He grabbed hold of it with all his might. He lifted her into his arms and settled her on their wedding bed. They would not stay another night but he needed to love her. He needed to know she still wanted him as she did last night. He had to erase the memory of Sergei leering at her naked vulnerability in this very room where she had lost her virginity. He would replace ugliness with love. He had to know if she was completely his. He would have her no other way.

As he slowly began to loosen the dressing gown, making his intentions known, he peered deep into her eyes. He saw love, he saw pain but he also saw relief. "Tatianya, your innocence is something I cherish. It is not a weakness. Do not feel humiliated that you do not have a mind for deception."

As his words filled her heart and mind with love, she felt an aching for him to fill her body with his love. She kissed him with more assurance now. It took so little to ignite his need. His body was screaming for her but his mind was screaming louder to rebuild her trust. Slowly he caressed her, removing her dressing gown as she moved closer to him, exploring. He had already dressed for their travels but tore himself free from these constraints.

He held her gently. He wanted to impress upon her that he would never stoop to the depths that Sergei had. He gave silent thanks that he had won her hand. He could see now that her life under Sergei's roof would have been an unhappy one.

Lost in his thoughts he barely heard her whisper. "Love me." They had been lying on the bed as they had last night while she had slumbered on his chest. She had her fingers entwined in his chest hair. This small gesture, so new and yet now so familiar, let him know she was his. As she lay there straddling him, her blond curls caressed his face. She sat up to meet his gaze. He raised her hips and drove himself deep. She gasped as he now moved to possess her completely. She arched her back and held her hair in her hands, forcing it to cascade down her back. He feasted on the sight of her. As his caress of her hips became more possessive, he drove further and more forcefully deep into her core. She accepted his loving, driving all thoughts of Sergei from her mind. He would ensure no one else would ever enter her mind, her soul, her body. As she crested, he allowed himself to explode within her sweetness. He had righted his world. He had secured his place in her heart, her life.

Nikolai pulled her down to his chest, remaining deep within. Gone was her uncertainty. He was relieved they had weathered their first hurdle as man and wife. He knew there would be many. He had just not expected it to happen so quickly and with so much potential for disaster. "How about that bath now my love?" Tatianya looked up at him. "Will you bathe me?"

As she lowered herself into the steaming waters, rose petals scenting the air, Nikolai gently sponged her fragile shoulders. She looked so calm and peaceful; he couldn't resist. For the second time today he disrobed, need overcoming reason. She had been lulled by the waters, the scent of roses and had drifted off. She had not heard his clothing dropping to the floor. As she opened her eyes with a start, she felt Nikolai entering the bath. His manhood throbbed for her. She caressed him, causing him to moan her name. He pulled her to him not caring that water was splashing, soaking his travel clothes. "If we don't stop this we will never get to France, Nikki." Unable to think or speak, he kissed her, demanding she claim his passion. Regaining his composure, he suckled a rose scented breast, grateful that she was again his angel, trusting in him fully. "France can wait. As far as I can tell it's not going anywhere." She giggled and he arched an eyebrow in playful reproach. She felt emboldened, her confidence soaring once more. "Teach me Nikki." He stroked her contented face. "I will. We have time. Just promise you won't ever leave me."

For the third time today, Nikolai dressed. "Maybe I will make it out of this room sometime today" he wryly thought to himself. Tatianya's governess had helped her dress. In light of this morning's ugliness with Sergei, the duke had released the governess to accompany them on their honeymoon. Nikolai only relented and accepted this unwanted burden when the duke had agreed to his total control over the governess who would now function as a lady in waiting. Nikolai insisted that under no circumstances would she contact the duke or duchess. He had already assured them he would be in contact and that would have to be enough.

Nikolai adjusted Tatianya's bonnet which echoed the color of her eyes. He was overcome knowing he had almost lost her already so many times. This would have to stop. He placed the muff over her delicate hands and smoothed the velvet lapels of her travel suit. Tatianya stood at the threshold to their honeymoon suite, gazing around the room, gazing at the bed which held the secrets to her lost virginity. Nikolai smirked and pretended to be taking his jacket off for another passion driven encounter. Tatianya giggled, they both knew they had to be on their way. They had raised enough eyebrows for one day.

Alexi had been sent up to see what was delaying their departure. He hoped they were fully clothed. They were but Nikolai was embracing Tatianya, flexed muscles visible thru his jacket. Alexi took Tatianya by the shoulders and whirled her around. "You are going to have to learn to say no to him!" Tatianya now in a playful mood, flashed her baby blues at Alexi. With a naughty look, she said "Maybe I don't want to!" Alexi was dumbfounded. He hadn't seen this side of her yet. Maybe she wasn't such a baby after all. "You've been warned!" He joked with her.

Nikolai was happy to see his wife and best friend finding their way with each other. He had hoped she would find common ground with his friends but had worried about the age difference. He had suspected she could hold her own.

As they made ready to leave their sanctuary, Tatianya reached up to encircle Nikolai's neck. "Carry me Nikki." Last night she had been carried over this threshold as a wife but still a child. Today she wanted to be carried back over as a woman. Alexi felt awestruck watching her unabashed love for his friend. Her innocence kept her from worrying about what some might think. It freed her to love and be loved. He thought to himself he could take some lessons from this baby. Humbly Nikolai picked her up. He had carried her over the threshold last night in the throes of passion. Today he was carrying her over with renewed promises to cherish and protect.

As Nikolai carried his bride down the stairs, Tatianya's sisters tore her from his arms, showering her with kisses and tears. Her mother looked deep into her eyes and found the peace and happiness that had been there since their engagement restored. She was relieved to see no traces of Sergei causing concern. What a blessing to be so innocent her mother mused. Tatianya had simply trusted her husband and left the unpleasantness behind. The duke hung back until the sisters were done with their hugs and kisses. He finally took Tatianya's face in his hands. "Are you happy, really happy?" She looked up at her father and then stole a glance at Nikolai. Solemnly she nodded and then whispered, "I will bring you another grandchild, father." The duke was shocked at this and her sisters screamed with laughter, hugging her tightly. "Maybe you already are!" The duchess hugged her husband, knowing he was having trouble letting go. Thinking of his baby carrying her own child was more than his poor heart could handle. As Nikolai turned in alarm at hearing the screaming, he saw the duchess caressing the duke. He was glad she was being attentive to him. He had no idea what the commotion was about, but he didn't really care. He also had sisters and they were always screaming about something. He just saw that his wife was contented which contented him.

As Nikolai's family embraced him, there was no screaming. Alexi, Olga and his larger circle of friends were wishing the newlyweds well but their eyes did not match their gaiety. Nikolai never asked how or who but he sensed from their somber undertones that Sergei would no longer be an issue for Tatianya or any other woman for that matter. Not wanting to tarnish his happiness, Nikolai fought the urge to demand the morbid details of Sergei's demise. Deep in his soul he knew he should have been the one to silence Sergei's demons. He knew he should have secured his future, stained his hands with the blood of this monster. But his family and friends did not want his new life tainted and in a rare moment of weakness he acquiesced to their well-intended meddling. Just for a moment, Nikolai had veered from his path. He turned from the dark cloud of doubt that was welling in his soul. He turned a blind eye to the truth. He knew a misstep had been taken. He knew a mistake had been made. He clung to the hope it was not fatal.

Nikolai drew his mother aside. He kissed her cheek, calling her mama, something he hadn't done in a very long time. He had grown up so fast, she had felt cheated. "Mama I love you. Thank you for what you did for Tatianya this morning. And for me. I thought I was losing her." Nikolai's mother was touched, she had so much she wanted to say, the words now suddenly choked by emotion. She held his face. It was rare that he allowed his family this opportunity to touch his soul. His cold calculating cunning so engrained into him over the years had made it difficult to reach him and she had contented herself with what he could offer. Thru her tears she managed to whisper, "Be happy. Love her. Her innocence is good medicine for you." She hesitated but then allowed a sly smile to broaden, "Bring me a grandchild and your father his heir!" Nikolai let his head rest on hers. It felt good to let go of the past. It was a relief to now have someone where he could safely let his guard down. He knew he could always melt into Tatianya, no matter what the situation. His businesses had made him cold and hard. His inability to find love over the years had also strengthened that unyielding exterior. He thanked God he had led him to Tatianya. He thanked God he had been able to let her in. He prayed to God the ugliness with Sergei was truly behind them......

Something told him otherwise.

Chapter Six:
The Honeymoon and
Nikolai's Second Misstep

Tatianya was finding her new husband to be full of surprises. It amused her to watch the wheels constantly spinning in that complicated mind of his. She knew she had a tiger by the tail. She loved his boundless energy, the way he went after what he wanted. Just looking at him gave her goosebumps.

Ever on the prowl for an opportunity, Nikolai shrewdly saw their honeymoon as a chance to give some much-needed attention to his business ventures abroad while showing off his bride. Tatianya didn't care what they did or where they went, just as long as they were together. Although much younger than all of his associates and their wives or mistresses, Tatianya's aristocratic upbringing served her well. Her manners were impeccable. She was an avid listener. She showed true interest, asking questions when she felt confident. Her youth was obvious, but she was able to enchant effortlessly.

She seemed to enjoy these meetings which always took place at a grand estate. Growing up the daughter of a duke, she was accustomed to the finer things. She appreciated luxury but did not lose composure, gawking at grandeur. In truth, most of Nikolai's associates were impressed with the simple fact that Tatianya was the daughter of a duke. It helped smooth over a lot of questions or mockery of Nikolai for taking a baby for a bride. Just as Alexi had seen, Tatianya was young but not stupid. She had a quick wit and an easy laugh. In her innocence, Tatianya would be distracting, giving Nikolai the edge.

Not all of Nikolai's meetings included Tatianya. He grudgingly had to admit he was relieved to have brought along a companion for Tatianya. The incident with Sergei was never far from his mind. In strange surroundings when facing a particularly predatory business associate, he would shield her. These associates would none too kindly ridicule him about his choice for a wife. They would crudely joke about her sweet demeanor, insinuating that she hadn't much to offer a man with his needs. They assumed he was still afflicted with his restlessness and roving eye. He would smile, never giving away her secrets, letting them think what they wanted. It was only to his advantage that they were so off base regarding his bride. Nikolai would safely ensconce Tatianya and her former governess within the household of an aristocrat eager to entertain his effervescent glowing bride.

On occasions when he did decide to include her, Nikolai would dress his angel in blue. He would have her wear her hair in a simple cascade, delicately enveloping those alabaster shoulders. Her gown, her jewels would be of his choosing, as she always trusted him with these details. They would arrive just late enough to ensure a grand entrance, all eyes on the striking couple he knew they were. These fools would then be shocked to see his beloved, not such a baby after all. Jealously, they would stare, gallantly trying to recover, much to the annoyance of their dinner companions. Nikolai knew the devastation she could wreak, he being her truest victim.

But the small hours of the morning belonged to Tatianya and Tatianya alone. If an associate, longing to continue leering at his bride would suggest ways to defer their parting, Nikolai would chide them that they were on their honeymoon. Tatianya would reach out, making these predators feel special, cooing how they had torn themselves away to spend a few hours in their company. She would sweetly smile, big blue eyes carelessly disarming another foe. They would gracefully take their leave. They would depart; their victims awash in quandary. Tatianya's beguiling demeanor would give false hope that Nikolai had lost his edge. In truth, his cunning, his ruthlessness, his business acumen only seemed to be gaining momentum. The reality of the matter was that he now had a purpose in life, and it drove him to be his best.

Night after night she would set his world on fire, having an appetite for any and all of his fantasies. Although he felt more in control of his life, having total dominance now over her destiny, Nikolai had fallen prisoner to a burning desire to ensure she soared to higher and higher heights with him. As they crested over and over again, he didn't give a damn about anything but searching her eyes for that look of contentment. It was worse than an addiction.

Tatianya had taken to sleeping draped over Nikolai or tucked deep within his embrace. She was unable to sleep unless wrapped tightly in his arms. He slept only after she slumbered, drifting off to sleep, spent and sated by his all-consuming craving for his heaven on earth. He worried that he was too rough but the look of satisfaction on her face told him differently. No one would believe him if he had been lecherous enough to divulge her secrets. He would wake before she did, aching to love. He adored her responses to him, still drowsy in the early morning hours. He had yet to free himself of the worry that somehow, someday she would turn from him. It consoled and soothed his tortured mind that during these early morning trysts, barely awake, she would savagely cling to him. He would explode with abandon, his heart soaring, confident in her love, at least at that moment.

Most of the ruling houses in Europe had met Tatianya, many knowing her since childhood. All had tried in vain to secure a betrothal or at least a courtship for their aristocratic son. Some were pleased with her happiness. Others were frustrated that, even before the last note of the last waltz at her ball had sounded, Nikolai had snatched her for himself. Most felt cheated that this ray of sunshine was not to shine her lovelight on their son, bestowing them with a beautiful grandchild and an heir in the process.

It was quickly apparent that Nikolai's once wild and restless ways were gone. His roving eyes had finally found their home. It was a mystery to those who truly knew Nikolai that his love had come down for such a sweet soul. They marveled that this once selfish, hard-living man had become so concerned with another's needs. His calm, satisfied countenance led them to believe she must be a tigress. He did little if anything to hide his happiness. But he ferociously guarded her secrets. All could see this little aristocrat had him eating out of the palm of her delicate hand.

Tatianya enchanted young and old alike, one by one, with her kindness, her warmth, those infectious giggles. When visiting an aristocratic household, invariably there was an elderly relative, brought to the gathering but then discreetly settled into a corner of the room, cast aside as if they no longer had anything to offer. Tatianya would seek them out. She would sit with them holding their brittle, withered hands as they recounted their youth to her. They would reminisce about their own honeymoons. She would fuss over them, giggle at their oft-told and repeated jokes and stories. She would flash those baby blues, giving an old man once more the illusion of a woman's interest. If her confidant was a woman, her youth would bring them fond memories of when they had effortlessly turned a head. Tatianya had so easily conquered Nikolai. She was now doing the same, leaving a trail of wistful admirers.

Nikolai's friends also fell under her spell. Knowing him and his past inclinations, many had initially voiced concern about her age, about her being a child. Nikolai waited patiently for the moment his friends would look into his eyes, acknowledging what he already knew. As they left each household, all were smitten and understood the spell she unknowingly cast wherever she went. She wielded her innocence like a weapon. With great care Nikolai worked tirelessly to ensure nothing would jade her mind, dampen her spirit, causing a cynical streak to threaten his world. He had seen the effects of Sergei's assault on her delicate mind. He had no wish to ever again see misery replacing trust in the depths of her vast blue oceans. But he couldn't shake the feeling that their happiness was not secure.

Nikolai not only lavished physical love on Tatianya, but he also enjoyed spoiling her in any way he could. He spent wildly on jewelry. Each evening she would find an ornate box dressed with a satin ribbon on her pillow. She would look up at him, "Nikki, you don't have to do this." He would smile sheepishly, "I know, I want to." She would then giggle in anticipation and clap her hands as he slowly pulled the ribbon free of its moorings. With a flourish, he would place his unopened offering in her lap. She was finding being cherished and spoiled not the worst thing in the world. She was also finding she had a penchant for jewelry. Each evening after the latest bauble had been revealed and thousands of kisses bestowed, Nikolai would affix her newest treasure. If the piece was a jewel-encrusted hair clip, Tatianya would carelessly gather a handful of her gorgeous locks, securing the piece in a jumble of curls, looking stunning effortlessly.

Nikolai had undressed his bride on their wedding night which was now their custom. When the last garment had fallen from her frame, now clothed only in Nikolai's latest symbol of love, Tatianya would dance around the room, showing off her latest acquisition. Nikolai would lie naked on their bed, awestruck by his latest acquisition. Entranced, he would watch as the pale moonlight filtered thru the flimsy curtains billowing in the night air, caressing her youthful exuberance. Eventually, a devilish smile would descend. He would crook a finger in her direction, beckoning her to him. She would fly into his arms, smothering him, drowning him with her unbridled devotion.

During one of their outings to a palace in Paris, Tatianya had found yet another forgotten soul to cheer. Nikolai had smiled at the sight of her tenderly stroking the arm of an elderly gentleman. He had felt secure she was safely tucked away. A group of his comrades had gathered in the garden, enjoying a brandy in the crisp evening air. Tatianya seemed content with her companion and Nikolai saw no harm in slipping out to join this group. One member of the party had captured the spotlight although he had positioned himself in the shadows. Despite being the center of attention, this man had no desire to take the stage. Nikolai thought this odd. It rankled Nikolai that this man had accepted a snifter containing a rare and prized vintage of brandy, but made no move to imbibe. The stranger eyed the brandy, occasionally swirling the amber liquid as if longing to enjoy this luxury but was somehow unable.

This man, this creature, was describing in glowing detail the tremendous opportunities in America, specifically New Orleans. While business was a questionable topic for a gathering of gentlemen, this stranger was igniting interest in them all about bourgeoning ventures that would surely produce vast wealth.

Nikolai was always interested in a new business venture. He was always keen to hear an opportunist plead his case. But this man was different. He was not trying to obtain backing for a personal venture. He seemed content to merely spark curiosity.

Nikolai and this man eventually spoke. Slyly the man began discussing Mardi Gras, New Orleans, and the mysticisms that surround this exotic city. He became excited, almost agitated when he began to probe Nikolai's knowledge of the demonic underworld, specifically the landscape of the vampires and the gatherings they held on the eve of Mardi Gras. Nikolai responded that he did have some cursory knowledge of these demons. He had heard tales that these demonic beings held vast powers and were not to be taken lightly. But Nikolai went on to say most dismissed these tales as nothing more than fantasy.

The man laughed softly, almost to himself. "My friend I fear you have been led astray. I assure you; vampires are very real."

In a hushed tone, the man confided to Nikolai that just before Mardi Gras, the vampires of New Orleans host a gathering for a fortunate few in which they bestow something called a **Searing**. The man continued that in exchange for vast sums of money, the vampires could be coaxed to confer superior abilities. Nikolai was shocked at what he was hearing. He broke into laughter at the absurdity of this conversation. Nikolai could not resist the opportunity for debate, "So if these vampires are so powerful and fearsome, why have we never seen any evidence of their dominance?" Nikolai could see he had struck a nerve. The man's breathing was becoming rapid as his voice became strained, "So, you admit you have never been to New Orleans, never walked its darkened city streets on the eve of Mardi Gras. And yet here you are, a self-proclaimed expert. I had been led to believe you were a man of superior intelligence. What proof do you have that their influence is not at work? Perhaps you prefer to leave the truth unknown."

Nikolai was taken aback by this man's urgency to assure him of the vampires' existence. It piqued Nikolai's curiosity that this man seemed so certain that these beings truly existed, that they could be convinced to bestow superior abilities, albeit for a price. The man paused for a moment to gauge Nikolai's reaction to his staged outburst of indignation. The creature turned his head briefly in the direction of where Tatianya sat. In a voice that was somehow tinged with poignancy, he murmured, "Your lovely bride seems satisfied beyond all measure with her groom's abilities." Nikolai felt a wave of panic as this man had obviously been studying his wife. "How sad that you scoff at the powers of the vampires, that you dismiss an invitation to not only increase your business holdings but to also ensure no one could ever please your little angel like you currently seem able to do. Are you that certain of her affections?" Nikolai made no reply as a cold sweat began to trickle down his spine. That nagging worry that their happiness was in jeopardy blotted out all reason.

Nikolai's obsession with power and conquest had made him an easy target. This creature knew he had successfully planted the seed in Nikolai's mind that he would receive huge advantages from a single encounter with a demonic vampire. This man went on to assure Nikolai that the encounters, called **Searings**, were brief. He assured Nikolai that only a very small pinprick upon the wrist with a rose thorn followed by a quick **Searing** of the site was all that was required. The man cajoled Nikolai that surely a man of his strength and power would find this small discomfort of no consequence. "To someone such as yourself my friend the biggest inconvenience would be the vast sums of money you will need to part with for this privilege." Nikolai had a growing apprehension about this man, this idea. He wished he could have searched this man's eyes, his soul. There was something both familiar and foreboding. That voice, he could swear he had heard it before. Resolutely, this stranger remained in the shadows, despite numerous attempts to draw him out. He avoided attempts at further familiarity, ignoring requests to divulge his name. Nikolai thought it peculiar he could not remember seeing him at the dinner reception earlier. Silently the man drifted away from the group. Nikolai watched as the man abruptly became reclusive, craving solitude, letting the night close around him as he escaped into the deeper recesses of the gardens. Nikolai felt uneasy and made no move to follow. But he was mesmerized by the idea of heightened powers. And he suddenly felt insecure, wondering if he truly did rule Tatianya's world.

Despite a glorious honeymoon, Tatianya came home discouraged she had not conceived. Both of her sisters had come home glowing. Never for a moment did Tatinaya think it was not her destiny to follow in their footsteps. She was inconsolable when she bled periodically, sobbing she would never have a child. She would climb into her husband's lap who stroked her tears away, consoling all was not lost. But secretly, Nikolai was relieved. He just wasn't ready for the changes a baby brings. He had worked so long and hard to win Tatianya's hand. He just couldn't seem to get enough of her. And he was deathly afraid that an infant would change his perfect world.

About a week after returning home and settling into a routine, Nikolai paid Alexi a visit. Immediately Alexi saw the restlessness in Nikolai. He was stunned to see this so soon. He thought Nikolai had already tired of Tatianya. But Nikolai had other ideas which were even more of a shock.

"New Orleans? Are you mad? You just got home! What are you going to tell Tatianya?" It was now Nikolai's turn to be shocked. He quickly reassured Alexi regarding Tatianya. But he was a man who needed conquests. With a personal life more satisfying than he had ever dreamed, his energies were turning to business conquests. He explained that Tatianya would be accompanying him. He had no intention of ever missing one rapturous night in her arms. But he chose not to explain the siren's call to attend a gathering of the vampires that had made New Orleans their stronghold. He chose not to explain his fear of losing Tatianya's love.

Alexi never did understand this side of Nikolai, his longing for constant challenge. But he also knew that when Nikolai got around to discussing something, it was a foregone conclusion that they would be moving forward with his latest scheme. Alexi knew he never won these arguments, his protests only politely endured. He smiled indulgently at Nikolai. Some things change and some things remain the same. He was just grateful Tatianya had not been cast aside.

Nikolai had no success obtaining approval from either set of parents. He hadn't expected it. They all knew Nikolai no longer needed anyone's approval. It was merely a polite nod to deference. They had no real chance of winning any argument with him. Gone was his need to please the duke. Tatianya was now under his care, his protection, her future his to decide. Both fathers could see his mind was made up. Both men said very little except to voice their disappointment.

Tatianya was surprisingly ready for another adventure. It was difficult to be around her nieces and nephews. It only made her obsess about a baby all the more. Nikolai's fascination with the vampires' gatherings held a foreboding which he was choosing to ignore. The tales that an encounter with a vampire would heighten the senses, the abilities, became a silent obsession. He was already a successful businessman, a satisfying lover. He savored the idea of even more successes in both areas. He found it hard to believe he could derive any more pleasure from his loving with Tatianya, but the thought just wouldn't let him go. His mind screamed to abort this folly, be satisfied with his perfect, idyllic life. His soul screamed louder to reach New Orleans before Mardi Gras. He was powerless to fight this obsession. He wished he had never had that brandy in Paris, that conversation in the garden. Unaware of the subtle changes that stranger had ignited in his soul on that fateful night in Paris, the infection, the transformation had already begun.

Chapter Seven:
Separations of Death
and Distance

Nikolai wasted little time arranging for their passage to New Orleans. He had every intention of attending the vampiric annual gathering. He shared this facet of the trip with no one. Logically, he knew this need for secrecy, for deception, was reason enough to resist the temptation. But the pull to participate only grew stronger. He found he had no will to fight this dangerous undertaking. His pragmatic mind continued to scream, pleading with him to abort this treacherous plan. His soul also continued to scream, begging him to proceed. His soul had little difficulty triumphing over reason.

Shortly after Nikolai had announced that he and Tatinaya would be leaving again for an extended time, a fever fell over Moscow. Nikolai, terrified that Tatianya would succumb, ferreted her away in their home, allowing no one to visit. He refused to even let her leave their chambers, denying anyone access to her. He alone would bring her meals to her, anxiously surveying her countenance for any signs of the fever. She felt his concern was being taken to the extreme, but she acquiesced to his demands, not wanting to further agitate him.

Devastating news had come from Alexi's home. Olga, Anastasia, and little Nikolai all had come down with the fever. Anguish for Alexi consumed Nikolai, but now having his own wife to think of, he was unable to do anything but hope and pray from afar. The fever was vicious, causing much pain and destruction. Young and old were falling prey with the numbers mounting daily. It seemed the whole city was under siege. Physicians shuttled from home to home, exhausted by the never-ending pleas for help. Despite all efforts, they were finding there was little to be done but pray. Those that were surviving were few and far between. These lucky souls survived out of sheer determination, medical attention having a negligible effect.

The duke and duchess begged Nikolai to bring Tatianya to St. Petersburg, which had escaped the fever's onslaught. But he was afraid for her to venture out. She was safely tucked inside her new home. Nikolai felt it best she stay hidden away from this evil. He feared the exposure this trip would necessitate was not worth the risk. He adamantly refused to let her travel, keeping her secure within the fortress he had built around his bride. The duke and duchess had little choice now but to hope and believe in the efforts of their newest son-in-law.

Several days into the siege, Alexi received the first devastating blow. Early in the morning, it was discovered that his little daughter Anastasia had taken a turn for the worse. Her fever-soaked body lay limp in his arms. He crawled into bed with her, desperate to still the violent shaking from the alternating chills and fever that wracked her rail-thin frame. She clung to him, "Papa help me. Make it stop." Her normally radiant smile was now subdued by the overwhelming effects of the illness.

Anastasia was a spunky child who drove him to distraction. She was a handful; naughty in a way that only made her dearer. They had a special bond and she was the apple of his eye. He loved the way she would wrap her delicate arms around his leg or pull on his coattail when she wanted his attention. He would sit with her in her nursery as she studied his face. He would endure her childish efforts to affix her hair ribbons to his hair, confident that it needed her best efforts. He would then take tea with Anastasia, her nanny having great difficulty suppressing her laughter. She had known Alexi for a long time and never thought she would see the day he found himself wrapped around a child's finger. Quietly, she stood by, watching the devastation unfolding, helpless to do anything but pray.

As the morning wore on, Anastasia began slipping in and out of consciousness. The doctor had been sent for and as he witnessed her current condition, he knew she was lost to Alexi and Olga. Alexi vainly tried to encourage her to fight, promising her anything she wanted. He stroked her sweat-covered face, chiding her gently that she owed him another tea party. She weakly opened her eyes and met his with a look of defeat. Her tiny, honey-infused lilt was no more than a whisper, "Papa, I so tired. I go seep."

Alexi wanted to scream at her to fight. He held her as close as he dared, hoping to fill her fever-wracked body with his strength. As she slipped into deeper and deeper sleep, the doctor motioned for Alexi to come with him into the hall. Alexi was reluctant to leave her side. Her nanny was close by and assured him she would call for him if any changes occurred. The doctor took Alexi's arm and began to prepare him for the worst news a parent could receive.

Alexi broke free, trying to escape the words that would ruin his life. The doctor and Alexi's father were holding him now, forcing him to face the inevitable. He clutched at his clothing, tearing at his shirt, sobs choking his efforts to breathe. He was on the verge of hysteria. His father held him close, urging him to regain his composure. His father didn't want Alexi to miss out on the little time she had left. He didn't want Alexi scaring his dying granddaughter.

As Alexi returned to Anastasia's bedside, she opened her eyes and reached out for him. "Papa hold me. Papa, say you love me. Say I pretty." Alexi mistook her words for a rally. For a moment he felt victorious that the doctor's predictions were unfounded. As he began to stroke her hair and coo these truths to her, she relaxed. He thought she was now peacefully sleeping, the worst of the fever freeing her from its clutches. As he stroked her hair, she released a long sigh. She looked deep into his eyes, "Papa I sorry I so naughty." Alexi clamored to dispel any cares she had. As he cursed himself for any reprimand he had ever delivered, however much deserved at the time, her last breath passed over his cheek. Alexi ran headlong into the realization that he had witnessed his daughter's death. His sweet baby now lay peacefully in his arms. He looked for signs of life, desperately willing the rise and fall of her tiny chest which would not come. Hysteria finally took hold. He howled in agony; his soul slashed with the razor-sharp reality. Olga heard his agony thru her fever-induced haze. She knew one of her children was gone.

Alexi gathered their daughter into his arms. He knew Olga would want to see her one last time. He wanted her to see Anastasia while she still had a semblance of life trailing across her innocence. He stumbled trancelike towards Olga, tears blinding his way. He approached the entrance to their chambers where they had conceived this precious gift and found Olga clinging to the doorway. As she looked upon the small lifeless form in his arms, she wailed and fell to her knees, the fever preventing her from reaching her child.

Alexi collapsed beside her. He supported both mother and child, one newly dead, one closer to death than he knew. Olga stroked the now calm face. "She is so pretty. She looks like she is just sleeping. Alexi, how did this happen to us?" As Olga sobbed into his shirt, soaking him with her tears and her fever, he prayed she and their son would survive.

Anastasia's tiny body began to grow cold and her nanny gently pried their little treasure from them. Silently the nanny took the child into her embrace and mourned her loss as well. The household staff had loved her like their own. Her infectious laughter, her constant questions, her inability to sit still or behave had driven them to the ends of their patience but had also made them smile with delight. This house would never be as bright without her smile.

Olga looked up at Alexi. With alarm, he saw the telltale signs that the fever was winning its battle. She wore the same distracted countenance as Anastasia had as she slipped thru his fingers. Alexi desperately wanted to settle her into their warm bed, but she was determined to see her son. She had been robbed of the chance to say goodbye to Anastasia. She longed for the gift of time Alexi had been given. She would not lose this chance with her baby boy. A growing dread was filling her that he too would succumb. Alexi relented and carried Olga to their son. Raspy breathing was audible from the hall. "Why didn't you come for us?" Alexi screamed at the nanny who had been watching over little Nikolai. She shook her head in confusion. Her face swam with tears, grieving Anastasia.

As they knelt by their son's cradle, they saw he was no longer covered in the sweat of the fever. Olga hoped with all her heart he had beaten this demon. Alexi gently set her on the pale blue chaise where she had nursed their son. He swaddled the child and laid him in her arms. Alexi hovered at her knee, letting their sight and scent sink deep into him.

He held one of Anastasia's hair ribbons. She had only recently fastened the pale pink ribbon to his shimmering blond waves at their last tea party, before the fever had struck her down. He trailed the ribbon softly across his cheek, her scent still fresh. For a moment, he forgot she was gone.

As the morning passed into afternoon, the shadows grew tall in the nursery with the coming of the early Russian winter night. Little Nikolai had not roused as Anastasia had. This child had his mother's calm composure. He had often studied his surroundings with a thoughtful gaze, making Alexi laugh. Little Nikolai would stare at his sister as she romped or threw a tantrum, depending on the dilemma at hand. He would have had a quiet way, an easy way. He had won the staff over effortlessly, his large eyes drawing them in. His death, it now appeared, would be similar to how he had lived. Gone was Alexi's hysteria, and Olga was too ill to mourn. Little Nikolai, even in death, was a soothing salve to his grieving parents. By early afternoon, they had also lost their son. He had slipped thru their fingers as well, never once opening his eyes.

Olga was devastated. She had been robbed of saying goodbye to both of her children. She had cooed to him and lavished fevered kisses on his face which had long grown cold. She hoped he had known she was there. Alexi laid his head gently in Olga's lap and prayed she would survive. No one could ever replace these two angels, but he dangerously gave himself hope that they would embrace another child. He had no way of knowing that by midnight he would have lost them all, she was too ill from the fever and too overcome with grief to continue her fight.

As the nanny pried a second lifeless child from his parents, again mourning the unthinkable, Olga turned ashen. The devastation had taken its final toll. She looked into her hero's eyes. He had not moved from her side as the nanny had removed the now cold corpse that had been their son. "Alexi, take me to our bed. I want you to hold me. I have never felt such cold."

140

The shivering and fever convulsed her body. Alexi held her to him, trying desperately to warm her with his own warmth. The shadows were now long and the chill of the evening pervasive. As he tucked her into her coverlet, she held onto him with a fevered hand. She fought to keep her death at bay.

"Alexi, sit with me. Hold me. You know you were the love of my life." Looking down into her eyes, he realized she was saying goodbye.

"No Olga no, I can't lose you as well. Fight. Don't leave me here all alone."

Alexi's eyes were wild with pain and the refusal to lose the last of his universe. She was his anchor. He would be adrift without her. She weakly smiled at him, "If only I could my love."

Alexi held her to him, crushing her, willing her to seep into his soul. "Forgive my foolishness. I wasted so much time at our beginning. This is God punishing an unworthy soul."

Olga used the last of her strength. She caressed his face as had become her custom. It would be her last time reaching deep into the farthest recesses of his soul. She wanted him to remember all the good that had been in their marriage. "Alexi you have to know how happy I have been these last few years, how happy you made me. You were a good husband, a good father. You have to go on. For me."

As he leaned in to kiss her, she willed herself to return the kiss. As their lips met, he felt the now familiar spark that had eluded him for so long in their early years. He cursed himself for not being open to her from the very start. As their love and longing for each other shone brightly one last time, Olga had no choice but to let go of life. Her caress became weak and then fell away from his face. He reached out to steady her hand, cherishing this intimacy. He wanted to remember everything about this last embrace. It would be all he would ever have.

As word reached Nikolai that Alexi had lost everything he held dear, Nikolai crushed his own reason for living to his chest. In just one day, he had received 3 letters from Alexi's father that first Anastasia, then his namesake little Nikolai, and then finally Olga had died, all three in the span of one short day. It was unthinkable. The normally self-assured Nikolai was at a loss as to what to do for his dearest and oldest friend. What would there be to say? All he wanted to do was shut out this ugliness. Only this year had he finally found love. He was driven insane by the possibility of losing what had eluded him for so long.

As the last letter fluttered to the floor, Nikolai sunk into a chair by the window. He gazed out over the hills separating his home from Alexi's nightmare. As he ran his fingers thru his hair, Tatianya encircled him from behind, laying her head on his neck, golden curls falling into his face. He clutched at a stray tendril, thinking the unthinkable.

"Nikki, you have to go to him." He turned to look into her face with misery. "I can't leave you." She kissed his neck, "Then I will go with you." He turned to hold her shoulders "No, No, No, there is too much sickness there." She held his gaze until he slumped into her. "I will go. Promise me you will stay hidden away where I have the illusion you are shielded from this terror."

Nikolai reached Alexi's home in the early morning hours. He found the front door unlocked. So many people had been coming and going, the staff eventually just left it open. As he entered the main salon, he found Alexi lying on the floor, staring at the latest family portrait he had commissioned. "They are so beautiful" Alexi stated with a flat affect. Nikolai lay down next to his brother. "That is true. It is a beautiful painting.....what can I do?" Alexi looked at him with a torrent on the verge, "Bring them back."

Alexi threw himself into Nikolai's embrace and the two brothers sobbed. Nikolai held Alexi until the sobs no longer wracked his grieving soul. Eventually, he sat up, Nikolai along with him. He looked at Nikolai, "Tatianya?" Nikolai hung his head, ashamed now that he had not flown to Alexi's side when the first letter had arrived. "She is fine, at least for now. I have forbidden her from leaving our chambers." Alexi nodded, if only it had been that easy for him.

Again, Nikolai asked, "What can I do for you? Anything." Alexi said, "I want to dig their graves. Will you help me?" Nikolai was shocked at this request but fought to show a calm exterior. He nodded. He would help his friend grieve. Although the hour was now approaching 3 am, Alexi got to his feet and stumbled towards the door. "Now?" Nikolai asked. "Now," was all Alexi could reply.

Nikolai and Alexi climbed the hill to the private family cemetery at the far corner of Alexi's estate. The cemetery held many long-gone relatives but there was plenty of room for 3 new graves. Alexi surveyed the cemetery for their final resting spots. He seemed immune to the howling Russian winter winds lashing at his heaving chest thru his open coat. He pointed, "Over there by that tree, I expect I will be sitting here a lot and that tree will shade my misery." Nikolai wondered how they would manage to dig deep enough thru the frozen ground.

But Alexi was driven by grief. His anger, his longing all focused on forcing the icy frozen ground to give way. Nikolai had no choice but to join the attack on the silent hill alongside his grief-stricken friend. Nikolai knew Alexi was strong, but it was a shock to see the depths of strength grief could unleash. As Alexi dug deeper and deeper into Anastasia's and then little Nikolai's and then finally Olga's graves, Nikolai worked tirelessly, silently by his side. No words were spoken. Nikolai now saw that no words had been needed. It was his presence and support that Alexi had needed from him. Nikolai faced the somber truth that words are useless when all is lost.

As the sun crested the winter frozen hillside, the last of the graves were deep enough. Silently the two men trudged back down the hill. As the household saw the two men coming from the direction of the cemetery, the staff realized they had been out in the winter cold for hours, digging into the frozen ground. They were stunned that they had attempted this. They were more stunned that their mission had been accomplished. Nikolai and Alexi entered the main hall, muddy and sweaty from their exertion. Alexi's staff offered to draw a bath for both men to fight off the chill, fearful that these two would also fall ill. Nikolai declined; he had not intended to be gone so long. He needed to wrap himself around Tatianya, assure himself of her vibrance.

As he hugged Nikolai, Alexi told him he planned to bury his family the following morning. Nikolai nodded. He would be there. Riding home, he struggled with what do to about his planned trip to New Orleans. As much as he was still drawn to this deception, he knew he was needed at home. He would cancel the trip. He would postpone it until the following year.

Tatianya had been watching for her husband's return. She too was stunned when she heard that he and Alexi had spent hours digging the graves in the subzero temperatures. She insisted that he sink into a steaming hot bath, fearing for his health. As he laid back, eyes closed from lack of sleep, Tatianya lowered herself onto him. He forcibly embraced her, burying his head in her breast. He found he only needed to hold her, his efforts from the night before exhausting him to the core. Tatianya melted into him, giving him whatever it was he needed. As her warmth and scent surrounded him, he stirred. Silently she straddled him and he found the solace his soul was crying out for. His need was tender, almost prayer-like, thankful, that she had been spared Olga's fate and he, in turn, Alexi's.

In sharp contrast to the homecoming Nikolai was receiving, Alexi stood in the grand salon of his home, confronted with 3 open caskets. They looked so peaceful now. Gone was the convulsing from fever, sweat dripping down their faces, matting their hair.

Alexi spent time in turn with each one. He first knelt before Nikolai's tiny white coffin. He gently tucked in his son as if there was a chill in the world that could touch him now. Alexi placed a small toy in the coffin along with a golden bell. Alexi vainly hoped to hear the bell tinkling, somehow cheating death. As he stood by Anastasia's slightly larger white coffin, he stroked her sweet face and fussed gently with a stray tendril. He smoothed the lapels of the velvet dress he had selected. It was her favorite which had instantly made it his favorite. He smiled wistfully as he remembered the trouble she had had saying velvet. Tears slipped onto her cheek as he remembered she had never had trouble saying Papa. It had been her first word. He tucked her favorite doll and two teacups into her coffin. He wrapped a golden bell around her wrist, just in case. Standing before Olga, his sobs became uncontrollable. He placed tiny portraits of them all within her grasp. He laid one of Anastasia's ribbons and one of Nikolai's toys on her chest. He wound a tiny chain around her wrist with the same golden bell he had placed with their children.

Tatianya insisted that she attend the funerals. Nikolai had no desire to fight with her. He had no desire for harsh words. Fear gripped his heart that he would also be digging a grave before too long. He agreed she could attend only if she remained inside their carriage, safely tucked away from the cold and the disease.

As they arrived at the gravesite, Tatianya silently pointed to the cluster of mourners standing in the bitter cold. Most were far older than she. Nikolai relented and against his better judgment, escorted her from the carriage to the edge of the 3 open graves that he and Alexi had dug the night before.

Alexi stood alone at the forefront of the group of mourners. As the earth slowly filled the pit covering his son's coffin, Alexi stood resolute in his determination to grieve as was the custom of the day, silently holding in his pain. But as the earth was now obscuring the second coffin from sight, his composure began to slip. His shoulders shook violently with the sobs he could no longer muffle. Tatianya looked up at Nikolai. She motioned to him that his place was with Alexi, his brother. Nikolai hated to break away but knew she was right. He bent down and kissed the top of her fur-covered head. Silently he stepped forward and put a tentative arm around Alexi. They watched the dirt obscuring Anastasia's coffin, silencing her forever. Nikolai had never thought he would miss Anastasia's constant chattering, her interruptions, her tantrums. But he found himself wracked with grief, sobbing uncontrollably. As the final words were being said over Olga's coffin and it was being lowered into the ground, Alexi picked up the bouquet of roses he had selected to lay on top of her coffin. His intention had merely been to step forward and carefully send the flowers into the ground after his beloved.

But as grief drove him past the borders of sanity, Alexi found he could not let the cold hard earth separate him from his beloved. He jumped down into the grave after her. He lay face down on her coffin, sobs wracking his body. He pounded on the lid where her name had been delicately carved. He screamed "Wake up! Get up! Don't leave me!" The gathered crowd stood stone still, shocked by this unexpected display. Nikolai could feel all eyes boring into his back, knowing what they knew. He would be the only one Alexi would listen to. Nikolai looked down into the pit where his friend lay sobbing, flowers in one hand, the other hand fisted and pounding with all his might. Nikolai saw no alternative. He jumped into the grave after his lifelong friend.

The gathering gasped as the two men disappeared into the pit with Olga's coffin. Nikolai wrapped his arms around Alexi who was wailing an unearthly plea, "No, no, no. Listen. She is only sleeping. We have made a terrible mistake!" Alexi was on his knees, pleading with Olga to fight, to ring the golden bell, letting him know she needed his rescue. But the bell remained silent. Gently Nikolai drew Alexi into his embrace. Alexi was fighting to free himself, his grief driving his strength, making it difficult for Nikolai to maintain his grasp. "Alexi, her sleep is not that kind of sleep. Let me help you. I will do anything with you. But not this."

Alexi's emotions were now spent and he had no wish to further shock Olga's parents. They too had lost too much too soon. As Nikolai climbed out of the ground, his face hardened by the effort it took to stay strong for Alexi, he sought out his own angel. It had unnerved him to see Olga's name etched into her coffin. Tatianya's eyes met his eyes. They shone with pride. She knew his actions were difficult. They belonged to a true friend, a brother. His loyalty was something Alexi would need in the coming days and she was only too glad to share him. Alexi now realized with alarm and shame that he was standing on his wife's coffin, a battered bouquet of roses in his hand. He hung his head in shame and bewilderment.

Alexi had no choice now but to say goodbye. He kissed each letter in Olga's name. He lovingly rearranged the bouquet and tenderly placed it below her name. Lingering just a moment longer, he gently fingered each letter in her name. It was then that he noticed a thorn from a rose had pierced his wrist. He watched as his blood trickled down his sleeve and silently surrounded Olga's name. Alexi hastened to wipe away the blood before it could stain the coffin and then stopped. A small smile mixed with his tears. He would allow his life force to lie with her forever. It somehow gave him hope. He pulled a rose from the bouquet and tucked it into his coat. "I will love you forever. Wait for me." Alexi looked up and saw Nikolai's outstretched hand. It was time. With an easy motion, Nikolai pulled Alexi into his embrace. Silently, they stood arm in arm as the earth closed around Olga, and Alexi's universe was lost to him.

Tatianya came forward and encircled Nikolai's waist. He clutched her to him and Alexi forlornly looked at them, still able to feel each other full of life. He hung his head as his mother and mother-in-law embraced him. Olga's mother spoke first, her eyes full of pain but also full of love for this grieving man who had just buried her daughter. She had been disappointed in him for so long, but the last few years had been full of love and laughter for Olga. Alexi had brought her 2 beautiful grandchildren and he had not been embarrassed to show his love for them. He now one last time had made her proud, not afraid to wear his heart on his sleeve. It had taken a long time for Alexi to grow to love Olga. But when his love finally came down, he had fallen hard and had not been ashamed to show the depths of his emotion. Alexi's own mother had also been disappointed in him at the beginning of this marriage. He had agreed to court and then marry Olga, but the commitment had been slow to truly manifest. She had been full of sorrow for this sweet girl who had so obviously yearned for her son to shine his lovelight on her. When he finally realized everything he had ever wanted was already his, he made up as best he could for lost time, sparing no expense to lavish her with love and her heart's desire. But in truth, all Olga had ever wanted was to feel Alexi's arms around her, loving her senseless into the early morning hours. Alexi had come to crave her more than she craved him. He now cursed all those lost nights when he had foolishly scoffed at her requests, begging him to stay home. How he wished he could recapture just one of those wasted nights. As they turned from the freshly dug graves, just for a moment, Alexi could have sworn he heard a bell's tinkling being lifted by the wind. Against his better judgment, he fought the impulse to cause another scene.

As Nikolai made plans to cancel his travels to New Orleans, Alexi found he was looking forward to the space this would place between him and Nikolai. It was simply too difficult to see him with Tatianya. It was too difficult to see the satisfaction, the contentment that was forever shining in Nikolai's eyes. He didn't begrudge his friend this hard-won love. He just couldn't face them and then go home to a house that was now hollow and devoid of any happiness. He needed them to go to New Orleans. He knew this would pass but right now it was all too raw. Night after night he roamed from silent room to silent room. Nurseries once filled with delicious smells of lotions and freshly bathed cherubs anxiously awaiting his nighttime stories and goodnight kisses were now darkened and already wearing the stale smell of disuse.

Olga's pianoforte she had so dearly loved stood furtively waiting for her graceful fingers to release its magic. Alexi would wander with brandy in hand, wondering how he would ever survive this. He would trudge up to the cemetery in a drunken stupor, lie face down in the snow, hoping for the fever that never came. He cursed his health. He made Nikolai promise to forge ahead with his plans, stating pouring his grief into their businesses would be the best medicine for his aching heart. Nikolai worried that this would be too much for Alexi, but his growing urgency to get to New Orleans made it easy to agree to Alexi's irrational request. Nikolai and Tatianya boarded their ship as planned. Alexi saw them off. As he turned for his dark and desolate estate, he was relieved that the love so palpable in Nikolai would not be haunting him, taunting him, as he tried to reconcile himself to this new life now only filled with an unending deafening silence.

Chapter Eight:
New Orleans, Devastation

Tatianya loved the constant movement of the waves. She loved leaning over the rail, allowing the spray to kiss, sometimes even drench her face. Her infectious giggles would take flight with the blustering winds that took her breath away. She was mesmerized by the shifting of the waves, the deep blue cresting into whitecaps for fleeting moments before retreating into the depths. Nikolai would stand behind her, arm crooked around her fur-covered shoulders, alert for unexpected rouge waves. At night, the creaking of the ship was like a lullaby she wished would never end. She drowsed tightly wrapped in her protector's embrace, the sea air filling her mind with curiosity of what exotic New Orleans would hold. Her spent and satisfied body vainly fought against succumbing to the ocean's call to slumber. Despite the devastation they had left behind, she sensed something wonderful was on the horizon.

Nikolai was relieved to see Tatianya so buoyant, no trace of the fever evident. He teased her that the sea air must be good for her appetite; that her finicky palate had vanished into the rolling sea's murky depths.

And then it hit him one evening. As she lay naked in his arms, he realized something was different. By now he knew every inch of that sensuous willing body. The curve of her belly seemed to swell under his large hand. Lazing dreamily in his arms, she felt his caress stiffen. She misread his reaction for hunger. As she reached out to return the caress, he brought her hand to his lips, kissing it gently. Silently he held his universe in a way he never thought he would. Tatianya attempted to pull away but possessively, he reined her in. She whispered in the darkness, "Nikolai what is wrong?"

When he finally spoke, his voice was shaking. "Tatianya, do you feel alright?" He was haunted by the suffering that had plagued Olga. He had thought for sure he would have sensed something if his angel was with child. True, she was tired, but she had assumed it was from the rocking of the ship. It seemed to lull everyone with its mysterious cadence.

As Nikolai held her gaze, a tear-streaked down his face. He couldn't believe how much he found himself wanting this child. It shocked him, all those months he had been relieved, thinking she hadn't conceived. He was going to be a father and Tatianya would bear his firstborn, his heir. Gently, very gently, he took her hand and placed it over her slightly swollen belly. He showered her face with kisses that were wet with tears. "Tatianya, you are carrying my child." At first, his words did not register. But as the curtain of confusion lifted, the knowledge sent joy and peace sailing thru her soul. She curled into her protector's embrace as he shielded their child with a gentle hand. Tatianya relaxed with this dawning knowledge. Nikolai thought of Alexi's heartbreak and the vampire summons he was powerless to resist.

The months at sea flew by for Tatianya. She screamed with delight when she felt the first signs of life deep within her belly. Soon after, she came to see this child was every bit as aggressive as his father. During the long ocean voyage, her belly had swollen with a child as feisty and robust as his father. She was sad to leave the ocean behind but was glad to reach dry land. She desperately needed a new wardrobe.

After settling into a beautiful old mansion with a view of the Mississippi River, Nikolai secured a seamstress for Tatianya. A creole woman, Angeline, had come highly recommended. He instructed this woman to make Tatianya whatever she wanted and assured her that money would be of no issue. He also instructed Angeline to make some new clothing for herself. Nikolai could see Tatianya was uncomfortable requesting a lavish new wardrobe for her expanding belly while this woman was clothed in little more than rags. Angeline was grateful to this foreign couple. No one had ever shown her much in the way of compassion. She would do her best to please. She had somehow felt an immediate connection to these strangers.

Nikolai watched for a moment as Angeline and Tatianya began to discuss the new wardrobe. It touched his heart to see Tatianya holding some of the expensive fabrics up to Angeline, encouraging her to take whatever she wanted for herself. He smiled and nodded his encouragement to the young creole woman who nervously met his gaze. Her shy smile melted his heart. He surmised her past must have been anything but happy. But her dark brown eyes glowed with a knowledge that made Nikolai wonder just who she really was.

Nikolai kissed his wife and gave Angeline another nod of encouragement. Satisfied that Tatianya would be occupied for hours, he set out to secure a doctor. He knew she would be giving birth in New Orleans. He wanted everything arranged before he broke this news. He knew she would be distressed to give birth in a foreign land, surrounded by strangers.

Nikolai followed up on a suggestion and arranged for the doctor to pay them a visit in the morning. He then set out to see if he could uncover any truth regarding the gatherings held by the resident vampires of New Orleans. Being a man of wealth made it simple. It wasn't long before he found a man willing to talk.

He was quickly put in touch with a liaison for these gatherings. The cost would be very high Nikolai was warned. He assumed the gentleman meant financially. Nikolai had no way of knowing that sunny afternoon just how high the cost would ultimately be.

A meeting was arranged for later that evening. Nikolai meandered the streets to better acquaint himself with his new surroundings. He wanted to have an escape route planned if he detected any danger. His wealth had made him vulnerable. Proof had been required that he could pay the exorbitant admission fee before his contact would arrange the meeting. A nagging worry continued to grow but his fascination and curiosity were overruling his common sense. Persistently, he ignored his gut reaction to abort this folly.

As the shadows descended across the city, Nikolai made his way to the designated establishment. The contact had only been described as someone who would be easy to pick out in the crowd. As the tall figure moved in his direction, Nikolai immediately understood. It would have been difficult to describe this man. His movements were measured, calculated, and yet had a fluidity of ease. He silently sat down opposite Nikolai. When Nikolai offered to buy him a drink, he moved his hand gracefully to wave the waiter away, exposing a nasty scar encircling his wrist. It unnerved Nikolai. It looked identical to the one he had seen on Sergei's wrist. He longed to question this man about the origin of the scar but found he lacked the courage. Nikolai wondered what made this man so feared. When their eyes finally met, Nikolai understood. The man was clearly not human in the truest sense of the word. He had looked human from a distance, but now face to face, there was definitely a menacing quality to his demeanor. There was the faint but unmistakable stench of death and decay about this man. And yet, somehow, he managed to elicit excruciating longing in the women at the surrounding tables. He managed to seduce Nikolai into trusting him as he had never trusted anyone.

The man eventually spoke, "So I hear you have come a great distance to satisfy a curiosity. Why don't you tell me what you have heard? If you curry my favor, perhaps I will tell you if you have been misinformed."

Nikolai found himself giving much more information to this stranger than he had intended. He hadn't wanted to tell him about Tatianya, their honeymoon, their child, but the words just tumbled out. He had laid bare before this stranger the most intimate details of his life. The stranger stroked his finely chiseled chin with an equally aristocratic hand. He eyed Nikolai with an intense dead gaze. These lifeless, soulless eyes fixated on him were completely devoid of the light he had grown accustomed to in Tatianya's eyes. They were nothing like those vast blue oceans he adored.

The man could see that Nikolai was a man of wealth who liked a challenge. He too understood that allure and had also once relished the pursuit. It was obvious by the cut of Nikolai's garments that he could pay any sum requested. The man wanted Nikolai to bring Tatianya, but there Nikolai drew the line. The man appeared agitated but reluctantly agreed. He resisted baiting Nikolai, his ego, and his lust for power. He would allow Nikolai this small victory.

Just as quickly, the man released his agitation. He smiled seductively at Nikolai, "My inquisitive neophyte, what you request is called a **Searing.** You were well informed in Paris. It is but a trivial inconvenience for one so strong as yourself. You will barely feel a thing, a mere pinprick upon that beautiful masculine wrist of yours. But afterward, you will never be the same again. That I can promise you, my courageous power-hungry friend."

He then informed Nikolai coolly that payment in advance, in full, was required. Nikolai meekly questioned having to pay the entire sum upfront. He received no reply. He chose to blindly trust a man he barely knew, another bad omen Nikolai readily ignored.

Nikolai was shocked to learn the gathering would be held the following evening. He had wanted more time in New Orleans to prepare. The stranger purred, "My friend, tomorrow night is Mardi Gras. Special things can only happen at special times to those who are worthy." He leaned in close, the aroma of death becoming an elixir. "Nikolai, I think you are special, deserving. The question is now, do you?" He stroked Nikolai's beautiful high cheekbones and lingered just a moment. It didn't even occur to Nikolai to pull away. The scorching heat exuding from this gentle embrace only left Nikolai craving whatever this creature possessed.

Nikolai warily agreed. Money changed hands and the location was finally revealed. The man then abruptly departed, leaving Nikolai in a cold sweat, seriously questioning this decision. He became embarrassed realizing how intimate he had become with this stranger in a public setting. He found his waiter timidly inquiring if he needed anything. The look of alarm on this young man's face did nothing to allay his fears but only confirmed his suspicions. He was standing on the brink of disaster.

Nikolai walked home slowly. He needed to regain his composure before falling into Tatianya's embrace. He couldn't risk alarming her. He had never lied to her before and would do so for the first time. He knew this was reason enough not to attend the gathering, but he was compelled, no longer able to trust his instincts. His contact was an intriguing quietly powerful creature. Nikolai hungered to wield this type of power. He envied men whose mere presence was enough to send fear thru their opponents. He pushed reason aside. He knew he was going to attend. He knew nothing was going to stand in his way. Darkness gripped his soul, chilling him to the bone.

Relief washed over Nikolai as he entered the mansion. The gentle candlelight bathed him, dispelling the shadows. Tatianya was waiting for him in the parlor. She looked radiant but as the weeks wore on, her growing belly made it difficult to get comfortable. As he knelt before her, she smiled and stroked his cheek. She didn't seem to notice the pervasive scent of death from the stranger's recent caress.

"Nikki, I need to lie down. Your son is going to be as demanding as you are, I fear. He is kicking a lot tonight. Do you want to say hello to your heir?" When Nikolai placed his hand over the little foot that was yearning to break free, the connection seemed to calm the infant. Tatianya loved how their child could respond to his father in such a way. She thought to herself how quietly powerful he was in so many ways.

Nikolai placed his head gently on her swollen belly. He felt she must be close to her time. Tomorrow they would know more. As he carried her up the stairs, he felt their loving would now have to wait. He had wanted so badly to love her tonight. He feared what would transpire tomorrow night. He needed to drown himself in her for courage.

Tatianya reached for him but Nikolai made no move to possess her love. The look of hurt and reproach in her eyes told him she feared he no longer found her desirable. He spanned the distance between them holding her to him as closely as he dared. Her imploring blue pools shimmered in the candlelight and his composure slipped. Tonight, his loving would be that of a husband and father adoring a woman in full bloom. He caressed her rounded breasts that were now swelling with milk. He gently suckled. He willed himself to control his need, his desire.

Tenderly, he loved her as he should have on their wedding night. Their gentle rocking lulled their child to sleep.

As they lay entwined, Nikolai told Tatianya he had found a well-respected doctor who would pay them a visit in the morning. He also chose this moment to tell her he would need to attend a business meeting tomorrow night. His heart broke as he lay next to her stroking her belly, telling her this lie, trampling her trust. Even as he held his reasons for living close to his heart, now heavy with deceit, his resolve to attend the gathering only burned brighter with each passing hour.

The following morning the doctor came by as promised. After the examination, he informed them that due to Tatianya's small frame it was difficult to tell how far along she was. Nikolai paced, running his fingers thru his hair. He demanded the doctor make an educated guess. When pressed, the doctor stated she was close to 8 months. Upon hearing this, Tatianya was ecstatic. It meant she had conceived on their honeymoon. She couldn't wait to tell her sisters. The doctor then broke the news that she would not be going home anytime soon. Tatianya was crushed she would not give birth on Russian soil. She wanted her family around her and this was not to be. There would not be enough time to send for them. They decided they would hold off with their good news until after the baby was born. Nikolai would merely send word they were extending their visit.

As night closed in around the city, Nikolai readied himself for the gathering. He kissed Tatianya and then knelt to caress her belly. She ran her fingers thru his hair. Momentarily he wavered, but tore himself away, venturing out into the night. His mind filled with darkness. It sadly chastised his heart that he was a fool.

Nikolai made his way to the address for the gathering. He knew this was folly. Every fiber in his being begged him to go home. Never one to ignore a gut feeling, Nikolai found himself stubbornly turning his back on instincts he had trusted his entire life. He was unable to veer from this path he was almost certain spelled disaster. Grasping the elaborate brass knocker on the finely carved door, a moment's hesitation lingered before he allowed the sound of brass on wood to signal his arrival.

Upon entering, Nikolai was given a glass of champagne. As he sipped, the room began to spin. He knew he had been drugged, heavily drugged. He clumsily attempted to retreat, find his way back to his perfect life, cursing his obsession with this power. But he knew it was too late to escape. Instead of finding his freedom, he had found his demise.

The creature from the previous evening approached.

Nikolai's drug-induced stupor could not mask the man's vicious intention to do more than **Sear**. He leered at Nikolai. At first, this creature merely clasped Nikolai's wrist, trailing a finger along the finely tailored sleeve of his jacket. He sighed in feigned resignation, "Such quality. Almost breaks my heart to inflict my damage." Thru a drug-induced haze, Nikolai watched as the creature broke his own skin with the thorn from a rose that was heavily caked with dried blood. A small trickle glistened in the candlelight before it dripped onto the floor, pooling. The creature then tore at Nikolai's expensive garment, exposing his muscular forearm. A sinister smile crossed his predator's face as it filled with longing, making no attempt to hide the desire to possess. The man's caress suddenly turned to imprisonment, whirling Nikolai into his arms, pinning his back to the creature's chest. With a vengeance, he plunged the blood-soaked thorn deep into Nikolai's wrist. He melded it to his own gaping wound, forcing their blood to mix. Horrified, Nikolai watched as his own blood ran in a torrent. The being then encircled Nikolai's wrist, his grasp revealing the intention to dominate from within as well.

At first, there was no pain. The creature slowly, maniacally let loose with crazy laughter in anticipation. The warmth of skin on skin suddenly roared into an unbearable inferno. As the creature's grasp became a death grip, this roaring heat encircled Nikolai's wrist. Nikolai's assailant then placed his hand over Nikolai's heart, attempting to sink his hand deep into Nikolai's chest. In an effort to rob Nikolai of his essence, his soul, his assailant was attempting to rip out his heart.

The creature hissed into Nikolai's ear, "Give me what you no longer own." The demon trailed his tongue along Nikolai's neck, seeking out the pulsating vessel, rich with the elixir a vampire eternally craves. He found his quarry and sunk ravenously into Nikolai's neck.

Nikolai struggled against this creature's efforts to crush his chest; each breath now filled with excruciating pain. He fought valiantly to break free of the teeth deeply entrenched in his neck. A scorching, burning pain shot thru his entire being. His knees gave way as the creature continued his assault, tightening his grasp. The vampire had released his fury, his skin now blazing with the desire to own Nikolai's very essence, his soul. Wildly, futilely, Nikolai tried to free himself of this aggression. When the vampire had nearly drained Nikolai of his essence, the being broke free. Nikolai gasped. "Why? What have you done to me?" He had expected only a small pinprick, a quick **Searing** of the site, to bestow the coveted powers. His vast sums of money had only purchased disaster for his ego and those he loved most. He barely noticed the gaping hole in his chest where his heart and soul had once resided, his neck viciously splayed open. He was unaware that this creature had all but drained him of his lifeforce, that he was standing in a pool of blood, his own blood.

The demon had heard this all before. "Why not? How does it feel to have thrown it all away? Tell me, my foolish friend, do you now feel more powerful than before our paths had crossed?" The vampire attempted to continue toying with his prey, but the being was clearly frustrated. This assault had not been as satisfying as he had hoped. Nikolai had been able to hold back, retain a shred of his decency, the epicenter of his essence so desired by this relentless vampire. The creature's best efforts had failed to possess the farthest reaches of Nikolai's soul. He had succeeded in retaining a shred of his essence and in turn, had thwarted the vampire's desire to dominate and consume.

The demon now sneered at Nikolai, death edging ever closer. "So, it seems you have two choices. You are very strong, stronger than I expected. I can finish you off if you like. Surely death is speaking to you tonight, so great is your loss of blood. I apologize, but I am not known for having much self-control." The demon waved his arm still dripping with their mixed blood, bowing to Nikolai with mock remorse. "Or, I can **Restore** you. But you must decide quickly as you haven't much time left my friend. You must quickly choose between death or a murderous life. From this day forward, you will desire to possess another's soul, ingest their fragile essence. You will thirst for blood. It will be a constant desire you will never truly be able to quell, to quench, but it is the only way you will survive. Murder will ensure your existence. Poetic don't you think?"

The two were now in the center of a circle of vampires, some centuries old, some newly minted tonight. He was aware of someone screaming as they also futilely attempted to escape certain doom.

Nikolai's only thoughts were of Tatianya and their child. In desperation, he chose to be **Restored,** not fully understanding. He just knew he couldn't leave his family defenseless in a city full of demons.

The vampire nonchalantly held out his wrist to Nikolai as he chose between death or **Restoration**. With the last of his strength, he tore into this monster, seething, "**Restore** me, you son of a bitch."

The vampire had not expected Nikolai to accept the invitation. Somehow Nikolai managed to encircle the demon's wrist with his own searing heat. With every ounce of hate he possessed, Nikolai would make this demon suffer whatever pain he could inflict. As the lifeforce flowed back into him, Nikolai's eyes focused enough to see his assailant writhing in unexpected pain. Finding himself to be the one on the brink of death, the vampire flailed about, desperate to escape this humiliation. Nikolai had never killed anyone. Aside from Sergei he had never even wanted to kill anyone. This was a hatred that went so much deeper. Confusion warped his instincts but he sensed Sergei was somehow a part of this. He could almost feel his presence. Hatred spurred him on. He sunk his teeth into the demon's neck, drinking deeply.

The vampire struggled against Nikolai's grip as the other demons began to chant and laugh. Nikolai attempted to continue his assault, but his maker was ultimately too strong and broke free from Nikolai's clutches. He commanded the others to throw Nikolai out into the street. He would follow Nikolai home. As their blood and souls had mixed, he had seen how much Tatianya meant to Nikolai. He had never loved someone like this. He had been disgraced tonight by this aristocratic Russian. He would make him pay as he took his wife and child from him. Nikolai's **Restoration** ensured he would have eternity to grieve. As Nikolai's head collided with the cobblestoned street, he could have sworn he heard Sergei's voice mocking his fall from grace.

Nikolai lay in the stinking water of the gutter for hours. He tried to think of Tatianya and what to do but his mind was screaming to feast on the blood of living souls. He dared not go home until he sated this overwhelming desire to kill. He pulled himself together and stood. With each step becoming steadier, he made his way to the seedier side of town. His initial attempts at feasting were not as clever as the one who had **Restored** him, but it got the job done. Victim after victim succumbed to the tall blood-thirsty stranger.

Eventually, he had feasted enough. He felt it safe to go home. He knew he looked different, was different. He knew he would frighten Tatianya, but this could not be helped. He hoped to God he could come up with a plan they could live with. He closed his mind to the fear that he had lost her by his own doing. He closed his mind to the countless murders he had committed. Wave after wave of nausea wracked his body, his mind unable to blot out all those dead eyes. He tried to feel remorse for all those chests, all those necks savagely torn open, now devoid of their blood, their souls by his newly murderous hands. He tried. Remorse was but a fleeting memory.

As Nikolai staggered into their mansion, he saw Tatianya out of the corner of his eye. She dropped the candle, starting a small fire. With lightning speed, he knelt at her feet and put out the flame with his bare hand. There was no pain. Tatianya shrieked. His clothing was tattered and covered with blood. She saw the ugly wound encircling his wrist. She gasped as she saw the gaping hole in his chest, the blood still oozing from his neck. His eyes were familiar yet somehow different, darker, tortured. Her large blue eyes beckoned to him as never before. As the souls of his wife and their unborn child were crying out to him, Nikolai fought against possessing their fragile essences. Somehow, his love for her overcame the excruciating longing to feast.

When she fainted, he had no choice but to break her fall. It was torture not to possess her soul, feel her blood coursing thru his veins; so much worse than resisting her virginal love. He carried her to their bed chambers and gently laid her down. He sat in a chair on the far side of the room unable to trust himself not to harm her or their child. Miserably he cursed his ego and his deception. He alone had ruined their happy life.

Tatianya woke to find Nikolai in fresh clothing but soon saw that it had not been a nightmare. Her life was now a nightmare. She found herself fearing the man she had thought would be her fortress. Nikolai slowly approached the bed and gingerly sat at a distance. He dared not touch her. He ached, realizing she was not reaching out for him. As best he could, he confessed to his folly which had gone so terribly awry. Slowly, the fear left her eyes. She was confused. Her innocence was making it difficult to grasp the gravity of the situation. All she knew was he still loved her. And she loved him. Her sweet words assured him they would find a solution. For a moment Nikolai's eyes lit up, letting himself be fooled into believing there was a way. As they sat there, the vampire who had transformed Nikolai perched silently on the balcony outside their bedroom. He was entranced with this gentle innocent still able to love Nikolai. He was fascinated. He had never seen such love. Or restraint. He waited until they seemed to be coming to terms with Nikolai's devastation.

Jealously watching something he had never attained, the vampire's desire to consume this innocent's essence and make Nikolai suffer for eternity took hold. He flung the balcony doors wide. Nikolai jumped to his feet and lunged at the creature who was eyeing Tatianya. "No!" Nikolai screamed. The demon merely sighed. He lifted Nikolai off his feet with one finger and flung him against the ornately carved stone fireplace. Nikolai slumped, dazed. His body failed him as he attempted to scramble to his feet. He could do nothing more than listen as Tatianya screamed while the demon assaulted his universe.

Eventually, the creature seemed sated. He had wanted to finish her off but was more interested in making Nikolai suffer, watch her slowly fade away, entombing his child in her withered womb. Tatianya now understood what had happened to her husband. She pleaded with her assailant to **Restore** her as well. Nikolai tried to object but found he had no voice. The vampire sneered in Tatianya's sweet face. He cynically stroked her swollen belly that was now strangely still. He let loose with a sinister laugh. "You are of more interest to me as a woman, almost a mother, dying just on the cusp of producing life. Think how your useless husband will weep for you. Just as you let poor Sergei weep for you. Still does weep for you." The vampire stood for a moment to casually admire his havoc. He then slowly descended the stairs and strolled out into the night, whistling, satisfied with the misery he had inflicted.

Nikolai made his way slowly over to Tatianya who lay on the bed close to death. She pleaded with Nikolai to **Restore** her. She pleaded it was the only way to try to save their child. Nikolai stroked her belly. There was no movement, no connection like before. He feared their child was gone but couldn't bring himself to say those awful words. Tatianya was now clinging to him. He knew she didn't have long.

As their eyes met, she cried a single tear as she melded his hand to her wrist that was already viciously torn open. Urge overcame reason. He would sentence her to this hell. He placed his hand over her heart and sunk deep into her chest. She held his gaze, too weak to even gasp, as he descended to pierce her neck with a mouth now intent on possessing her in a way neither had ever imagined.

Nikolai drained the last of her essence. He felt the pulsing of her magic flow thru him but he also smelled the death of their child. Silently he held her wrist, waiting for her decision.

Tentatively she nodded, "**Restore** me, Nikolai." He allowed his fury to blaze. Selfishly he prayed she would survive this ordeal. It was the last prayer he would ever allow himself to utter.

As they lay on the bed together, Nikolai's mind was racing. What do they do now? Where do they go? He knew going back to Russia was out of the question. He just hoped their child was still alive.

Instinct told him his son was gone.

Excruciating pain shot thru Tatianya's core. The bed became soaked with the blood of an untimely labor. Wave after wave tore thru her body. Accusation flew from her eyes, but she never uttered one word to shame him. He wished she would scream at him, something. But she was too consumed with laboring to deliver his son.

As the child slid from her body, the room failed to fill with an infant's lusty cry. Dead silence was all that rewarded Tatianya for her efforts to love this man with all her heart. Nikolai held the tiny perfect child to his chest. He cried out that he had failed those he loved the most. Tatianya motioned for him to give her their child. She vainly attempted to encourage her son to suckle. Milk flowed from her breast but death rejected her best efforts.

Eventually, Nikolai put his hand on hers, stilling them. "My love, he is gone. How can you ever forgive me? Tonight, my lust for power has caused you to lose all." Nikolai took the child from her breast and hung his head. As their eyes met, Tatianya's were awash in misery and confusion. But Nikolai could not deny a trace of love remained. He was startled, humbled, grateful. He had not totally lost her.

Tatianya spoke well beyond her years for the first time in her life, "Nikolai what you did was unthinkable with devastating effects. You have turned us into murderers, the lowest of the low. You have cost us our son, our lives. We need to bury our child."

Nikolai watched her innocence die a little more, "And I need to rob someone of their essence, their soul. I desire the taste of blood upon my lips."

Nikolai could only nod his head in agreement. Silently he cleansed the tiny body and gently wrapped it in the blue blanket Tatianya had waiting for their son. He helped her dress. As they stepped out into the murky night air, they were greeted by another vampire. Nikolai instinctively jumped in front of Tatianya.

But the creature spoke quickly. He gave his name, Torrin. "You have nothing to fear from me. I witnessed your demise tonight. Come, I will help you bury your child in a safe place. The waters in New Orleans claim the dead. I know of a crypt that will keep him from being swept away. Also, do not fear your maker. He is gone. He went too far tonight and we have destroyed him. If only we had gotten here sooner. You must not stay here for long. You have made enemies. Go into the swamp. There is an old mansion. Stay there until you decide as to where you will go." Torrin stopped for a moment, there was more. "Be forewarned, the dawning day is no longer an ally. Its strength will combine with your newfound heat, igniting a flame that is not ours to snuff. I can see you already know that human essence, human blood is the only sustenance you will ever crave, be able to ingest. I am sad to say the killing will get easier with time. Finesse will come."

Torrin held Nikolai's scarred wrist. "This will not fade. Each time we **Restore**, we bear the mark." He smiled at Tatianya, trying to comfort her in some small way, "Sweet innocent, your scar will fade. I doubt you will ever choose to **Restore**. Your chest wounds will also heal, no one need ever know. I know it is small comfort. I wish I had more to offer." His lack of ability to comfort, make up for her losses didn't matter. She wasn't listening. His words were falling on deaf ears.

Torrin was stunned to watch Tatianya consumed with bestowing love on the silent child. It broke his heart knowing Nikolai was powerless to turn back the hands of time. Large blue eyes were drowning in misery that was of her protector's hand. The bereft mother whispered, "His name is Nikolai II. Let it be known how much I love him, how much I wanted to be his mother." Her vast blue oceans were pulling Torrin, along with Nikolai, into their depths.

Chapter Nine:
Alliances

Angeline heard rumors that a **Restoration** had gone terribly wrong last night. She feared it was her Russian couple. As she continued to work on the clothing for Tatianya, tears ran down her face, certain the baby was gone. Even with the language barrier, she could see how much this child had been wanted by both parents. How could Nikolai have been so misguided? This would remain a mystery to all but Nikolai. He now knew this course toward destruction had been set in motion on their honeymoon, in that beautifully manicured garden on that star-lit night, in Paris.

The elusive, disturbing man in Paris had been a vampire. Nikolai was fairly certain now it had been Sergei. That voice. The reluctance to show his face, give his name. He cursed himself for not killing Sergei when he had had the chance on his wedding night. He knew this man, whoever he was, had used his powers to plant the seed in Nikolai's mind to head for New Orleans, for devastation. Nikolai's intelligence and business savvy had been no match for the vampire's superior abilities who had found it fairly easy to influence the wealthy power-hungry Russian, drunk with ecstasy from loving Tatianya.

As night fell, the two newly minted vampires feasted well, devouring blood, claiming soul after soul before attempting to approach Angeline. Nikolai now understood those dark brown eyes. She appeared to know about such things. He hoped his instincts about her were correct, that she would believe their story. She was their only ally in this dangerous city. He had to be careful not to frighten her away.

Nikolai explained to Tatianya he saw no choice but to attempt the **Searing** with Angeline, bestowing what had been denied to him. It would endow superior abilities, improve their communication and forge a bond. Tatianya was adamant they were not **Restoring** Angeline but saw the logic in attempting the **Searing**. She just prayed he could stop. She knew she couldn't. Tatianya was afraid to even go near Angeline despite being sated. Her grief, her anger was making it all but impossible to control her wildly vacillating emotions, her need to kill.

Silently, they made their way toward Angeline's ramshackle home by the river, keeping to the shadows. They were acutely aware of other vampires in the vicinity. It was obvious why these demons lurked in this God-forsaken corner of the city. Living here was little better than dying at the hands of a fiend.

Angeline was not surprised to see them and quickly ushered them inside. She kept the room dark. She couldn't bear to see their changes. Tatianya's figure saddened her. The rumors had been true. While she was afraid, these were the only people that had ever shown her any kindness. She had already decided she would help them if they came to her. As Nikolai hesitated, Angeline silently stepped very close to him.

Tatianya feared for her. They were definitely not in full control of their needs. But Angeline had long known about the **Searings**. Slowly she pulled back the sleeve of her tattered dress. She held her wrist inches from Nikolai. She produced a rose she had stolen from the market. The merchant had turned a blind eye as if he had known she needed it more than he. She had stolen an ornate box to house the thorns. Again, the merchant had simply looked the other way. "Kind sir, if you please." Large brown eyes implored Nikolai to proceed.

Nikolai was stunned. He searched her face. "Are you sure? You must be very certain." Momentarily she wavered in her decision. She saw just how much he had been affected. But she was so very grateful to this couple. She trusted that the kindness at their cores had not been diminished. She would accept the servitude that came with the abilities. With a small smile lighting up her face, "I wish to serve you, kind sir. I accept you as my master."

Nikolai and Angeline now turned to Tatianya. All three had to be in agreement. Nikolai had made a solemn vow to himself that he would never again do anything without Tatianya's knowledge. He owed her that and so much more. Tatianya was afraid Nikolai couldn't stop but as she looked around the squalor in which Angeline lived, she knew anything would be better than this. Even death.

Tatianya sighed and nodded. She watched Nikolai pierce his own wrist with the thorn Angeline had placed in his hand. He then turned the bloodied thorn on the creole wrist, tainting her blood with his, releasing his **Searing** heat upon the tiny wound. Tatianya regretted her acquiescence seeing Angeline's eyes go wild with pain. But true to his word, it was over almost before it began. He hoped it had been enough. Angeline crumpled into his arms and together they sank to the floor. He took the beautiful box he knew Angeline had stolen to house the thorns. She seemed to think he would need them again. They waited in silence, not knowing what to expect.

Eventually, Nikolai spoke, first in Russian, then Creole, and finally in English. Although Angeline could not respond, she was shocked to see that she could understand most of what he said. She merely nodded that she understood. Nikolai outlined that he was formulating a plan. He knew they could not remain much longer in New Orleans. He intended to head west, to San Francisco. He smiled and said they would return the following evening. This would give her time to adjust to her new powers, pack her few worldly possessions.

As they made their way back toward the swamp, Nikolai took a chance and wandered the streets, listening in on conversations.

He was fascinated that their hearing was so acute now. It was overwhelming that they could understand any language they happened upon in this cultural melting pot. English, French, Russian, African dialects, any and all were understood.

Tatianya was relieved to see that Nikolai was again taking control of their lives. She was having trouble controlling her raging emotions. Last night she had lost her life and her child. She ached to see that little rambunctious foot yearning to break free, make his own mark on the world. She hadn't known of the dangerous game her husband had been playing. She had trusted him completely and he had thrown everything away for power.

Tatianya was torn between hating and loving Nikolai. If she was in Russia, she imagined never wanting to see him again. But she wasn't. She was far from home, reeling from her changes, her losses. She had no choice but to stand by him, for now. She would wait for her new path to unfurl, reveal her destiny. She wondered if it would include her husband.

As they wandered the streets, a certain thread of conversation was repeating all over town. There had been a murder-suicide. A plantation owner had taken a beautiful slave as a mistress. His wife had been a fragile soul with a delicate mind.

This blatant disregard for her feelings had caused her mind to finally fracture. It was believed that she had stabbed her husband and his unwilling mistress before turning the knife on herself. Not wanting to bring further shame on her family, the slave's husband was expected to be charged with all 3 deaths. Today, however, this slave had escaped into the swamp. Speculation abounded as to how long this man would last. Nikolai smiled to himself. His new abilities reached out, seeking the essence of this slave. He sensed this man's vibrance. He also sensed the man's pain.

Nikolai fingered the ornate box holding the thorns. He began formulating a plan to enlist this slave in his plans to head west. It would be the beginning of the alliance with Isaiah.

Chapter Ten:
Isaiah

On impulse, Isaiah had started walking toward the far reaches of the plantation, toward the swamp. At first, no one had noticed. By the time it was obvious he was making a run for it, Isaiah had placed a substantial distance between himself and his vicious captors. Their shots failed to shatter his skull, explode within his brain. Their dogs snapping at his heels failed to sink their teeth into his flesh. He almost wished they had been more successful.

Isaiah finally allowed himself to slow his pace. Fear of what lurked in the shadowy swamp had caused his captors and their dogs to pull up short on the fringe of the putrid waters. As he propelled himself deeper into the swamp, the sound of dogs barking and shots whizzing by his head faded away into the stillness, the gloom. Even in broad daylight, the swamp was cloaked in darkness. As Isaiah's eyes adjusted, he grimly thought to himself, "Now what."

Wandering the swamp, Isaiah could not blot out the sight of his beautiful Kawanaa draped over that monster, blood trailing everywhere. Even in death, that lunatic had continued to clasp Kawanaa's inviting breast. Just as the scars from all those countless whippings were etched into his strong broad back, this new nightmare was now forever etched into his mind. He no longer cared what happened to himself. He had escaped the humiliation of a trial for murders that were not of his hand. He had managed to preserve his dignity. It was all he had left. For now, it had to be everything.

Occasional snatches of dappled sunlight danced across the swamp, obscuring any semblance of a path. Isaiah found himself standing knee-deep in the murky, stinking waters. He spotted erratic movements just below the surface, careening in his direction. With nowhere to hide, Isaiah knew gaping jaws would soon emerge. Watching the alligator make its final approach, intent on crushing his body, Isaiah made no move to elude this death. There would be no more running. He imagined Kawanaa waiting for him where there was no fear of beatings or abuse. He closed his eyes and made his peace.

Isaiah heard a horrendous attack ensue but felt nothing, He was not in this fray. He tore his eyes open and witnessed a beautiful woman ripping his assailant to shreds. He was stunned to see this elegantly dressed, obviously wealthy woman fearlessly dominating a creature that should have easily been her own demise. He had heard stories of such creatures, quickly dismissing these tales as the workings of overwrought imaginations or drunken rages. But it was impossible to deny the assault she had unleashed. He was unsure she knew he was there, witnessing.

She knew.

After Tatianya and Nikolai had left Angeline, Tatianya had found herself yearning to dominate another soul, her own essence reduced to shambles. She had stumbled upon Isaiah in the swamp and had followed him. She knew he was the slave that had escaped the plantation, 3 murder charges on his head, his innocence inconsequential. This innocence had spoken to her, struck a familiar chord, reminding her of a life now lost to her. But her need for his essence had spoken louder. Kindness had not prompted his redemption from those gaping jaws. Tatianya had merely saved him to sate her soul screaming for his lifeforce. She now turned cold murderous eyes towards him with this intent. Isaiah felt death would not be cheated a third time. Once again, he closed his eyes, waiting.

Isaiah heard a masculine voice with an unfamiliar accent, "Tatianya, please, not this one." An eerie calm descended. The quiet stillness was deafening. Isaiah had no choice but to open his eyes. He shrieked, recoiling in fear. Barely inches away were the remnants of a man looming over him, the woman now sulking like a scolded child. The woman had a trickle of blood staining her delicate chin. It belied the strength and intent of this fragile-looking creature. Her breath smelled of death. Her eyes were cold, dead. By contrast, the man's eyes were full of fire, darkened by deep sadness. Isaiah gasped and recoiled, falling against a nearby mangrove.

Isaiah watched the man turn to his companion and whisper, "Thank you, angel." His eyes were full of love. His heart was on his sleeve. She was obviously his everything. He gently reached out to wipe the blood from her chin. She cringed at this tenderness. A silent tear slipped from the man as she turned and wandered aimlessly toward a decrepit structure in the distance. The being ran frustrated fingers thru thick dark hair. Isaiah felt a kinship with this being. He knew what it was to worship someone. He also knew what it was to be powerless to reach them, protect them.

Isaiah faced Nikolai, each man sensing the other's heartache. He somehow trusted Nikolai. He made no move to run. Calmly, Isaiah stood his ground as Nikolai opened an ornate box and removed a thorn, caked with dried blood. Isaiah felt a strange peace watching Nikolai gently prick his own wrist and then just as gently turn the thorn on Isaiah's willing wrist. He felt a small jolt as their blood mixed, a quick flash of intense heat as Nikolai's thumb **seared** the wound, scarring the site. Isaiah sensed this

175

gentle assault was binding him to Nikolai. Curiously, he felt no fear. He had been subjected to far worse.

Nikolai released Isaiah after bestowing the **Searing**. He looked deep into Isaiah's soul, the one he had saved from Tatianya's hunger. He saw that the servitude was taking hold. He smiled as if in welcome. Nikolai turned and started toward the mansion in the swamp. Isaiah quickly fell into step. Silently, they followed Tatianya. Nikolai had known Isaiah would follow. He now would have no choice.

When they reached the mansion, Nikolai motioned for Isaiah to join him on the dilapidated verandah. "What were you doing in the swamp?" Isaiah was shocked he could understand the unfamiliar language. Patiently Nikolai waited as Isaiah collected his thoughts. At last, Isaiah began to recount his sordid tale, unleashing his sorrow, lamenting his overwhelming losses.

As Isaiah finished detailing the events leading up to his escape into the swamp, Nikolai probed Isaiah's mind. He was an open book. Nikolai's new ability to search another's mind found nothing untoward. He had to be certain from this day forward those he held close, those he rebuilt his future with were beyond reproach. He had made one huge misstep. There could be no more. Try as he may to discern any major flaws, he found only goodness, loyalty. And misery.

Nikolai understood Isaiah more than Isaiah could possibly know. Out of courtesy, Nikolai proposed his alliance.

He knew Isaiah had no choice but to acquiesce. However meaningless in the grand scheme of things, Isaiah was grateful for this show of respect. Isaiah nodded his acceptance. He could see that Nikolai would do his best to treat him with dignity. Isaiah vowed to deserve this honor.

As the two men sat huddled on the porch and Nikolai divulged his plans to head west, Tatianya slipped away. She thought Nikolai would not notice her withdrawal. But ever since the day he had first laid eyes on her, nothing about her had gone unnoticed, was forgotten. Nothing had changed for him. If anything, his changes had made him only want her more. But he knew she was furious with him and rightly so. He was grateful she was still with him at all. He accepted she was only with him as she had nowhere else to go. He had a sinking feeling that one day soon she would simply walk away and never look back.

As difficult as it was, he let her go. He hoped she would return. As much as he was also grieving their son, the loss for her was so much worse, compounded by his deceit. If he lost her, he would have no one else to blame. He wouldn't try to hold her against her will. She had come to him once before of her own free will. It would have to be her choice again.

For the first time, Nikolai was unsure what Tatianya needed from him, if anything. He had become her whole world. He had thrown this away for power, ego. He had always been as flawed as any man, but in her eyes, he had been perfect. She had adored him. Until last night Nikolai had not really understood the depths of her love for him. He wished with all his might he could turn back the hands of time. The best he could do now was to ensure she would never hurt again. It stung deeply to know the only person who had ever truly hurt his blue-eyed angel was himself.

Nikolai thought about what their families in Russia would need to be told. He had only sent one letter, to Alexi. His terse letter requested Alexi meet them in San Francisco, bringing the remainder of his vast fortune. He had not found the words to describe their changes, their losses. He was glad he wasn't seeing Alexi just yet. It would buy him time to adjust and formulate a more permanent plan. He would know by then if Tatianya would still be by his side. He didn't know which was more crushing, his need for a stranger's essence or his need to know where he stood with the love of his life. But he had no intention of pressuring Tatianya, letting her know he was dying to take her in his arms and love her, that his need for her had only grown. He was fearful that this precious part of their life was over. If it was, he would accept whatever she could offer. He would once again pursue his wife and let her decide what their marriage would be, for him, and for her.

Tatianya found her feet beating a path back to Angeline's ramshackle little world. She desperately missed her sisters. Her need for female companionship, a confidant, was overwhelming. She found the door ajar. Tentatively she crossed the threshold, finding Angeline sitting, waiting, her few possessions already packed. Tatianya took a chance and held Angeline's hand. Both women locked eyes as Tatianya's skin was so much warmer than Angeline's. She began to sob as she told Angeline what had happened. She told her one of the vampires, Torrin, had helped them bury their son. He had told them they had made enemies and were in danger.

Angeline looked deep into Tatianya's eyes, trying to reach what was left of her soul. She stumbled over carefully chosen words in her newfound language. But she made it clear to Tatianya that she would follow them wherever they went and do what she could for them. In truth, Angeline was very lonely and cared very little about what might happen to herself. She had nothing to lose. Even without the bondage forged by the **Searing**, Angeline knew she would have followed Nikolai and Tatianya wherever their paths might lead.

Tatianya helped Angeline carry her precious few belongings. They carefully made their way thru the city, hoping not to attract too much attention, revealing their refuge in the swamp. They spent hours meandering the city until it was almost daylight, Tatianya resisting the crushing urge to dominate another soul. She had no desire to see revulsion replacing friendship in Angeline's trusting eyes.

Tatianya toyed with telling Angeline about Isaiah but ultimately held her tongue. She would let nature take its course. She had had enough of nature being interfered with by meddlesome hands. She secretly felt Angeline and Isaiah could be good for one another. But Isaiah had recently suffered a great loss. He may not now, or ever, be open to another love and Tatianya suddenly felt very protective of Angeline. She didn't know Isaiah well enough to risk this tender heart, hoping something might develop. She herself had just been deceived by a man who had promised to protect and cherish. Her mind was spinning with her own misery and felt it best to leave all their paths to the fates. No, if Angeline and Isaiah were meant to find each other, it would have to happen on its own.

By the time Nikolai sensed Tatianya returning, he was out of his mind with worry. She had shut herself off to his new ability to read another's deepest thoughts. She too now had abilities. When she finally entered the decaying mansion, he could not help himself. He swept her into his arms. She did not respond, but Nikolai pushed fear aside, satisfying himself that she had not pulled away. He would need to content himself with these small victories. So overwhelmed, Nikolai missed her sighing softly as she allowed herself a moment's reprieve, breathing deeply of his musk.

It was then that Nikolai noticed Angeline standing in the shadows, Isaiah's eyes riveted to the lovely creature in the doorway. He also hoped these two would find their way to each other. But Nikolai knew it would be a long time before Isaiah would truly be ready to once again open his heart. He smiled at Isaiah's gaze upon this beauty but also vowed not to interfere. He had done enough of that. His hands were more than full trying to win back his universe and secure a safe means of getting them out of New Orleans and on to San Francisco.

Chapter Eleven: San Francisco

Nikolai swore he would never come back to New Orleans. Nothing good had come out of this sweltering mix of vile nuance and inconceivable treachery. Nothing except for a murdering irreverent demon with a raucous laugh that made Nikolai fight the urge to smile. A maddening turn of events had started to give Nikolai hope.

Torrin. This vampire would turn up at the oddest times, as if on cue. By now, Nikolai knew enough about this richly intricate underworld to know none of their casual meetings were anything but coincidental. He knew Torrin was keeping tabs on their progress to flee the city. But Nikolai could not deny a friendship of sorts was on the fringe of their guarded repartee.

"San Francisco! Ah, not going to venture a return home I see...." Torrin nodded his agreement as if he understood all too well. His thick Irish brogue seemed to take the sting out of this dismal reality. He turned his head ever so slightly in Tatianya's direction. "Coming around any yet?" Nikolai didn't answer. He knew Torrin also had powers and knew the answer. The Irish in Torrin longed for light banter and this was as close as they would come, for now.

Torrin lowered his voice, knowing Tatianya had powers at her disposal. He was disturbed to see this young beauty so isolated, so disconsolate. Her pain was like a magnet. Nikolai's mind was still an open book to him. He could see how much promise had been thrown away. He longed to encourage Nikolai, throw an arm around the younger Russian, cajole him into believing the worst was behind him. He resisted the urge. But he was delighted Nikolai would lean on him for advice. Together they concluded that it would be best to first travel north up the Mississippi by private riverboat and then head west over land by private means. It would be more discreet.

Torrin found himself amused that Nikolai had already enlisted Isaiah and Angeline in his plans to rebuild his life. He smiled knowing Nikolai was fast gaining control over his unwanted powers. Less than a week into his **Restoration**, and already two successful **Searings** and a **Restoration** to his name. Torrin knew that the day would come when Nikolai would once again be someone to respect. But it would take time. He doubted San Francisco would be much of a challenge for Nikolai to conquer. It was a good plan.

Torrin knew nothing about Isaiah aside from what his scattered grief-stricken mind would let itself reveal. But he had heard of Angeline. This frightened young girl had powers of her own that no one had ever cultivated. Despite now being bound to Nikolai through her **Searing**, Torrin felt it had been her good fortune to come under his care. He knew Angeline, having the most knowledge of demonic ways, would be an asset to Nikolai and Tatianya. He suspected Nikolai already knew Angeline had more to offer than just her ability to make a beautiful gown.

Isaiah was not as enlightened by his **Searing**, having no innate powers simmering beneath the surface. Isaiah found himself in awe of Angeline, her intuition when it came to what was going on with their newly **Restored** masters. He found himself drawn to her strong quiet ways. He was shocked, disappointed in himself that he felt a growing attraction. His Kawanaa was barely gone, and here he was, tempted by those soulful brown eyes. He berated his longing, another disappointment to a wife he had so miserably failed. He had no idea just how attracted Angeline was to him, how flattered she was with his stolen glances. But she was more concerned with Tatianya to show any reaction. Although she found Isaiah very alluring, she was obsessed with getting them all safely to San Francisco, especially Tatianya. Her primary goal was to firmly establish herself with her new mistress. Not one day had gone by in her young life when she hadn't worried about finding her next meal. Sleeping in a soft warm bed with a full tummy were luxuries she was holding onto for dear life. She wouldn't allow herself to dream of sleeping in Isaiah's strong embrace.

Upon learning of the plan to head north by boat, Isaiah had pleaded with Nikolai to find another way. "Nikolai, master, they will kill me. I cannot stand trial for murders I did not commit. They will recognize me. I will never make it to the boat." He waited for the pain a **Reading** would ignite. Instead of pain, Nikolai placed a hand on Isaiah's shoulder and smiled, "Trust me. Trust Torrin."

Isaiah soon came to see that money silences most if not all concerns. Under Torrin's watchful eye and Nikolai's deep pockets, no one seemed to notice the tall black man with the handsome foreign couple. Nikolai's wealth had cloaked Isaiah in a shroud of anonymity. Eerily, he walked among a silence that gave him the courage to believe he had a future. He was beginning to understand that somewhere deep inside that demonic body, Nikolai was clinging to goodness, loyalty, even as his taste for murder was becoming second nature.

The resident vampires of New Orleans watched closely as Nikolai and Tatianya prepared to leave. It was best for everyone that they move on. No vampire among them had ever intentionally caused the death of a child. They felt they owed it to Tatianya to help her leave behind the city that had caused her so much loss. The vampires had silently vowed to watch over her son's tiny grave. It was the least they could do. Even the most hardened vampires were finding themselves haunted by those now soulless blue eyes. Starkly beautiful, she somehow struck a chord, eliciting guilt from beings not accustomed to examining their actions.

Walking in the shadows towards the waiting boat, Torrin couldn't resist. He clasped Nikolai in a brotherly embrace and then gave him a good shove, tickled he had caught Nikolai so off guard. "Don't give up. It doesn't become you. You have certainly made a mess of things. Now find a way to right your world." He caught Nikolai's raised hand that was poised overhead. "Fight for her. Your fire rages ever brighter for her." Suddenly serious, Torrin held Nikolai's face between his surprisingly soft hands. With a cultured voice Nikolai had not heard during previous encounters, Torrin whispered, "Get the upper hand. Others are lusting after your angel. She has stirred demons like none I have ever seen. It wouldn't be long before she belonged to someone else if you allow this. But I sense she still loves you." Torrin's mouth quirked into a lopsided smile, lightening the blow he had just delivered. Nikolai nodded. He would miss this man.

Chapter Twelve:
Olga's Kiss

Alexi read and reread Nikolai's letter over and over again. Slurred speech whispered in the darkness, "San Francisco! First New Orleans, now this. What is really going on my brother? What is keeping you away?" In his drunken stupor, Alexi was at a loss. Nikolai's cryptic, terse letter all but commanded him to sail halfway around the world.

The night was falling. It was the hardest part of the day to endure. The servants were no longer tending to their duties. The hush over the house was deafening. During the day, Alexi could push aside the realization that little feet no longer echoed in his grand home. He could quell the waves of nausea as he passed Olga's now silent pianoforte. But at night their ghosts would not let him rest. He wandered nightly into each child's room and sobbed as he clutched a favorite toy. He would stand in the archway to the bedroom he once shared with Olga. He now slept wherever a drunken stupor overtook. He could not bring himself to crawl into that bed. He found it easier and easier to crawl inside a bottle, letting the liquor soothe his soul.

Alexi had sent word to Tatianya's and Nikolai's fathers that he had received an odd request from Nikolai. Both families were alarmed that there had been no word from Nikolai. Alexi would discuss with them just what to do. He wanted to go. Escape the hell his home had become. But he needed solid advice. His mind had not cleared since he had watched those three caskets disappear into the ground.

Tonight, he found himself outside despite the chill that remained in the air. He carried the crumpled letter, a crystal decanter of brandy as he silently stumbled up the hill to the cemetery. He drank the last of the brandy and then hurled the empty decanter, shattering it against a nearby tree. He then looked at Nikolai's letter. Carefully he folded it, kissed it, and placed it in his vest pocket close to his breaking heart. He threw himself onto Olga's grave and dug his fingers into the soil. "Olga, my love, I fear Nikolai is also deserting me. Was I that evil to deserve so much abandonment? Please ask God to come for me. He doesn't seem to hear my prayers. Ask God why he withholds my solace. What good am I to anyone? I bring no peace or joy to this world." He knew it was folly to sleep on the dew-soaked earth. He prayed for the death that would reunite him with his family.

Eventually, a fitful sleep overcame his restlessness. As he slept, Olga's beautiful calm face came into view. She lay on the ground next to him, cooing, chiding, "Alexi you need to stop this wallowing. You need to stop hiding in a bottle, drinking shamelessly. You have been spared for a reason. It is time for you to walk your path. Rest assured my handsome husband that I am safe, and your love is safe with me. I will wait for you forever. But for now, you are needed in this world."

Olga smiled at Alexi, time holding no meaning for her now. She confided that Nikolai and Tatianya needed him. He needed to rise above his grief for their sakes. She encouraged him to go to San Francisco and confirmed his fears that they were in trouble. As she drifted away, she kissed his eyelids and for the first time in months, he peacefully slept, knowing there was a purpose to his empty existence.

The following morning, both fathers arrived, their haggard expressions etched by weeks of worry. Alexi let each man read Nikolai's letter. Alexi announced that he intended to go to San Francisco. Both fathers nodded. It would be good for him to escape his torment. But Alexi was shocked when each father informed him that they would also be going to San Francisco. They were hurt and alarmed Nikolai had only contacted Alexi. Alexi did not have the energy to fight them and quietly agreed. They made plans to leave the following week. They grimly prepared to bring the vast sums of money Nikolai had requested. For this reason alone, Alexi finally agreed that it was better not to travel alone.

As their journey brought them closer to San Francisco, Daniil and Grigorii spoke to Alexi as if he was their own son. Nikolai's father especially was concerned about Alexi who had always been so stable. They had allowed him this time to mourn, endured his nightly drunken rages. Alexi knew they were right and struggled to regain control over his life and his drinking. It was time.

When they finally reached San Francisco, Alexi arranged to meet with Nikolai. Alexi was taken back when Isaiah arrived at their hotel to escort him to Nikolai's temporary home. He had hoped to see an exuberant Nikolai stride into the hotel lobby, taking command over the room with his palpable aura. Alexi stared at the tall, elegantly dressed black man. He saw Nikolai's hand in the finely tailored clothing this man wore with confidence. The perfect command of Russian was an unexpected shock. Isaiah had now been with Nikolai for months. Knowing this day was coming, he had drilled Isaiah until every nuance of the new language was perfect. When Alexi arrived at the mansion, he eagerly ascended the staircase leading to the main foyer. Again, he was startled to come face to face with yet another stranger. Angeline welcomed him, also in perfect Russian. She led him directly to the dining room and proceeded to set out the dinner while Isaiah poured him a stiff drink. Alexi was stunned only one place had been set. Trying to contain himself, he questioned Angeline about this. He knew she had heard him, understood his concerns, but offered no reply. Solicitously, she smiled and continued to serve him his meal.

Eventually, Nikolai and Tatianya appeared in the doorway. They did not make a move to embrace him and seemed oddly more comfortable in the shadows. Alexi was now confused more than ever. Something was obviously wrong. Alexi slowly got up from the table and walked over to his lifelong friend, "Nikolai, what is it? What has happened? You can tell me anything." He heard Nikolai sigh.

As Nikolai stepped out of the shadows, the two men came face to face. Alexi looked directly into eyes that should have been alive with excitement, that look of satisfaction. But all he saw was pain and something he had never seen before, doubt. His knees gave out and Nikolai carried him to a chair. Alexi began to sob. As Nikolai sat with Alexi, Tatianya lingered in the shadows. When she finally stepped into the beautiful room's soft glowing candlelight, he looked into her eyes. He could see that she was also transformed. Her eyes looked dead, her demeanor stoic. By contrast, Nikolai seemed much less affected. His eyes still blazed with that familiar fire even if it was now tempered by a deep-rooted sadness. "Alexi, my dear, dear friend, Alexi, I have been such a fool. I don't know where to start. I fear I have ruined everything. I can no longer pray, but I can hope. I hope you can forgive me. I hope you can still love me as your brother."

Nikolai recounted his deception to Alexi. He introduced Angeline and Isaiah. He assured Alexi that they had not and would not be **Restored.** When Alexi heard that Nikolai had been able to **Restore** Tatianya, he shocked Nikolai when he begged for

Restoration. Alexi's desperate plea seemed to jolt Tatianya out of her stupor. When she finally spoke, she gazed at Alexi with agony in her eyes, "Why would you want to be like us? We don't want to be like us." Her changes did nothing to shake his resolve. He was determined to be by his brother's side. "Nikolai, you are all I have to live for now. Please, give me a reason to go on." Nikolai merely shook his head, "You don't understand."

Alexi could see it was useless to pursue his plea. He slumped into the richly brocaded chair and informed them their fathers were also in San Francisco. Nikolai merely nodded; he had peered into Alexi's mind as he had begged for **Restoration**. But Tatianya was stunned that their fathers were only across town. They both longed to see them but were loath to face them as blood-sucking demons. Nikolai knew they would eventually have to face them but not tonight. It had been enough to face Alexi as a monster. He knew this next confession would not go as well.

Alexi again begged for **Restoration**. He stated he did not want to return to Russia. Nikolai stroked the cheek of his friend who recoiled from the shock of the extreme warmth in his caress. "Why would you want to be like this? This will not make you forget your losses. It will only sentence you to carry them for all eternity. At least as a mortal, your suffering will end. Take comfort, my dearest friend, that one day you will join your family." Alexi then further shocked Nikolai.

"If you will not **Restore** me, you must kill me! Claim my soul for sustenance. Steal my soul! I have no use for it. It appears this is the only way I can remain with you as before, no boundaries between us."

Again, Nikolai refused. But he tucked Alexi's request to be **Restored** into a corner of his racing mind. He would cherish having Alexi with him. But he would need Tatianya's blessing.

He was just now slowly regaining her trust. He would do nothing to jeopardize these small strides, not even for Alexi.

Nikolai then changed the subject and asked Alexi if had brought the money he had requested. He outlined his plans to Alexi. He wanted to buy land and lots of it north of San Francisco in the Napa Valley. He did not know what he wanted to do with the land just yet. But felt it would be a good place to settle, far from prying eyes. So far no one had questioned the mysterious wealthy aristocratic Russian couple. Their odd ways were only seen as eccentric. He felt it best not to push their luck.

Nikolai and Isaiah had been out to Napa several times and had selected large tracts of land. They had wandered over the rolling landscape in the moonlight for hours until the fog rolling in from the Bay signaled the coming of another dawn. Most of the land was flat but a good portion of it was hilly with cave systems running throughout. Whatever they ended up doing with the land, Nikolai felt the remote location would provide good protection. The cave systems would allow them to avoid the sunlight Torrin had warned was now their enemy. Isaiah had a great deal of knowledge when it came to land cultivation and Nikolai knew a portion of his new business would be agricultural in nature. He was toying with the idea of planting a vineyard. The climate, coupled with his long-held interest in viticulture made this an obvious choice. He shook his head, lamenting the irony that he would never be able to enjoy the fruits of this labor.

Nikolai and Tatianya decided that they would have no choice but to face their fathers and be truthful about their new lives. They both wrote letters to their fathers which Alexi would deliver. Nikolai knew that Alexi was very lost. His heart ached for his friend. Even though he had made devastating mistakes, Nikolai still had his wife by his side. Nikolai embraced Alexi, "My brother, nothing would please me more than to have you stay here with us. But I need you to really look to the future. For if you are to stay, I need to know that it is permanent. Alexi, I am rebuilding all our lives. It seems we are all adrift. You have always been my anchor. It gives me hope that you will be by my side as I try to rise out of this tragedy of my own creation."

Alexi told them Olga had come to him in a dream, that she had told him Nikolai and Tatianya were in need of his help. Alexi held Nikolai's face in his hands, absorbing his inferno, "Nikolai, there is no place I would rather be. My home, Russia, no longer offers me solace. Olga was right. My place is as it has always been, by your side. But you sadden me. I am no longer truly by your side. **Restore** me, dammit, **Restore** me! No matter what you think, we will never truly be brothers again until you do."

Anger overcame Alexi. He viciously attacked Nikolai, stunned to see his assault resulted in nothing more than a smile. "I promise you, Nikolai, whatever you have become, I want this for myself. Rest assured; I will not let this plea go unanswered."

Chapter Thirteen: A Father's Love Is Tested

Alexi ran his fingers over Nikolai's familiar seal. Even the cooling wax felt different. Distant. Empty. And betrayed. Staring at the black man sitting next to him in the carriage, he had never felt so alone. He thought he had escaped his nightmare. He had merely traded one nightmare for another. He wasn't sure of anything now. He muttered into the silence, "You stupid fool." He could feel Isaiah wince.

A vampire? Before tonight, Alexi had always dismissed such beings as fantasy, a whimsy of the sickest kind. **Searings? Restorations?** It was all so insane. He wondered how Nikolai could have been so completely duped.

Snippets from the evening's conversation, dosed with accusation, pleas for forgiveness and remorse grew louder and louder in his mind. Nikolai quietly had confided that he was certain the stranger in Paris had been a vampire. Lowering his voice even more, hoping Tatianya wouldn't overhear, "I am beginning to think that man was Sergei." Eyes glowing with agony, he continued, "I am certain that Sergei was close by the night I sold my soul." Betrayal had hung in the air, "Alexi, you led me to believe Sergei was no longer a threat." Those piercing dark eyes.

"No, Nikolai, he slipped away. Like a phantom. We assumed he had fled the city; overcome by the shame he had brought to his father's name." Alexi sighed, "Be reasonable Nikolai. We didn't want to mar your happiness."

"Why didn't you tell me? Didn't you think I deserved to know?" The obvious answer hung in the air. "No, you chose to mar my future." Those piercing eyes stared at the golden blonde curls just out of reach.

Alexi had no words. Another loss. He didn't know just how much more he could take. "I don't know what to say."

His tone had made Nikolai stop his badgering. He hugged his brother, letting his inferno ignite. "We cannot let any of this come between us. I need you more than ever. And I suspect you feel the same." An impish grin had appeared out of nowhere, spreading across Nikola's face. "Only you would ever forgive me such deceit. And only I would ever forgive you the same. Another bond between brothers?"

Alexi searched Isaiah's face. He could see he was a good man. He knew he had courage, facing a life bound to an unpredictable demon. "Isaiah, I can't do this alone. You have to help me. You can make Daniil and Grigorii understand."

Isaiah said nothing but shook his head.

Alexi found himself clutching Isaiah's face, "How can you refuse my desperate plea?"

"It is not my place to speak for my master." He calmly peeled Alexi's fingers from his face and looked away.

Alexi laid his head back among the carriage's luxurious interior, closing his eyes. The strain of the evening taking its toll, "I am begging you. I barely understand myself. Perhaps you can find a way. You have been with them now for months. There must be something you can do to help." He neglected to warn Isaiah that the duke was an irrational man, even under the best of circumstances. He imagined the duke hurling vicious accusations, throwing salt into an already festering wound.

"Tell me about Tatianya. She seems far more affected than Nikolai. Is that even possible? Their united front was just that, wasn't it? This must be killing Nikolai."

Isaiah found himself opening up to Alexi against his better judgment. "You still know your brother well, better than you realize. She doesn't even seem to see him."

Isaiah had wanted to scream at Tatianya. It was time that she either forgave Nikolai or walked away, allowing him to go on without her. But in his heart of hearts, Isaiah knew that would never happen. He knew that Nikolai would give up without her. He would find a way to end his existence. He so lit up when she entered the room while Tatianya barely noticed his comings or goings. Isaiah described her constant cold forbearance toward Nikolai. It broke Alexi's heart listening to Isaiah. It was obvious she was still Nikolai's everything.

When Alexi and Isaiah entered the hotel, they were accosted in the lobby by the waiting fathers. Alexi introduced Isaiah. The two older men had the same reaction he had had earlier in the evening when Isaiah's perfect Russian flawlessly rolled off his tongue. It broke Daniil's heart listening to the cadence of Isaiah's newly adopted language. Alexi knew what he was thinking. Nikolai's fastidious care was written all over Isaiah. The clothing, his carriage, everything down to the last syllable of each and every word, Nikolai's hand was evident.

The fathers were anxious for news, but Alexi would only confirm that he had seen Nikolai and Tatianya. He chose to say little more. Their faces lost all color as Alexi grimly stated he wanted to continue the conversation in private. The four men somberly made their way to the suite, Alexi fingering the letters in his vest pocket. He was dreading the reactions they would elicit.

Before Isaiah could close the suite's door, Daniil and Grigorii began to hammer Alexi with questions. He said nothing, solemnly handing them each two letters, one from Nikolai and one from Tatianya. By now Isaiah had grown accustomed to the luxury wealthy men lavished on themselves. He surveyed the expansive room and found what he was looking for. He immediately went to the banquet and poured four snifters of brandy. Isaiah was not a drinking man, but he raised a snifter and took a generous mouthful before silently serving the other three men.

As the fathers read and reread the letters, their reactions ranged from shock and disbelief to anger. The duke became enraged. He had entrusted his youngest and most cherished child to this man who had turned her into a monster and had cost him a grandson. He cursed Nikolai and smashed his snifter against the wall.

The duke's temper was now getting the better of him. He paced the length of the suite's parlor cursing Nikolai for his treachery. He cursed himself for allowing this poor excuse of a man to infect his family with this tragedy. The duke was almost beyond reason when he caught sight of where Alexi's and Isaiah's attention had turned. Nikolai's father had slumped in a chair. He was silently sobbing knowing that his son had made such a horrendous irreversible blunder, causing unimaginable consequences. They all knew the ripples of this catastrophe were only beginning to gain momentum. No one could deny that Nikolai alone had hurled them all headlong into unchartered waters. The duke calmed himself. Even in his frenzied state of mind, he knew the time for blame was long gone.

All eyes turned to Isaiah. He was now unsure he wanted to discuss anything with the duke. He was leery of this man's intentions. He decided not to elaborate how viciously Tatianya had been able to tear apart that alligator in the swamp. Instead, he focused on how Nikolai and Tatianya had struggled under their dire circumstances to treat him and Angeline with kindness and dignity. While this was true, both he and Angeline had a healthy respect for the newly **Restored** vampires. They were both constantly on guard, extremely mindful not to cause any untoward reactions.

Isaiah carefully chose his words, doing what he could to soften this catastrophic blow.

Isaiah recounted how over and over Nikolai bemoaned the fact that despite numerous misgivings about attending the vampire gathering, he had simply been unable to stay away. Both fathers began to understand that Nikolai had been bewitched in Paris. This knowledge helped bolster Nikolai's father. Alexi was relieved to see Daniil regaining his composure. He was relieved to see that the duke was also coming to realize that Nikolai had not acted entirely out of selfish greed. Alexi neglected to mention Sergei. He didn't see the point.

The fathers turned their letters over to Alexi and Isaiah. It was gut-wrenching to read the letter Nikolai had been forced to write to the duke. As the duke now calmly reread the letter, he remembered why he had come to love Nikolai as a son. He realized he still did despite being furious that he had caused so much devastation.

Alexi had been permitted by Nikolai to arrange any meeting the fathers might still want to have. Nikolai was determined to bridge any obstacle that he possibly could. He fervently hoped that this would be another stepping-stone back into Tatianya's heart. He wondered if the **Restoration** during her pregnancy had been too much for a trusting, innocent heart, so full of love and hope. He obsessed that her **Restoration** had taken a toll to the extent that she had nothing more now to look forward to except wandering thru each day a mere shadow of her former self. He knew himself well enough to know that his own **Restoration** had not been as devastating. He had been stronger, had been able to resist surrendering the entirety of his essence. More and more often, he was catching snatches of his old self. There were fleeting moments when he caught hold of glimpses of the once self-assured Nikolai attempting to reemerge.

As all four men stood in front of the fireplace in the suite, each father reluctantly littered the grate with the torn-up pages of the letters from their now murderous children. They knew no trace of any evidence could remain to incriminate them as vampires.

Isaiah departed with verbal messages. He was instructed to tell Nikolai and Tatianya that their fathers would visit the following evening. Isaiah felt he had been somewhat successful in deflecting the duke's initial explosive reaction. He reasoned that Nikolai must have expected this, given the eloquent letter he had written the duke, taking full blame for the disastrous turn of events. Isaiah just hoped Nikolai would not feel he had spoken out of turn. He knew Nikolai had been searching his mind as well as Alexi's for Daniil's and Grigorii's reactions. He had felt Nikolai's stranglehold on his mind. The brandy had done little to ease this pain.

Chapter Fourteen:
Loyalty

"Isaiah! Don't lie to me. This is important!"

Angeline was in a panic. She was determined to do what little she could to ensure this reunion would go as well as could be expected.

"Are you sure it tastes good enough?"

Isaiah could only nod, he couldn't get the food into his mouth fast enough.

Angeline had fretted all morning over the meal she would prepare for Daniil, Grigorii, and Alexi. For months she had only to cook for herself, Isaiah, and the odd occasional guests Nikolai would feel compelled to entertain. And now she was cooking for a duke! She tested recipe after recipe on Isaiah who was thrilled to death to be her guinea pig. As Nikolai did not care what Angeline spent on the household budget, her culinary skills had soared, much to Isaiah's delight. It was the only part of her that he could reach. He was taking full advantage. He hoped Kawanaa would understand.

On the surface, Angeline and Tatianya had very little in common. But their emotions, frozen inside their hearts for very different reasons, had created a bond no one else would ever understand. Angeline had never known true love or even kindness before Nikolai and Tatianya. It shocked her on a daily basis that her first gifts of kindness and respect had sprung from the hands of two murderous vampires. She knew they caused devastation outside their fortress overlooking the dank San Francisco Bay. She knew they haunted the cliffs perched just before the swirling waters, enrobed in fog, met the vast Pacific Ocean. She chose to use her growing powers and see the goodness that was screaming for release, even as they murdered with a vengeance. She hoped in some small way, her food, shimmering with her love, would somehow help tonight's reunion, help Tatinaya find a way to smile again.

Tatianya had known true love but had lost so much. She was terrified to ever let her guard down again. Angeline felt fairly certain that if Tatianya was going to leave Nikolai, she would have done so by now. But Tatianya was unable to reach out or allow Nikolai to reach in for her. Angeline hoped this reunion would culminate in some sort of resolution to the stalemate that now sat squarely between the two breathtaking Russians. So much was at stake. Isaiah jumped as she attacked yet another poor unsuspecting onion.

True to his word, Nikolai had not once pushed Tatianya any further than she could go to reach out to him or for him. He was beginning to feel this was as far as they would ever go on their path towards reconciliation in the truest sense of the word. Even after months of being regarded with a cold aloofness by his young wife, Nikolai still held out the faintest hope that he could break down the walls that now surrounded her heart. He knew he had caused her to be greatly wounded. He would wait forever if that was what she needed. He now had forever to give. He was finding he could be a very patient man.

As much as he held out hope, nothing about her spoke of invitation. Previously, her blue eyes had been alive with love and trust, sparkling only for him. Now, all he saw was the misery, anger, and betrayal placed there by his inability to resist the need for power. Gone was her innocent willingness to shower him with her love, to receive love, his love. His empty arms ached for her. His hands longed to caress her face, her body. He wondered how long she would remain with him. Silently he accepted his prison. She alone held the key to his joy, his love. How could he so blindly have thrown all this away for power, for personal gain? She had every right to her anger. By attempting to increase his already substantial power, Nikolai had rendered himself powerless to reach her heart. Bitterly he saw he had had it all. Falling into the depths of remorse, he had only to look into Tatianya's cold dead eyes to see he and no one else had caused the loss of everything important in his life.

Nikolai was overcome with shame, but the competitor that lived on within him refused to give up on their love. He would wait. He would do anything to rekindle her love light. He resolved at the very least to reignite her will to live, see her blue pools shimmer once again. He would do his best to reopen her heart to love. He hoped it would be for him. He doubted it would be his to recapture and nurture a second time. If another would ultimately restore her faith and be the one to make her love and kisses rain down, he would be eternally devastated. But he would let her walk away, knowing he had done all he could to ensure any happiness their new and confusing existence could offer her.

Nikolai envisioned himself accepting a lonely future. At night after he had sated his desire to steal yet another essence, the telltale traces of blood washed away, he would lie awake, alone in the dark. Anguished tears would kiss the pillow that had once been hers. He would make himself take small comfort that she had again found love, albeit in the arms of another. It would kill him knowing another was now taking her to her ecstasy. He resolved that if she left him, he would never take another. He would cling to the hope that one day, she would return.

Nikolai knew he shouldn't allow such thoughts of this desolate and very likely future to take hold. He forced himself to quell these fears. His rational side reminded him she was still by his side. Daily, he sought ways to shower her with any love she would accept. It seemed, for now, this would only be in the form of patience. Any small advance to touch her, any small caress was met with guarded tension which only subsided when he withdrew.

At night after their murderous rampages, she would sadly undress. She would lie next to him, her back and long cascades of curls shutting him out. He would lie inches from her, taking in her scent. He would gently clutch the end of a curl, careful not to disturb her repose. It was the only touch she would allow. He wondered if she even felt this loving caress. He resisted the urge to **Read** her, search her mind. He was afraid of what he might see.

It had killed Nikolai that first night when she had silently dropped her garments to the floor, carelessly leaving them in a pile. This had been a gentle pleasure for them both, he slowly removing the fabrics that had kept his love at bay all day. She had felt cruel stripping him of this beloved tenderness. The pain in his eyes and his humble acceptance of the restrictions she was lording over him simultaneously brought her vindication and deeper sorrow.

He would lie next to her, she just beyond his reach. He would wrap a curl around his finger, rolling and unrolling it just as she had done with that blue satin sash in her gazebo not so long ago. She felt this gentle gesture and cherished it, but could not bring herself to just turn around and throw herself into all the love she knew was waiting for her. She ached for him somewhere in her depths. But the part of her that could accept love and give love had been stolen from her. And Nikolai had been the cause of this thievery. She questioned if she could ever accept him back into her embrace. She cried silent tears thinking how he had lavished her with everything he had and knew it was still hers for the asking. Confused and angry, she had no way to reach out for his love. She alone held the keys to both their prisons.

Tatianya was thankful she had insisted on bringing her cachet of jewels Nikolai had showered her with night after night on their honeymoon. Each afternoon she would slip away to their bedroom. She would sit with her treasures, fingering each piece. She would remember how Nikolai had anxiously awaited her approval of his latest offering and then watched as she danced in the moonlight filtering into their private oasis. She smiled wistfully as she recalled how he would eventually get that devilish look she so loved and beckon her to him. She had loved flying into his waiting arms knowing how much he wanted her.

She would place a jewel under her pillow. When night had fallen, she would finger this treasure for comfort until her need for sleep overtook. Somewhere in her depths, she knew this was a cry for rescue. But she kept Nikolai ignorant of this small innocent attempt to reach out to him. In his efforts to reach her by showering her with patience and respect, he failed to secure his anchor. He had not won her the first time with patience or even respect. He had fought, fought hard. Unknowingly, by veering from his true path, he was widening their abyss. Once again, he was the architect of their demise.

As night began to descend across the bay, Nikolai finally signaled Isaiah to retrieve Alexi, his father, and the duke. He had been restless all evening. He and Tatianya had robbed victim after victim of their essence, hurling their limp, soulless bodies into the waiting choppy waters of the bay. They could not risk the slightest interest in predatory actions clouding all reason and judgment. Nikolai knew that he was going to have many, many questions and accusations flung at him tonight. He needed to be as clear-minded as possible. He and Tatinaya had stalked their prey far longer than normal and with a vengeance neither had previously known. Both were worried about how the evening would unfold.

When the freshly sated demons had returned home, both Isaiah and Angeline had been shocked at their appearance. Both Isaiah and Angeline knew that when they hunted, there was destruction and death, but had never seen any evidence of it. They had chosen to turn a blind inner eye to the truth staring back at them out of Tatianya's cold soulless eyes and Nikolai's tortured soulful ones. It was an odd contrast to see how full of love Nikolai was and how devoid Tatianya had become. It was a sadness that hung over the house, no one knowing how to rescue her from the depths to which she had sunk.

Both vampires had attacked with an abandon neither had ever allowed. Their clothing was soaked with the newly spilled blood from an unknown number of victims. As they silently re-entered their home, their eyes were wild and held an unfamiliar intent. Isaiah and Angeline said nothing and helped the pair to change. Without a word or look of reproach, Angeline took the clothing and began to wash away any telltale traces of what must have transpired.

Before Isaiah returned with their guests, Tatianya and Nikolai had regained their composure. They looked about the table laden with the fruits of Angeline's efforts with the familiar detachment they now held for food. As Nikolai and Tatianya heard the approaching carriage, they once more retreated into the recesses of the parlor's shimmering candlelight.

Isaiah escorted the three men directly into the dining room. Alexi was now ready for the pair to remain in the shadows. His stomach twisted as he knew what lay ahead. He knew the two fathers were anxious for this reunion which had an uncomfortable remoteness hovering about it.

Angeline greeted the men and did her best to make them feel welcome. Alexi encouraged them to eat as he knew it was expected. The two fathers had no interest in food, but as Angeline looked so eager to please, they surrendered to the course the evening would take. They began to enjoy Angeline's superb efforts. They relaxed while Isaiah poured wine and brandy, hoping to soften the coming blow.

Slowly, the presence of Tatianya and Nikolai could be felt on the periphery of the dining room. Both of them had wanted to observe their fathers. They knew it was possibly the last time they would see them. They wanted to feast, not on their essence, but simply on the sight of them.

As the men sat savoring their brandy, complementing Angeline on her efforts, she shone with pride and contentment. She would never get tired of being appreciated. It took so very little to ignite her gratitude for any kindness. All three men found her endearing and were curious as to how she and Isaiah were able to survive in a house dominated by inhuman creatures shackled with a horrifying hunger. It was a strange and intricate dance.

As the last of the shadows fell over the city, further dimming the ambiance of the dining room, Nikolai and Tatianya stepped into view. Again, Alexi was taken with the change in their appearances. But tonight, he was able to look further than the obvious. He found them both more alluring than ever. As mortals, they had been a striking couple who had turned heads wherever they went. But their immortality had bestowed a riveting aura. He now understood how Nikolai had been so easily seduced in Paris. There was an allure, almost a compulsion, which drew you in. He now understood how easily, almost willingly, their victims would fall.

But the fathers were in a state of shock and horror, much as Alexi had been last night. The duke lost no time flying into a rage which he launched with as much fury as he could muster. All day, he had fought to remain composed so as not to lose his chance to see his daughter. But now that she remained in the shadows of this grand room, he was no longer able to remain seated. In another life, she would have run to him with abandon and thrown her arms around his neck. Her infectious giggles would have filled his ears with song and his heart with love. As she stood wooden-like, coldly regarding him, he could no longer contain his fury seeing the extent of the damage Nikolai had inflicted upon his precious daughter. He strode across the room and struck Nikolai squarely across his face. Nikolai reeled as he had not expected this. Angeline and Isaiah were aghast. They fully expected Nikolai's wrath to flare.

But Nikolai's only reaction to this affront was to hang his head. He probed the duke's mind that was too overcome with grief to focus. The duke then faced Tatianya and her countenance caused him to stop short. As their eyes met, he saw she was a ghost of her former self in every way. He roughly grabbed her arm and began to pull her away from Nikolai's side.

"Come Tatianya, you are coming home with me. I don't know how we will proceed, but you are not staying here with this poor excuse for a husband. I should have never agreed to this foolhardy marriage. I knew there was something wrong with this union. You will come home with me and we will figure something out." The duke spat in Nikolai's face. He then turned to Isaiah, "Call for the carriage. Take us back to the hotel. Now. I will not stay another minute in the presence of this failure."

All present in the room held their breath, waiting for a horrendous response from Nikolai. He would never have accepted this attack from anyone else. Angeline and Isaiah had been standing side by side, watching. As the duke's attack on Nikolai descended further and further into chaos, Angeline became very frightened. She reached out to grasp Isaiah's hand. He was also in shock watching the duke coming perilously close to disaster. Isaiah welcomed the comfort of Angeline's warmth. Although he was also deathly afraid, his heart was soaring. She had finally turned to him. He would gladly hold this hand for the rest of his life. If only she would permit it.

Alexi and Daniil were now on their feet, not knowing what to do. Nikolai continued to eye the duke, but not with the cold eye of a killer. As tension hung in the air, Nikolai found his voice. "I deserved that and so much more. I know I have let you all down, and I will forever hate myself. I am doing whatever I can to move forward. I have tried to win Tatianya once again. It is very possible that I have lost her forever. I will not stand in her way. She is the love of my life and nothing has changed for me in that regard. She accepted me once before of her own free will. All these months, I have been waiting for her to again accept and forgive me. I will continue to wait for as long as I walk the earth. But I will not stand in her way if she chooses to walk away."

The duke was now clearly out of control. "I renounce you Nikolai Rozumovsky as a member of my family. I no longer feel the need to recognize the bond of matrimony between you and Tatianya. You do nothing but disgust me."

Furiously he commanded Tatianya to remove the rings Nikolai had placed on her hand. He again struck Nikolai. It was a testament to Nikolai's control and true character that he would not respond to the duke with the fury and strength that Angeline, Isaiah, and Tatianya knew he now possessed. Nikolai made no move to stop the duke's verbal or physical attacks. His newfound strength barely even felt the physical attacks, but the words had stung. He focused on Tatianya who had started to study her rings, the symbols of his love and commitment to her. He had taken small consolation these past few months that she had chosen to wear them. Occasionally he had found her admiring them, twisting her tiny hand to make the candlelight catch the fire in the diamonds he had chosen for her, a faint smile almost visible. He had hoped she was trying to remember, fighting her way back to him.

As tension clung to the very air in the candlelit room, it was Tatianya who finally broke the silence. For months she had let her heart turn to stone when it came to Nikolai. At first, she had been so filled with grief and anger. She had barely been able to be in the same room with him. But as the months went on and she observed his efforts to rebuild their lives and their marriage, her heart had softened towards him. As time dragged on, she had found herself painted into a corner just as her father had found himself when first confronted with Nikolai. She now looked upon her father with disdain and disgust. He had not seen her in months. Instead of trying to make the best of their desperate situation, he had chosen to attack her husband. Right or wrong, they were one. She found she could not deny she still loved Nikolai.

Tatianya now responded to the duke's cruel and heartless attack. It seemed this attack had shocked her out of the depths to which she had sunk. Anger flashed in her eyes as she jerked her arm free of her father's grasp. She flung her father a look that made him recoil. With contempt, she addressed the duke.

"Father" sarcastically she scorned, "Stupid man, you haven't seen me in months, and this is how you choose to act? I have no need for you if this is all you have to offer." She turned her back on the duke to fully face Nikolai. She seemed to be truly seeing him for the first time in months. Her heart now ached to ease the pain and defeat that was so deeply etched in his eyes. Tentatively she stroked his cheek, caressing the man that had never stopped loving her, despite her cold rejections. Slowly Nikolai met her gaze. He had become accustomed to her cold aloofness. He could scarcely allow himself to search her eyes. He had desperately waited to see the light return that had been there for only him. As he finally met her gaze, he saw that she had finally returned to him and they were truly one. In an instant, the coldness had left her eyes. The cold dead stare that had plagued her for so long was now replaced by fathomless blue pools shimmering in the tense candle-lit night. He was loath to trust this sudden change. But he couldn't deny she was looking at him in much the same way she had on that first night, with love, adoration, and yes, innocence.

Nikolai knew they were not alone, but he couldn't let this moment slip away. He wouldn't lose her again. Tentatively he reached for her, caressing a stray curl that had come loose as she had railed against her father. As she allowed this gentle touch and stood wide-eyed in front of him, he knew she had forgiven him. He crushed her to him and this time she responded with a vengeance. Months and months of pent-up love came tumbling down, but her motions were awkward, reminding him of their first kiss. In his mind, Nikolai was again holding the little blue-eyed angel in the gazebo.

With need born of desperation and fear, he savagely devoured her mouth not caring that he was creating a spectacle. He was in his own domain. If he truly had Tatianya again by his side in all ways, he would never fear anyone or anything again. Nothing except losing the love of his life.

Nikolai had to taste her love, feel the extent of her commitment. Her response to his demands made him gentle himself. It was as if she had been reborn, an innocent who would need tender nurture. She had been **Restored** as a woman, but this resurrection was coming from a place so pure, she was virginal to her new life and needs. Her mind had lain dormant all those months. It had taken the duke's violent outburst to free her from this cocoon. Nikolai could not believe he was being given a second chance. He would savagely protect her and the home he would rebuild around her, surrounding her with his love and protection. He would not need a third chance. There wouldn't be one. Her true essence of innocence would not allow her to survive another blow as great as this had been.

Alexi once again watched as Nikolai lost himself to this treasure. It was that first night all over again. But this time, it was Tatianya who had taken the lead. Nikolai had lost much of his will. His inability to reach Tatianya all those months had taken its toll. She saw for the first time how deeply she had injured him and felt a protectiveness she had never known. No one, not even her father, would ever come between them or hurt her Nikolai again. She would make sure of that.

Chapter Fifteen: Renewal

The past hour had Nikolai reeling. He had not expected Tatianya to turn on her father in his defense. He would be forever in her debt. More than ever, she was his salvation. The months of despair now seemed to have been a time of inward healing for her, waiting for just this spark. As the two vampires clung to each other, the duke realized his folly. He had sent his daughter back into Nikolai's embrace. Her adoring husband had not forced this turn of events. The duke, once more a foolish stubborn father, cursed his rash behavior. Again, Nikolai had prevailed at his expense.

The effect was now taking its emotional toll on Tatianya as she felt the shock of coming alive. Nikolai held her close as the walls that had surrounded her heart and mind came tumbling down around her, around him. She clung to him with all she had, stunned by the revelation that she was his as fully as she had ever been. He was not used to holding her possessively with his newfound strength. He prayed her **Restoration** had given her the ability to equal his desires. He knew his need to love would be far more than any mortal could withstand.

As the duo looked into each other's eyes, Nikolai whispered, "Angel, are you sure this is what you want? If you wish to reconsider, I will not stand in your way." Tatianya's eyes widened as his possession descended upon her. Nikolai held his breath, hoping that her feelings were truly aligned with his. Tatianya could do nothing but respond with the passion she had denied far too long.

Nikolai held her gaze and she smiled that sultry seductive smile. He crushed her curly blond head to his chest and the duo turned to face the duke as one. Moments earlier their eyes had filled with fire, heated by a passion that would soar far beyond the constraints of mortality. Now, as they eyed the duke, their gaze became cold, filled with hate. The duke was consumed by fear as his rage slipped away. He realized he had foolishly angered not one but two demons.

Nikolai knew he had the duke regretting his outburst. His casual command of the room sent a quiet but ominous message. There no longer was a need for Nikolai to fight for his place in his angel's heart. Quietly he whispered, "Tatianya, this is your father. As such, he deserves our respect. But we will not tolerate another such display. All in this room are either for us or against. We need to hear from each where they stand."

Nikolai's father had said nothing during the duke's tirade. He roused himself and approached his son and daughter-in-law. He reached out to caress both Nikolai's and Tatianya's faces. He winced as this touch scorched his hands. He made no attempt to hide his tears. He found the words he had been searching for all evening, reaffirming that they would always hold a place in his heart. Nikolai gently embraced his father. In turn, Tatianya also embraced her father-in-law. She shot a look of contempt at her own father over this welcoming shoulder of acceptance.

The duke knew all he truly wanted was to hold his daughter. Time and again, he let his temper win out over reason when it came to Nikolai. This man had replaced him in Tatianya's life and Grigorii found he could not accept this no matter how he tried. Daniil turned on the duke, suddenly impatient to be rid of the tension that was marring Nikolai's moment of triumph, "There will be no more blame or condemnation, Grigorii. You will either accept or forever turn your back." Reluctantly the duke nodded and sighed. It would be an uncomfortable alliance, but he would come to terms with it. He was left with no other choice.

Tatianya crossed the room and stood over her father as he slumped onto a finely brocaded chair. Defiantly she looked at him, sickened by his human shortcomings. Once more, she felt betrayed by him. Where was the man who had been her haven? Why couldn't he be like Nikolai's father and at least try? Tatianya reached out to the duke. Despite the heat that now pervaded her skin, he felt the chill in her caress. He flinched but endured. He knew this was his final chance to salvage their relationship. Once again, Nikolai had been the bigger man, and once again the duke had made himself look small. Tears of regret rained down on the indifferent hand holding out a final peace offering. The duke struggled to do his best and be the father she needed him to be. It wasn't easy. Tatianya gave her father a small kiss and whispered something in his ear. His mouth quirked into a cautious smile.

Nikolai feared the duke was once again attempting to wrench Tatianya from his side. He stilled his breathing and blocked out all but their exchange across the room. What had she whispered to the duke? He felt restrained to wait and hope she really had returned to him. Alexi had always been able to read Nikolai and tonight was no different. He knew his friend was aching to believe he had righted his world. Alexi took solace in seeing he could still find the pulse of their relationship even though Nikolai no longer had a pulse of his own. He gave Nikolai a smile of encouragement. It was like old times, almost. He could see it was best to quickly conclude the business that needed immediate attention and then return to their hotel.

Isaiah brought the carriage around and drove the three men back to the hotel. As the horses' hooves faded in the moonlight, Angeline said her goodnights. She was relieved that Tatianya had finally been freed from her prison. She was now allowing herself small snatches of what her own future could hold. She drifted off to sleep glowing, thinking how right it had felt to slip her delicate hand into Isaiah's.

As the house grew quiet, Nikolai led Tatianya silently to their bedroom. They had never made love since their **Restorations** all those months ago. Nikolai was tentative but Tatianya was on fire. She had been smoldering for him all those months. It took her father almost destroying her chance for resurrection to make her see things clearly. As Nikolai attempted to take things slowly, Tatianya ripped the clothing from his back. She had missed running her fingers along his broad shoulders and thru the hair on his chest. She drove her fingers possessively thru the dark shiny hair that hung seductively about his neck and in his eyes. Nikolai found it shocking that she was now the one breaking down his walls. He had locked this part of himself away, thinking this night would never come. He sat dazed on the side of the bed.

As Tatianya slowly began to remove her garments, his domineering nature came alive. He hated that she had taken this gentle pleasure from him, from them. He beckoned her to him. He laid his large loving hands on hers to still their motion. She looked up at him in awe. He had remembered. She thought he had forgotten. He wondered how she could ever think there would ever be anything about her he would forget. Shakily he let the clothing pile at her feet. When she was free, standing naked in the moonlight, he looked deep into her eyes. He found her calling to him. Her invitation encouraged and he began to explore what had been denied so long. He suckled and she responded, arching into his arms. Tentatively, he sought the soft golden hair between her legs as he had done on their wedding night. He wanted so badly just to sink into abandon and reclaim her in their new life. But just as on their wedding night, he resisted. He could no longer feed her chocolate-covered strawberries or champagne, but he could cherish and build her need.

Nikolai struggled to hold back, not certain her newfound strength would be a match for his. As she stroked and caressed his face, his body, he was overcome that this gorgeous creature was once more on fire, for him. This sanctuary had been devoid of love for far too long. He needed to heal the scars that her months of rejection had etched into his life. He needed to re-establish himself as her everything. With quiet joy and gratitude, he found her imploring him to make her his own.

Possession came with a fury. He threw caution to the wind. He dominated her as she reveled in his mastery of her needs, reclaiming her just before she crested. Tatianya screamed out in ecstasy. As shudder after shudder rocked her to her core, Nikolai released a desire born out of suffering and those long months of denial.

Wave after wave of need having been satisfied, they now lay for the first time in months ensconced in each other's arms. It was so reminiscent of their wedding night, their bed filled once more with the quiet joy of discovery and satisfaction. Nikolai was choked by emotion as Tatianya lay quietly on his chest just as she had done so many nights before all their pain, entwining her fingers deep into his nest of chest hair. Possessively he held her to him, humbled she would allow this closeness. She called him Nikki, the first time in ages. He took a chance, "Tatianya, what did you whisper to your father? I need to know."

Tatianya smiled up at him, relieved to see his need to dominate in every way was within her grasp. She snuggled closer, "I told that foolish old man I would never leave your side." She brushed dark locks out of her lover's face, intent on scorching him with her commitment.

"Nikki, don't ever let anything stand between us again. I couldn't reach you. Promise me you will always be strong for both of us. I wasn't strong enough." Tears of regret fell onto his chest. "I felt you caressing a curl each night. I wanted to turn to you but didn't know how." She cried her heart out releasing her anguish and sorrow. She recounted how she had taken a treasure to bed each night. She sobbed over her coldness. Nikolai held her closer. He would have waited for this moment forever. He stopped her flow of words with a fervent kiss. She had no need to apologize for anything, ever. He alone had caused their pain, their losses. He was more than ever her slave. He ran his fingers thru the long curls that had been his only connection to her for months. He felt renewed that thru those long months of rejection, her love light had continued to shine for him, however dim.

Their flame had never truly been extinguished. He would now guard her and their love with aggression. He cast aside his patience and swore he would make up for all they had lost. He would never again let her retreat into the recesses of her mind. He knew from this day forward he would accept no less than what they had at this very moment. He could see she depended on him for so much. It wasn't a burden. It was an honor. It humbled him to know she still completely trusted him to provide all she would ever need. He was thankful to be given this second chance. He vowed never to stray from his path again.

But as the passion slowly ebbed away, the specter of a child, his son, his heir, silenced before his first breath, sliced through the ecstasy of the moment. Thoughts of Tatianya's sad, dead, knowing eyes made Nikolai wonder if time truly could heal all wounds. He had no choice but to believe. Once more, he silently vowed, more fervently this time, never to stray from his path again.

Chapter Sixteen:
Napa Valley

Isaiah escorted Alexi, Daniil, and Grigorii beyond the glittering lights of San Francisco, northeast into the tranquility of Napa Valley. They were curious to survey the large tracts of land that had been scouted as the anchor for Nikolai's and Tatianya's new life. Isaiah and Nikolai had concluded that a vineyard would be the agricultural basis for the varied businesses Nikolai intended to establish in the sparsely populated valley with its gently undulating hills. It would fulfill a lifelong dream of Nikolai's to craft his own wine. The climate, the soil, even the timing was right, a bittersweet testimony to fate. But to the ever-practical Isaiah, it just made sense.

While Isaiah led the scouting party into the valley, Nikolai smothered Tatianya with caresses that were long overdue. As they lay entwined, Nikolai described Napa and the plans he and Isaiah had been carefully formulating. Tatianya questioned how they would sustain themselves in this beautiful but isolated valley. Nikolai was confident there were plenty of feeding grounds where little to no trace of their devastation would ever see the light of day. The budding vineyards were rife with migrant workers and other travelers passing through. He consoled her that their lightning speed would allow them to travel great distances if needed. He gently discussed the lost souls that seemed to find their way to the shallow coves of the San Francisco Bay. The element that was drawn to the surrounding cliffs were either criminal or pathetic in nature. Quietly he reminded her that no one ever noticed these disappearances. It shocked them both at how quickly they were adjusting to life as murderers. Torrin had been right. Finesse was coming with time.

Nikolai was captivated by the idea of founding a vineyard and winery. It was yet another challenge he could focus on dominating. He knew nothing about this type of venture, but Isaiah was confident with the right laborers and one or two people with experience, they could make a go of it. As Nikolai described this new venture to Tatinaya, his eyes lit up with excitement. His boyish enthusiasm drew her in. She too began looking forward to this new life.

With the blazing summer sun high overhead, the four men walked the rolling hills and surveyed the vast expanses. Nikolai's father looked at Alexi and smiled as he shook his head, "Always one step ahead of the pack, my son." Nikolai's enduring spirit was once more rising to the occasion. All four men had a good feeling about this idea, this location. The intense dry heat would make for good strong grapes which in time would make for excellent wine. The grapes would have to struggle to survive the dry excessive summer heat which would ultimately serve to intensify their flavors. Alexi returned the smile. He knew this wine would mirror the intensity that his friend always seemed to exude. He knew success was just around the corner. He hoped his brother had finally regained his footing on his path. Nikolai seemed oblivious to just how rapidly his powers were growing day by day. He was all but consumed with regaining his place in Tatinaya's heart. But Isaiah knew, and Alexi was also coming to see. Just like the wine that would one day bear his name, Nikolai had been thrown into the struggle of his life that now appeared on the cusp of bearing fruit beyond his wildest imaginings.

Isaiah continued to escort his guests around the valley, peeling back the layers of Nikolai's plans. Some of the tracts held underground caves which Isaiah described as ideal for wine storage due to the constant year-round temperatures. It would also allow for Tatianya and Nikolai to move around somewhat during daylight hours without arousing undue suspicion. Isaiah did not elaborate, but anyone who became too curious would not last very long. Nikolai would pay a very high wage in exchange for discretion and allegiance. He was loyal and fair but was becoming more and more comfortable with exacting retribution upon any who dared to cross him.

Alexi had been given the power to act on Nikolai's behalf when it came time to purchase the tracts of land. He wanted to secure as much as possible as soon as possible. Nikolai had taught Alexi well and he drove a hard bargain. Alexi secured all the tracts for a price that made Nikolai proud. He was glad Alexi was staying on. With Alexi and Isaiah at his side, the odd hours he was forced to keep were excused as eccentric, foreign. Nikolai was slowly learning to harness the power that had been lorded over him, first in Paris and then in New Orleans. He was slowly learning to exude that irresistible allure, the quiet power that had been his own downfall. Alexi was still attempting to convince Nikolai to **Restore** him, but he was seeing the logic in Nikolai's reluctance as well. He could still see glimpses of moments when Nikolai's eyes would cloud with uncertainty. He would be able to protect Nikolai and Tatianya better this way, still able to walk among the humans. Olga had been right. He was terribly lonely without his family, but this new land and new venture were just what his lost soul needed. He had grown immensely fond of both Isaiah and Angeline, but as far as truly trusting them, that was still to be earned.

As the land had now been secured, Nikolai spent hours with his inner circle planning the building phase of the project. He would want a large lavish home for Tatianya. He was insisting the underground caves be connected to the home. It was the only way they could move from home to the winery without the risk of sun exposure. It would be very expensive. It caused the architect to look closely at Nikolai, but no words were ever uttered regarding this demand. He suspected his latest client was some sort of demon. He found himself more and more believing he was in the presence of a vampire. The simmering heat that exuded at times in a handshake, the piercing dark eyes boring into the far reaches of his mind, the excruciating pain that this would inflict, all but confirmed his suspicions. But the architect was a savvy man who was being paid handsomely. He felt it best to let this go as an eccentricity of the wealthy, choosing to ignore what was staring him in the face. Doggedly he found himself protecting Nikolai, drawn to this man and his vision. He found himself almost compelled to squelch any rumors that saw the light of day.

While Nikolai busied himself with establishing new business contacts, Isaiah threw himself into working the land. It had been over a year since he had felt the dry earth crumble between his fingers. He had sorely missed the connection between himself and the land. He felt the soil speak to him as he coaxed life from it. His own heart was finally healing from the ordeal he had endured at the hands of the cruel plantation owner and then his captors. He often thought of Kawanaa, but these thoughts were more and more mingling with thoughts of Angeline. Nikolai and Tatianya had given him a new lease on life. He was the last person Alexi needed to fear would ever betray the Russian vampires. Both he and Angeline owed their lives to these demons who ironically took so many lives to survive.

Weeks were turning into months as the construction on the main house took shape and the fledgling vines took root. Isaiah spent his days looking down into the soil, checking the vines. His nights were spent gazing up into the heavens as he slept under the stars. He cherished the solitude of the valley but found himself missing Angeline more than he had expected or even wanted. During these clear, star-filled nights, he found himself talking to Kawanaa about how things were turning out. He told her about Angeline. He hoped she understood his loneliness. He hoped she knew no one could ever take her place. But he was a young man with a big heart who was finding he had room for one more.

Alexi often came out to check on the progress Isaiah was making. It was impressive to see how Isaiah had been able to take Nikolai's vision and craft the vineyard to his exact specifications. Alexi often brought along a little something extra for Isaiah from Angeline. Alexi never pressed Isaiah about his past, but the scars that were seared into his strong broad back from countless whippings spoke volumes. Nikolai had confided to Alexi how they had come to form their odd alliance when Alexi had voiced concern regarding trusting Isaiah with so much. Alexi knew that if he was going to remain with Nikolai, he would need to trust Isaiah and Angeline, completely, totally, utterly trust, as Nikolai's quiet gaze was pleading with him to at least try.

On one such visit, Alexi decided he would stay for a few days under the pretense of wanting to understand the vineyard. Isaiah was so proud to show the aristocratic Russian that he also had something to offer. He never suspected Alexi's true motives. Alexi worked side by side with Isaiah as the hot summer sun bore its intense heat deep into their bones. Alexi came to love this feeling and cherished being able to walk and work in this brightness. He more and more understood why Nikolai had refused his request for **Restoration**. He was saddened, understanding neither of his friends seemed destined to ever again enjoy this simple pleasure.

At night, Isaiah and Alexi would lie on their backs and silently study the stars for hours, lost in their own thoughts. One evening, Isaiah found himself compelled to know why Alexi would give up an obviously privileged life in Russia. He felt he and Alexi were at a point that he could pry, just a bit. Alexi had brought along a bottle of vodka which was now more than half empty. As he lay on his back, Isaiah saw tears run down the side of Alexi's face, pooling in the dusty earth. Alexi sighed. He rolled over to sit up and face Isaiah. He downed the last of the vodka. He wiped his face and recounted the story of his previous life. He described his tentative beginning with Olga, how he had not cherished her the way he should have right from the start. He cursed himself for wasting so much time on meaningless interludes with strangers whose names he no longer could recall. He sobbed that fate had cruelly cut their hard-won marital bliss so short. He smiled wistfully as he described his beautiful naughty little daughter Anastasia and his sweet serious son Nikolai. He stopped to collect himself when he thought of the fever descending upon his home, claiming its victims with little regard for the devastation left in its wake. Alexi then told Isaiah of the dream he had had that evening while lying on Olga's grave, hoping for his own demise.

Isaiah sat dumbstruck. He had had no idea what misery had lain behind those tranquil thoughtful eyes. He felt an immediate kinship with Alexi and retold his own sad tale. He surmised that Alexi already knew his story better than he let on, but Isaiah was glad to remember Kawanaa in happier times and to let Alexi know that she had been well-loved. He tentatively spoke about Angeline, that he found himself drawn to her, but didn't elaborate. He knew it wasn't their time, just yet. As Alexi listened to Isaiah pouring out his heart, he found himself trusting Isaiah and in turn Angeline. He knew he too had found his home, but his destiny remained elusive. He prayed someday his footsteps would fall with confidence upon a path that for now remained just beyond his grasp.

Daniil and Grigorii knew it was time to set sail for home. Months had passed. Autumn was fast approaching. They had been away far too long and needed to get home before the harsh Russian winter set in. One last time, they accompanied Alexi for a final look at the progress being made with the house and the vineyard. Both fathers saw their children were making a new life for themselves. In their own ways, the two fathers had come to terms with the horrifying reality of the situation. But it had taken months. They had put off going home, not knowing what to tell their families. Each man was still wrestling with what they were going to reveal, but each realized they had to tell the same story, perpetuating this lie to the ones they loved.

Chapter Seventeen: Russia

Nikolai's father and the duke boarded their ship for the long voyage home, knowing they had much to discuss. And once again, the two fathers found themselves at odds. The duke began sinking into rage after rage, constantly lamenting his decision to give Tatianya's hand to a man who had deceived them all. Nikolai's father became frantic that the duke's impulsive outbursts would expose the truth. He also was very disappointed that Nikolai had succumbed to the vampire in Paris but had come to terms with the present and chose not to dwell on the past. What was done was done. He had chosen to embrace Nikolai and Tatianya and not lose them even as they were now forced to live a murderous life half a world away. At least he knew where they were. He had vowed to make every effort to maintain some type of relationship. He quietly clung to the futile hope that one day a solution would be found to free his son and daughter-in-law from the hell Nikolai had chained them to with his power-hungry ego.

The duke was unpredictable. His reactions constantly vacillated, running the gamut from acceptance to outrage. Nikolai's father was very fearful that Grigorii would expose the truth which would be unbearable for all. It would disgrace both families, tainting the reputations of their other children and grandchildren. Nikolai's father tried to reason with the duke that enough harm had already come to their families. He felt that it would be wiser, kinder to tell all that Nikolai and Tatianya had succumbed to a fever much the same as Alexi's family. The duke alternated between seeing the logic in this and his need to expose Nikolai as weak, a failure.

As it turned out, the duke would no longer be a thorn in Nikolai's side. Shortly after setting sail, most of the ship's passengers and crew fell victim to a plague that spread quickly throughout the ship. Both men came down with the illness, but the duke could not seem to shake free of its hold. As time wore on, he became weaker and weaker. Both men came to realize that only one of them would set foot on Russian soil again.

The duke pleaded with Nikolai's father that he swear to tell both families the entire truth. As the sickness began to cloud his reasoning, he demanded Nikolai's father expose his son and his now murderous ways. He began to confide to the ship's doctor about the situation with Nikolai and Tatianya. At first, Nikolai's father was sick with fear that the situation was being exposed. But as the doctor spoke of the illness's worsening condition, it was clear that anyone who did hear the story only listened out of pity to a dying man. They merely assigned his rantings to one hallucinating from fever. Several days into the siege, the duke finally gave up his fight and the plague took yet another victim.

Nikolai's father was aware that the captain was being forced to conduct burials at sea to contain the outbreak. As the duke was royalty, Nikolai's father spoke with the captain and doctor, questioning if there wasn't a way to allow for a proper burial in Russia. Both men understood the situation but laughed at the idea. They were exhausted and overwhelmed from having had so much death on their hands. They wasted precious few words stating the obvious that sickness and death have no favorites. Nikolai's father had expected this response but felt he could truthfully inform the duchess he had tried in vain to return the duke's body to her. Nikolai's father was relieved, indeed delighted that this difficult man was out of his life. He attended the burial at sea and spoke the final words. But under his breath, he cursed this man who had caused so much anguish in the short time he had known him. Daniil felt Grigorii had gotten what he deserved. The elder Rozumovsky suspected the duke's pride and conflict regarding Nikolai had been his ultimate undoing more than the illness. The true cause of death was most likely a broken heart. Nikolai's father didn't care. He could now concentrate on getting his own strength back. He took comfort and solace knowing their awful truth was safe from further scrutiny.

Nikolai's father ultimately decided to confide the situation to his wife, Xenia. Together they would reach the decision as to how to proceed. He felt it best the truth go no further but was open to her opinion. Xenia was a fair and level-headed woman despite being high-spirited. It was she who Nikolai took after most. He would rely on her instincts, her never-failing ability to see things clearly.

Upon reaching home, Daniil gathered Xenia in his strong embrace. He could not meet her gaze as he ensconced them in their private chambers. She knew things were not as they should be. His letters had been short and evasive, speaking volumes of unknown heartache. He looked out the window over their beautiful estate he had always thought would one day pass to Nikolai.

He just didn't know where to begin.

Nikolai's mother sighed. She laid her head on her husband's back as she encircled him from behind. With a quiver in her voice she whispered, "He isn't coming home, is he." Nikolai's father shook his head. Xenia found the courage and asked, "Is my handsome baby dead?" Nikolai's father realized he didn't know how to answer what should have been a simple question. As tears ran down her face, he knew he had to speak the awful truth.

Daniil took Xenia in his arms and they sank to the floor. At first, his words came slowly but soon began to tumble over one another. Nikolai's mother was lost. He could see his turmoil was only making her pain and anguish worse. He stopped to collect his thoughts, this time laying out the whole situation, beginning with Paris.

After he had finished, he looked into her eyes for reaction, but they were closed. He gently shook her from her revelry, "Xenia?"

She smiled, "I was remembering their wedding day. They looked so happy. I remember thinking I had never seen my Nikolai so content. I am glad you were able to accept them and not add to their misery. God forgive me but I am glad that awful man is dead. We will have to go to the duchess, but Irina will never know what we know. No one will. We will tell everyone, even our own daughters, that Nikolai and Tatianya succumbed to the sickness; that the captain buried them all at sea."

Daniil and Xenia Rozumovsky steeled themselves knowing it was going to be very difficult to contain this lie but knew their sadness would be mistaken for grief over the deaths. Nikolai's parents vowed, that as soon as possible without arousing suspicion, they would go to Napa. Even if only for one more time, Nikolai's mother needed to hold her only son in her arms and assure him she too would never turn her back on them. It broke her heart thinking he had no way of knowing how she felt. She clung to the hope that he knew her well enough to feel her acceptance. It would have to be enough for now. A blinding pain descended, causing her to gasp for air.

Half a world away, a small smile trailed across Nikolai's face. Knowing the pain he inflicted as he searched another's mind, he let himself descend upon his mother's tattered thoughts. Just for a moment, he reached out. He had to know. He drew back the curtain and allowed his pain to descend. He smiled as he stroked

Tatianya's face, "She knows and is at peace. I should have trusted her. Spared her this added pain. But no one else will ever know. It is better this way. I have already caused too much sorrow."

The Rozumovskys set off for St. Petersburg. The duchess too had known something was wrong. As Irina heard the news that the duke, Tatianya, and Nikolai were all now gone, she clung to Nikolai's parents and howled. Nikolai's father had not allowed himself to anticipate this level of grief. He took much solace in knowing that the newlyweds were still walking the earth. He wavered in their decision. Xenia sensed his resolve dissipating and stepped in, showering the duchess with kindness. They sat together, two mothers grieving their children. The duchess mistook Xenia's grief to also extend to the duke, but in reality, Xenia was elated to be free of this horrid stubborn man. She held her tongue. She very much loved her own husband. She knew someday if his death preceded hers, she would also shed torrents of tears like this.

Nikolai's parents had no choice but to stay on for a few days. Memorials had to be planned. It was decided this would all occur at the duke's palace. The duchess became more and more distant from any and all. Immediately following the memorials, Nikolai's parents departed. They were becoming drained from the incessant lying. They could not continue to put up the façade with the duchess and her family. They felt it wise to depart under the guise of grief. As there was no need to continue contact with the duchess, they said their farewells knowing this would be the last. Nikolai's parents had no way of knowing that several weeks after the hurriedly planned memorials, they would again be summoned to the palace, but this time for the funeral of the duchess. No cause of death was ever revealed, but it was widely suspected that Irina had lost her will to go on when she had lost her duke and youngest daughter. While Nikolai's parents felt much guilt that they had contributed to the duchess' demise, they were at peace that Nikolai's and Tatianya's secrets would never be revealed. They would never betray their son and his wife. They would take their murderous secrets to the grave.

Chapter Eighteen:
Nikolai and Alexi

Nikolai made no attempt to hide his relief as Duke Grigorii Yusopov set sail for Russia. While it was true the two men had come to an understanding of sorts for Tatianya's sake, Nikolai was relieved to rid his household of this man.

But saying goodbye to this pariah had also meant saying goodbye to his own father. Once more, he was angry with the duke. Time and time again, Grigorii had managed to come between Nikolai and someone he loved.

Nikolai had not been up to Napa in quite some time. Business matters in San Francisco had kept him mired in the legal proceedings necessary to launch his burgeoning empire. It only added to his agitation that the precious little time he had spent with his father had been tainted by the duke's silent but ever-present accusations.

Tatianya saw his frustration and knew her father had been the culprit. She gently chided her husband that she and Angeline had never seen Napa. She playfully pouted, saying she felt cheated. Nikolai took her hand and lovingly kissed it. He knew what his angel was doing. Gallantly, he took the bait.

Alexi made the arrangements to take Tatianya and Angeline for their first glimpse of the beautiful rolling hills, now softly fragrant with the perfume of fledgling vineyards taking root. For Angeline, it was also a chance to see Isaiah. She had not seen him since shortly after the night Tatianya had found herself back in

Nikolai's loving embrace. She clung to the hope that Isaiah had felt their connection as much as she had. Tatianya's emerging powers allowed her to peer into Angeline's open mind. She too hoped that Angeline could find refuge with Isaiah. Tatianya was convinced they would be good for each other and in turn be good for the alliance Isaiah had accepted with Nikolai.

Everyone knew this visit to Napa was more for Nikolai than anyone else. He was again the center of Tatianya's universe. She realized that night as her father attacked Nikolai and he had restrained himself from lashing out, Nikolai had been thru so much for her. No one could ever love her the way he did. She felt remorse and guilt that she had turned from him for so long. She had not forgotten what had been taken from her on that fateful night by Nikolai's missteps. But she now understood it had not been out of cold-hearted, calculated malice. She would never forget her beautiful little son. It was a hole in her being she knew would never heal. It was a small part of her that seemed to have remained human. She found it hard to believe other vampires grieved as she did. She knew if anyone understood her pain, it was her husband. Although he never spoke of their lost little treasure, she knew Nikolai had not forgotten their son. Initially, his silence had done nothing but fan the flames of her anger. But as her anger subsided and she allowed Nikolai back into her heart, she understood. Tatianya came to realize Nikolai never spoke of their son for fear of awakening her grief. He was afraid his words would cause her to turn away from him once more. She knew that they would eventually need to face this pain, but they would do it together without fear of losing each other. They would grow from it, remembering their son as one.

As the shadows fell across the evening sky, they left the city's swirling fog behind. Nikolai was excited that the house in Napa was ahead of schedule. It wouldn't be long before they could make it their permanent residence. Nikolai had recently bought the home in San Francisco and would keep it for business. And for Alexi. He was trying to persuade Alexi to be open to a life away from the nightmare he and Tatianya were now forced to live. Nikolai knew Alexi wanted to be **Restored.** While Nikolai selfishly also wanted this, there had to be no doubt. He felt Alexi was still running from the tragedy of helplessly watching his family perish, leaving him alone to flounder in his grief. Nikolai needed assurance beyond a shadow of a doubt that Alexi would never regret his decision requesting the immortality and demonic hunger a **Restoration** would impart.

By now Alexi had moved into the large home overlooking the San Francisco Bay. He had adjusted quite easily to life in America. He was also adjusting shockingly well to living with demons. He did not fear for his life. Calmly, he regularly discussed with Nikolai his desire to be **Restored.** He understood Nikolai's reluctance to grant this request. Alexi knew he would miss feeling the sun's strength boring deep into his bones as he toiled in the vineyard. He knew he would need to learn to live with the heat that would constantly scorch from within. He knew he would need to master the never-ending need to quench this fire with a stranger's lifeforce. He had come to love the vineyard. He spent every possible waking hour there with his hands in the soil working side by side with Isaiah who had become a dear friend. But deep down, Alexi knew he was merely storing up cherished memories for the day he too would walk in the shadows. Ever since the day his world had come crashing down, Alexi no longer took anything for granted. He cherished each and every day, each and every moment. He understood far more than Nikolai what he was asking and what he would be giving up.

As the moon rose over the newly planted vines, Isaiah saw the little group approaching. He had been waiting all day to lay eyes on Angeline. Alexi alluded from time to time that Angeline would sheepishly ask about him, nervously giggling, anxious for any sign of encouragement. Alexi would smirk as he toyed with Isaiah that he'd better not wait too long or Angeline would find a city boy more to her liking.

As Angeline alighted from the carriage, Isaiah shyly came forward to help her down. He took the picnic she had prepared, savoring the softness of her hand as it lingered. Angeline had spent all day fussing over any dish she could possibly think that Isaiah might enjoy. Her efforts did not go unnoticed. Isaiah did his best to complement her thoughtfulness and show his appreciation. Nikolai and Alexi smiled at each other as they had hoped these two were finding each other. But Nikolai's heart ached for Alexi to also find some peace.

Eventually, the little group of five began to stroll about the vineyard. The vines were young, but Isaiah's instincts assured them the newly planted vineyard was vibrant, alive with promise. The dry soil crunched underfoot. The ground seemed to reach out to them, welcoming them to this slower pace of life. It was a sound they would all come to know and love. It would become the sound of home.

Nikolai then showed them around the house. Although Tatianya had never seen it she was enthralled. She threw her arms around Nikolai. He truly knew her every need. He had been able to capture every aspect of what she had always dreamed her home, their home, would be. Well, almost. He just hoped that as they walked from room to room, the glaring absence of a nursery would not be too much to bear. Although Tatianya noticed, she accepted this absence, the memory hanging heavily between them. Tatianya knew the time was coming that they would have to voice those unspoken feelings. But not tonight. Tonight, she would enjoy her new home and Nikolai beaming in relief at her pleasure.

As Tatianya and Angeline peppered Isaiah with questions about how he had managed to draw life from the hard dusty soil, Alexi drew Nikolai aside with two snifters of brandy. Nikolai raised a playful eyebrow but accepted the snifter. It was true that he could no longer enjoy his much-loved brandy, but he could still enjoy the aroma, the sensation of crystal in hand as he slowly swirled the velvety smooth amber liquid. He enjoyed seeing Alexi savor the brandy as it burned and settled. "Alexi, you know if I **Restore** you, this and countless other pleasures will be forever beyond your reach."

Sadly, Alexi replied, "I don't have anything left in this world that needs me. You are my brother. You are frozen in time and will walk the earth for a long, long time, maybe forever. Who knows? I want to do this with you as equals. I don't want to grow old without you." He looked at the brandy that had lost its appeal. "I could give this up today, all of it, to really be with you. You are my dearest friend, my brother. Why don't you want me with you as your equal?"

Nikolai picked up a stick and slowly drew a line between them in the dirt. "This is where I am, permanently, never to cross over. But you are walking between the two worlds. You have come to know our life. You have to know we are murderers, Alexi. We kill every night. And yes, we choose those that have caused pain and are evil, but nonetheless, we kill. We survive on our unfortunate victim's blood, their essence. But do you realize we absorb not only their lifeforce but also their blackness, their evil? Think Alexi think. Do you truly want to be a cold-blooded killer? You will need to be sure, really sure. If I am honest, the thought of drawing you into my darkness is like a beacon in this nightmare. I would selfishly **Restore** you tonight, freezing you in time with me. You will not only have to convince me but also Tatianya. I will not risk losing her again."

Alexi realized then that Nikolai was not against **Restoring** him and his spirit soared. Alexi demanded assurance that Nikolai was not simply stalling. Nikolai relented. "Five years. The vineyard will be producing by that time. Then we will revisit this madness." He commanded Alexi to make true efforts to find happiness as a human, ordering him to emerge from his self-inflicted reclusive lifestyle and make attempts with the young ladies in San Francisco. Alexi would need to prove once and for all he could truly find no peace except as a vampire.

Alexi was surprised to hear Nikolai's terms. He now knew that his **Restoration** was simply a matter of time. Nikolai's gaze let Alexi know he wanted this as well, but he needed to be certain it was the right decision. There could be no doubt. He knew how Nikolai had suffered all those months when Tatianya had shut him out of her heart. Alexi knew Nikolai feared this same retribution from him. He would agree to the terms, knowing five years hence he would be **Restored**. No one would ever touch him as Olga had. He saw that Isaiah was finding love again. But he was not Isaiah. His soul screamed he would never find love as a human. He was almost certain he needed to be **Restored** to love again.

Alexi triumphantly smiled at Nikolai, confident he had secured a rare and hard-won victory. Alexi's smugness caused Nikolai's temper to flare. His eyes flashed in Alexi's direction in a way Alexi had never seen. Both Tatianya and Nikolai were extremely careful to reveal their murderous natures and behaviors only when necessary. But Nikolai felt Alexi needed a dose of reality. With a speed Alexi did not realize Nikolai possessed, Nikolai was on the attack, Alexi the intended victim, or so he thought. As their eyes met, Nikolai's had turned black with desire. He held

Alexi in a death grip, the beautifully pulsating aristocratic neck and sensitive broken heart taken prisoner, his vulnerable essence exposed and beckoning. Nikolai had hoped to knock some sense into Alexi, but Alexi was the one with the surprise. He was ready for this, was praying for this, his own eyes now black with grief and loneliness. "Dear brother, I beseech you, bestow my **Restoration**. There is no need to prolong the inevitable."

Nikolai saw that his actions had not elicited the intended fear and revulsion. He released his friend, bestowing nothing more than a not so gentle shove. Tatianya had rounded a bend in the vineyard just in time to witness this battle of wills. She smiled and shook her head as she saw that the intended reaction had remained elusive. She knew that Nikolai had wanted to shock Alexi with a small insight into their true nature.

By now it was obvious that Angeline and Isaiah had benefitted from the **Searing** which had endowed each with certain superior abilities. Nikolai and Tatianya had discussed that bestowing a **Searing** would perhaps satisfy Alexi's obsession to be **Restored**. Their fondest wish was that this small window into their world would allow Alexi to give up his crazy notion of desiring a demonic life as a vampire. Alexi had sensed there was something special about Isaiah and Angeline. He had seen the tiny scars upon their wrists. Nikolai took his place beside Alexi and explained the **Searings** he had conferred.

Tatianya locked eyes with Alexi who instantly understood her thoughts, her intention. He watched as she transformed from a sweet innocent into her true nature. He had never witnessed anything so menacing. And yet he found himself mesmerized. He was shaking as Tatianya advanced with catlike prowess. Silently, she took his finely clothed wrist in her delicate hands. With a questioning glance, she traced her forefinger up and down the expensive fabric of his sleeve. Waves of nausea swept over Nikolai as he remembered his own assailant in New Orleans. It took Alexi a moment to realize Tatianya was requesting permission to bestow the **Searing**. He had assumed that Nikolai would be the master of this encounter.

Alexi nodded and Tatianya ripped the sleeve to reveal the pulsing vessel in his wrist. She ran her fingers over his skin so that a shiver ran down his spine. She seemed in a trance. She was hoping with all her might she could stop after bestowing the **Searing**. She was gathering all her will and control. She produced the ornate box cradling the blood-caked thorn. She pricked her own wrist, watching as the blood glistened in the moonlight, mixing with the earth of their dry dusty vineyard. She then sunk the thorn deeply into Alexi's wrist. She caught Alexi off guard. He howled as their blood mixed, her grasp burning with its intense heat, scalding this fresh wound. Nikolai worried that she could not stop. He agonized that Alexi would die tonight in their virginal vineyard or be **Restored** before his time. But he chose to trust her instincts. He would not interfere and betray her. Alexi had wanted to play with fire. This was only the beginning of his desired descent into hell.

Tatianya had sunk the thorn deeply, bearing down hard on Alexi's wrist. Her attack had been far more invasive than she had intended. She was not as gentle as Nikolai had been with Isaiah or Angeline. He possessed a subtle approach that she had not been able to master and doubted she ever would. She wished now she had insisted that Nikolai be the one. As her lifeforce flowed into Alexi, it was a sensual connection, much more compelling than the impulsive hunger when she took her victims. She resisted the desire to descend further into her chaos and rob Alexi of his soul. Instead, she sent Alexi flailing toward Nikolai who gently settled him against a vine bursting with life, ignorant of the pervasive evil surrounding this moment.

Tatianya struggled to regain her composure. She knew she had frightened Alexi and was both glad and remorseful she had been so aggressive. Nikolai was attentive to Alexi who was slowly regaining his composure. He looked at Tatianya and weakly smiled.

"Thank you Tatianya. I know that was difficult for you."

He stared at the wrist that showed the telltale evidence of the **Searing** he had just endured. His scar would not be as small as Isaiah's or Angeline's, but few would ever guess the truth behind this wound. Nikolai held Alexi's face in his hands, releasing his scorching heat, whispering, "Think very carefully my brother before you request any more than what you have received tonight. Now that you have had a glimpse into what you desire, I hope you can release this foolishness. I hope this will be enough to satisfy your hunger to be **Restored**."

Nikolai cradled Alexi as the powers bestowed by the **Searing** took hold. Whatever the outcome, another path had been chosen.

Chapter Nineteen:
Isaiah and Angeline

In the presence of Kawanaa's memory, a trembling Isaiah embraced Angeline as they exchanged vows. Kawanaa would always hold a corner of his heart. It was the place he retreated to when seeking courage. No one had been more courageous in his eyes. Today, he not only needed her courage, but he also needed her blessing. Both Nikolai and Tatianya repeatedly assured him that if Kawanaa had been half the woman he led them to believe, she would want him to be happy. She would want him to go on. It would be the ultimate revenge.

Things had moved slowly between Isaiah and Angeline. His commitment to Kawanaa kept Isaiah standing at a crossroads, unsure of how to step foot onto this new path beckoning to him. It was agony to believe Kawanaa was truly gone. It was hard to accept that this chapter of his life was closed. Oftentimes, he was blindsided by misery and guilt when he found himself feeling happy, content, full of life. Angeline would be gazing up at him and he would catch himself getting caught up in her, another woman. He had not known how to move forward, to permit himself to feel alive again. He was frozen by the knowledge he had not been able to protect Kawanaa. In his own eyes, he had been weak, a failure as a husband. He had vowed never to be that vulnerable again. Confusion and stubbornness had sealed off a willing heart.

But more and more, Angeline was in his heart, right alongside Kawanaa. He found his past and his future smiling at him, both trusting him to do the right thing, both urging him that it was time to once again walk among the living. It was not something he could reconcile. He chose to devote himself to the vineyard, despite a growing longing for Angeline.

But today was the opening of another chapter, finally. Isaiah had been dumbfounded watching Angeline descend the sweeping staircase of the home nestled among their flourishing vineyard. As the evening shadows allowed Nikolai and Tatianya a small measure of freedom, they greeted her at the foot of the stairs. They were beaming like parents, parading her around in her simple but elegant wedding dress.

The petite woman standing between the Russian vampires had looked questioningly at him, hoping for that smile of approval. Tatianya spoke first and giggled, "Isaiah, we got you a present!" Nikolai rolled his eyes. He knew this could offend Isaiah, but today Isaiah was beyond offense. Angeline was so beautiful. He had to agree with Tatianya. She and Nikolai truly had given him a gift, the gift of a second chance.

It was now almost five years since their move west. The vineyard was thriving. They were in the midst of a harvest that would produce their first vintage. The vines had needed tender constant attention during the first few years and Isaiah had not allowed himself the luxury of enjoying Angeline's company any more than he dared. Deep down he knew what they could have, but he couldn't bring himself to just let go and trust the fates. He ran from his future, choosing to bury his longing among the sun-dappled rows of their beloved vineyard.

Ultimately, Isaiah had been unsuccessful in running from his heart. He had missed this part of being a man, of being vulnerable to a woman who held the keys to his kingdom. Nikolai and

Tatianya's intimacy had become a burden to witness. Their open honesty with each other, the love that burned continually in their eyes sliced thru his heart with its intensity. He was getting older and wanted someone of his own to love and protect. He was stumped as to how to make this happen, his past suffocating his future.

Isaiah had felt somewhat avenged when Nikolai revealed that before leaving New Orleans, he and Tatianya had hunted down his captors. They had stalked each and every one, taking their time with their kills, striking fear into these black hearts before finally robbing them of their essence, leaving their corpses to rot in the hot southern sun. He had derived perverse pleasure knowing these evil men had succumbed to their dooms, crying like babies begging for redemption, for mercy that was denied. He could only imagine their horror. He couldn't help but let a satisfied smile spread across his face as he imagined Tatianya stalking and then attacking his assailants.

Tatianya and Nikolai had begun encouraging Isaiah to think about taking a mate. Of course, there had never been any doubt in their minds that it was to be Angeline. Nikolai's abilities had allowed him to see this future. And while he had promised Tatianya he would never again intervene without her consent, he had delicately steered Isaiah in Angeline's direction.

At first, Isaiah had been insulted, feeling Nikolai was suggesting he betray Kawanaa. He knew this was ridiculous, Kawanaa was long gone. Both Nikolai and Alexi reminded him that he was still a young man with hopes, dreams, and needs. Resolutely, it was his fears that he ultimately had chosen to address and nurture. He couldn't find the courage to walk this new path that was begging for his footsteps.

Tatianya also knew Isaiah was confused, incomplete. It broke her heart that he was so unsure of how to break free of the past.

She also wanted to steer Isaiah towards Angeline as what they both needed was right in front of them. In a move that surprised Nikolai, Tatianya decided to take matters into her own hands and play matchmaker. For all the killing and cruelty she had become capable of the past few years, she still possessed an innocence and naivety that kept Nikolai her slave. He had become a cold-hearted fearsome foe but when it came to Tatianya his devotion knew no depths. He made no attempt to hide the love he held for his angel. He wore this vulnerability like the hard-won badge of honor it was. Lucky for him, she was equally as devoted. They were truly one which only made Isaiah ache for more. Tatianya prodded Angeline to be more open, encouraging her to flirt with Isaiah. It had come so naturally to her with Nikolai, she found it amusing that these two were so inept at finding each other.

Nikolai took this cue and more boldly encouraged Isaiah to pursue Angeline. Isaiah had been appalled when he had discovered just how young Angeline was. She had been little more than a child when fate had opened her path to life with these demons. Nikolai revealed that Tatianya had not been 16 when he had asked for her hand. It was no different, except that Isaiah chose to see it as yet another stumbling block.

Tatianya knew Isaiah possessed a memory scarred by visions of a wife being repeatedly raped and then murdered, none of which he had found a way to prevent. She had finally spoken with Isaiah, "Angeline is an innocent, no tortured memories. She is a clean start for you. Be a kind, gentle teacher and she will never lose that sweet nature. She has no past, but you can be her future."

Tatianya had felt a connection with the poor creole woman right from the start during those first days in New Orleans, before the horror had descended. Over time as she watched Isaiah's furtive stolen glances, she came to believe Angeline could soothe his broken tortured heart if he could just let her in, let her enchant him with her charms.

Nikolai and Tatianya desperately wanted this union to consummate. They needed an heir to replace Isaiah when his time came. Long ago they had vowed not to **Restore** Isaiah or Angeline but their line needed to continue. As powerful as Nikolai had become, Isaiah and Angeline each possessed a power of their own. Their mere presence smoothed the way for their now demonic Russian masters to walk among the truly living. It kept the curious and their questions at bay.

And so now Isaiah took in the sight of Angeline as she stood before him as his wife. He knew she had never been with a man. A look of curiosity mingled with fear was etched upon her face. He would be gentle. It had been so long. He had not allowed himself to dream this moment would ever be his again.

Tentatively he came to her and took her in his arms. He was buoyed as he felt her relax into his embrace. Although Angeline had no firsthand knowledge, she and Tatianya had shared confidences like sisters in the night, giggling and giddy over love. Tatianya had confided that Nikolai was her one and only. She told Angeline to trust her instincts and not hold back. So much time had already been wasted. It was now time to grasp the future. Tatianya had fascinated Angeline as she came to understand that ever-present look of contentment shining in her mistress' eyes. She had begun longing for her wedding night, eager for that look of satisfaction Tatianya wore so well to settle in her own eyes.

Angeline was touched by Isaiah's gentle cautiousness. True to his way with her, reticence was plaguing him once again. She was emboldened with the freedom marriage had brought to her. Gone was her timidity. She began to devour his mouth, savoring his taste, his smell. She ran her hands over him and felt him come alive. She had finally struck a chord deep within his soul. Passion, desire, and want now overtook. He ripped the beautiful gown from her petite frame, stopping dead in his tracks. Kawanaa had been tall and strong while Angeline was diminutive and fragile. He worried that he would overwhelm her. It had never even occurred to him to hold back with Kawanaa.

Angeline sensed his confusion and smiled seductively. She beckoned her new husband to take his place beside her on their bed. As she quietly kissed his hand and placed it over her heart, Isaiah finally found the courage to trust his future. Angeline became all he could think of ever needing again. He cursed himself for waiting so long. He silently thanked the murderous demonic couple for opening his eyes to life and love again.

Chapter Twenty:
N&T Vineyards and Winery

Tatianya had come to love the valley, the mild weather, the sheltered life Nikolai was providing for them all. Long ago, she had lost interest in searching for the first silent snowflakes to caress her palace gardens. She had grown to love the fog rolling in from the San Francisco Bay. She felt safe behind the high stone walls surrounding their vineyard and her home. She loved the peace this slice of heaven had brought into a life now fraught with death and darkness. Gazing out over their vineyard, sometimes, just for a moment, she could forget she was a cold-blooded killer. Since they had settled among Napa's gently rolling hillsides, others had followed. The once barren land was now dotted with numerous fledgling vineyards. Nikolai's shrewd business intuition had landed them some of the best locations and soils. Their burgeoning vineyard and winery would surely one day be a huge success. Just this past fall, they had completed their first crush. Isaiah and Angeline had married during this time which had been madness. But it had been their moment. Tatianya was thrilled that Angeline had conceived so quickly. Nikolai had worried that this news would resurrect old hurts. His fears were unfounded. Her innocence shielded her from envy. Tatianya's sweet nature only saw Angeline's happiness. She was determined for Isaiah to have heirs to pass this secret way of life onto before his and Angeline's footsteps were silenced by the march of time. It would be a comfort to have someone of theirs to behold. It was another part of the alliance Isaiah had accepted years ago, chaining himself and now his descendants to Nikolai.

Tatianya loved the difference between the older and newer sections of the vines. She loved the feel of the supple young vines under her fingertips, tracing their strength and flexibility. The hue of green was vibrant, exciting, even happy. Their underlying resilience was deceiving.

Then her fingertips and gaze would move down the vines to the older, more established sections. Gnarled as if stricken and cursed by the decline of age, the thicker rough dull brown-gray sections hid a strength and wisdom about survival the younger more supple tendrils could have no knowledge. Yet here they were, the old and the new, anchored by the same roots in such opposite phases of their journeys. The older vines, sturdy to the point of paralysis, were trying to convey their wisdom to the grapes, the wine. The younger sections of the vines, while deceptively strong, lacked experience and flailed in the breeze or drooped under the scorching Napa sun. Both depended on each other to nurture their hidden treasures.

Roses the color of ecstasy had been planted at the end of each row. This was as much for the benefit of the vineyard as for Tatianya. She missed the rose garden of her childhood home. She loved to walk among the roses in the moonlight, stopping to savor their aromas when in bloom. She fingered the velvet soft petals and filled their home with fragrant bouquets. Nikolai would stand on their bedroom balcony and watch as she lost herself in the roses. He would remember the gazebo and the rose petals that had been strewn at her feet when he had asked for her hand. With his ever-present guilt and regret, he now also saw a darker meaning hidden among the petals that unfolded to release their aroma as well as their power to **Sear** and **Restore**. He fingered the box of blood-caked thorns that was never out of reach.

Far into the vineyard, Nikolai had built a gazebo for Tatianya identical to the one in Russia. Adjacent to the gazebo was an entrance to the underground caves that ran like a maze, safe from the unrelenting sun. Isaiah had prepared a portion of the caves for wine storage. Nikolai had prepared another section for Tatianya to move freely from the house to the gazebo. As ferocious as she had become as a hunter, when it came to men, she was still quite naïve. Her innocent mind along with her youthful beauty was forever frozen at 16. Alexi and Isaiah knew this could be a problem as there were now so many men on their land. While it was ridiculous to worry about Tatianya, Nikolai was protective, possessive, and worried about her as any husband. These cave passages allowed her to move about unrestricted away from prying eyes. It was the perfect solution to keep Nikolai's irrational jealousy at bay.

The winery was fully operational and the number of staff was growing which required a deft hand when it came to hiring. Nikolai was a very wealthy man with deep and generous pockets. Many men had come west looking for gold when the word had spread about Marshall's luck just on the outskirts of Placerville or Hangtown as it was also known. Despite huge fortunes being found in this area just east of Sacramento, most had only found hunger and disappointment. A growing vineyard and winery needed many hands to make it thrive. Nikolai was more than willing to be benevolent when it came to the wages he paid. Word spread quickly that the Russian vineyard was looking for good men. Alexi and Isaiah had the responsibility of screening the new employees. Their **Searings** had equipped them both with keen insight. These abilities were invaluable when it came to discerning which of these potential employees would work hard and mind their own business. The successful hand at N&T would be well rewarded if they knew to keep their minds and hands on the vines and out of their employers' personal lives. Suspicious speculation surrounded Nikolai and Tatianya. It was widely suspected that there was something odd about the alluring Russian couple, but as they were personable and generous, society and employees alike wisely chose to turn a blind eye.

The few unfortunates who would get curious and snoop around looking for clues simply disappeared without a trace.

There was a constant strain of worry about these disappearances, but no questions were ever voiced. Everyone knew that if you were summoned to see Nikolai, you weren't coming back and it was no use to run. As times were hard and the money was good, loyalty was forged as much from fear as from gratitude. Those that had made it thru the first couple of years were valued and Nikolai made sure they were well cared for. He provided housing and no one ever complained of hunger. He intervened when trouble broke out. An employer who stood by his employees in the burgeoning west was unusual and this further cemented unwavering loyalty.

The vineyard was peculiar in so many ways. While grapes were generally picked at night to protect their sugars, N&T required all work to be done at night. Most of the supervision was done by Isaiah and Alexi, but Nikolai enjoyed seeing the fruits of his labor in action. He rarely spoke to any of his employees; indeed, his mere presence was often cause for alarm. He enjoyed evoking this type of respect or fear, depending on the situation. This was the power, the quiet power that Nikolai had so desperately sought in vain from the vampire in New Orleans. Nikolai would smile ruefully at the fear he so easily evoked. He now realized he had always possessed the power he had once believed eluded him.

As word spread quickly that the vineyard had produced its first vintage, Nikolai was faced with handling the attention this was causing. The fine line between walking in the shadows and basking in the limelight was a new challenge that took finesse to traverse. It made Nikolai regret the promise he had made to Alexi to **Restore** him. Five years had all but passed. He knew the time was fast approaching when Alexi would demand his **Restoration**.

Alexi had kept his word. He had tried to make a new life, find another spark, but that had failed. Alexi had buried the only spark that would ever ignite his soul in a winter windswept grave. Both men knew this now to be true. Alexi was content to live in the past when it came to love but Nikolai had become a master at living in the present, planning for the future. He had left the past behind out of necessity, misery, and shame. It was coming close to the end of Alexi's promised five years. Nikolai would not deny Alexi the **Restoration** he continued to yearn for. Alexi had held up his part of the bargain. Foolishly, Nikolai was holding out hope that Alexi would ultimately reject their demonic way of life. While Nikolai would miss Alexi when he no longer walked with him, it was what he wanted for Alexi, to live a normal mortal life, free from killing, free from the ever-present lust for yet another victim's essence. The self-control it took to interact with mortals sometimes was almost too much to bear. It was a constant hum, which gradually built to a screaming raging pounding that drowned out all but the most desperate need to retain a shred of decency, dignity. It never faded. Try as he may to describe this torture to Alexi, sicken him with their violence and destruction, Alexi had quietly remained resolute in his decision.

Tatianya didn't want the stain of this **Restoration** on the vineyard. She felt Alexi should be initiated into his new existence in New Orleans, in the house they still kept in the city, in the very room where Nikolai had **Restored** her, simultaneously condemning her soul. When Tatianya had timidly outlined her proposal for Alexi's **Restoration**, Nikolai had been overwhelmed.

It had made him revisit his deception and the death of their son. She had looked at him shyly while she cautiously detailed her plan. She had no desire to resurrect his shame. Her plan had made perfect sense to Nikolai. They both knew Alexi would have great difficulty controlling his hunger and desires for quite some time and they would be there to guide him. Tatianya was very afraid for Angeline as the lust of an uncontrolled unprincipled demon had cost her a child. She vowed Angeline would never endure this unending despair. She knew Alexi needed to be kept away from Angeline while he adjusted to his hunger. Nikolai also worried that Alexi would lose control and decimate their workforce, revealing their closely guarded secret in the process. Yes, if Alexi was to be **Restored**, it would be in New Orleans, the city of their perdition, their downfall.

Tatianya knew it was time to bring the past out of the shadows. And she was one step closer.

Chapter Twenty-One:
Five Years Later, The
Past Makes a Demand

Tatianya could see Nikolai was never going to forgive himself. Once her mind had been freed from its prison, his constant remorse had made it so easy for her to forgive him. He had never mentioned their son since the night they buried him. She wanted desperately to bring this ghost that hung between them out of the shadows. But she didn't have the heart to shine a light on his misery and shame. She also knew the time was coming when they would have to face it and they would, together.

Tatianya chose a star-filled night to draw Nikolai into the far reaches of their vineyard. As she faced him holding both of his powerful hands, she began walking backward, drawing him past the rows of vines that were becoming gnarled with time and wisdom. Like an adolescent afflicted with puppy love, Nikolai allowed himself to be drawn into her magic. He was anticipating loving her under the stars.

Tatianya had other plans.

When they came to a small clearing beyond the vines, she looked deep into his eyes. He realized she was troubled, needing something beyond the physical. His chest grew tight. He feared she would say the words that would shatter his world. He had wanted so badly to remember their son with her. But cowardice had silenced his tongue. Not a day went by that he didn't give thanks that she would lie next to him, receiving him in any way he demanded. He walked in fear that one day she would be gone.

In the cool of the evening, they watched the stars dance across the sky. Tatianya sighed, "Nikki, don't you ever think about our baby? I think he would have been like you, tall and handsome, demanding and yet so loving. I miss him almost more than I can bear."

Nikolai knew the moment he had dreaded, had tried to avoid, was finally upon him. He was suffocating with regret, with self-loathing. This pain had been building for almost five years. It erupted in a torrent he couldn't control. He had no words, He showered her with tears and sobs that wracked his body and hers in turn. Together they lay in their vineyard openly sobbing, mourning their son.

He knew what she needed to hear from him. But Nikolai found himself mute with fear, strangled by disgrace. Patiently, Tatianya waited for him to find his voice. He knew he was trapped. Her innocent imploring gaze cut thru his emotional paralysis. He pinned her to the ground, anchoring her physically, mentally. He opened himself to her, letting her **read** him. But she wanted him to put word to feeling.

"Nikki, I need to hear you speak your pain. You have deprived us long enough. It is time."

Cautiously he began. His bitter regret built to a crescendo that he had cost them their son, their happy, perfect, mortal life. He confessed his never-ending fear of losing her. He confessed his fear that one day she would simply disappear without a trace, closing her mind to him, leaving a void he would never have the strength or desire to fill.

As he emptied his heart and soul of all his fears and regrets, he did not sense any withdrawal from her. If anything, he felt their connection strengthening. Nikolai was uneasy, deathly afraid he was simply seeing what he wanted to see, to feel. He savagely took her, desperately loving her. Nikolai made sure this loving scorched her being so that no other would ever be enough. As he sagged against her exhausted sweating body, she gently laid his head on her bare still heaving breasts. He cupped a breast as he pleaded with her, "Please don't leave me. I am nothing without you."

Tatianya stiffened. Her blue eyes flashed, feeling betrayed. Confused by her reaction, Nikolai cursed his candor. "Oh, Nikki, is that what you think this is all about? You are my love; I will never leave you. Can't you see that by now? The distance between us is the grief that has been suffered in silence far too long. We should have been grieving our son as one.

His ghost hangs between us. I want to go to New Orleans this year, on Mardi Gras. It's been five years."

What was he was sensing? If she wanted to go to New Orleans, he would make this happen. It was true that five years had passed. He was now a strong and powerful vampire, not one newly minted. He would make the preparations. He was in a position to make demands. And if that would keep Tatianya by his side, no one would stand in his way. She would get her wish.

He nodded that they would go to New Orleans. He quietly stated, "I will let Torrin know we are coming. We will bring Alexi with us. It seems it is time for many things."

Nikolai knew Tatianya's innocence prevented her from anticipating the level of shock revisiting New Orleans would rain down on her broken mother's heart. She then whispered, "I want to go every year. I want to openly mourn my child. I want to stand by his grave and sob. I want to lay flowers. I want to stay in the mansion in the swamp. I hope you understand. I need to retrace our steps. I need this, Nikki. Can you do this for me? With me?" Her blue eyes, her fathomless oceans, were awash in the throes of turmoil, a hurricane of emotion drowning him in the sorrow he had unleashed. Again, Nikolai simply nodded, relieved she was making no efforts to crush his soul.

Chapter Twenty-Two:
New Orleans

With their thoughts spinning out of control, Tatianya and Nikolai silently entered their stately mansion in the French Quarter of New Orleans. It had been five years since they had fled the city as newly **Restored** vampires.

Trying his best to be respectful and supportive, Alexi followed closely behind. He knew this was difficult beyond his comprehension. But at the same time, he was excited. He did his best to hide his curiosity. He had never seen anything like this before. It was all so seductive. The unfamiliar, at times revolting smells coming off the wide Mississippi River, the paddle wheelers churning up the murky water; they were mesmerizing to him.

Nikolai had retained several servants all those absent years and the home was ready for their arrival. He put Alexi to work discussing the details of their stay with the household staff. He steeled himself to face the room where he had **Restored** Tatianya. A lump was caught in his throat. This pilgrimage was far worse than he had allowed himself to imagine. Knowing the room where Tatianya had labored to deliver a son that had died along with her mortality was just up those stairs forced long-repressed fears to bubble to the surface.

Although Alexi was anxious to go exploring, Nikolai absolutely forbade him to venture out alone. Nikolai had arranged an uneasy truce with the resident vampires, making it clear he had no interest in a permanent residence. Nikolai had met no resistance to his announcement that they were returning to their city of horrors. He had made it clear to Torrin, who had become their leader, that they would be returning from time to time and wanted no trouble or in fact, very little contact with them. He reluctantly informed them that a human would be accompanying them. Once again, he felt he was placing a loved one in harm's way. But he was now wiser, stronger, and not afraid to use his finely tuned powers. The resident vampires saw that Nikolai had become a force not to be angered. Previously, his genteel aristocratic forbearance had fooled them into thinking him weak. They were shocked at how quickly he had grown into a formidable ruthless demon. They had no interest in any trouble either. Nikolai sensed a few harbored more than idle curiosity regarding Alexi. Although Nikolai had obtained assurance that Alexi would be able to meander the city unharmed, Nikolai had very little faith that all of their assemblage would respect this decree. The sooner they **Restored** Alexi and retreated to the decaying mansion in the swamp, the better.

Nikolai's nerves were much more on edge than he had anticipated. It was interfering with his ability to sense and **read** his surroundings. He knew he had to rise above his personal chaos for all their sakes, but especially for Alexi's. Tatianya had immediately gone upstairs. Nikolai knew he should join her but was dreading the coming scenario. He was cornered into facing the lowest point of his life. He had come so far. It would be a difficult emotional descent. He was torn between embracing the pain, communing with Tatianya on this primordial level, and the need to remain vigilant. He could not allow his vulnerability to be detected. Most of the resident vampires were sympathetic to Tatianya's need to grieve. Five years later, they were still appalled that one of their own had taken an unborn. But Nikolai sensed a darker evil beyond all their control.

Nikolai stood at the foot of the stairs, dreading Tatianya's reaction, fearing another rejection. Alexi said nothing, but jammed a finger into Nikolai's back, propelling him up the stairs. It was time. Slowly, Nikolai climbed the grand staircase, fingering the finely turned banister. He knew he was stalling. As he approached their bedroom, he heard Tatianya sobbing and speaking to someone. For a brief moment, it was five years earlier in his mind. He flew to her side, to protect her from the evil that he sensed.

But as he entered their chambers, he saw she was alone. She was crying out to her son. She was denouncing Nikolai's maker. Nikolai regretted coming back to this house of horrors. He took her into his embrace as she sobbed and clawed at the air. His heart was breaking over all the pain and destruction he had caused. But even in her darkest hour, Nikolai could feel her love reaching out for him. He found the courage to join her in this grief.

The grieving parents sunk to the floor. After what seemed like hours, Tatianya was spent from the emotional release that had waited five years to be recognized and claimed. She clung to Nikolai like a child frightened by a nightmare. He caressed her golden curls. His murderous angel seemed so small and fragile. She looked lost. Nikolai felt the need to protect her and she was grateful for his strength. She crumpled into him, allowing him to be her fortress.

Alexi had quietly joined them, careful not to intrude any more than necessary. As Tatianya remained ensconced in Nikolai's embrace, she listened while Nikolai shared more detail of their sordid past with Alexi than he had ever done before. She knew it was Nikolai's last attempt to dissuade Alexi from the madness he had chased these past five years. She surmised it was a futile attempt to save his soul.

Nikolai watched the stars making their way across the nighttime sky. He knew they needed to hunt. But he had made no move to rouse Tatianya from the cocoon his embrace was providing. Although still limp and exhausted from the emotions that had overwhelmed her, Tatianya finally realized her need to claim another's essence. This need was suddenly urgent, raging. Her eyes became wild and unfocused. Although Nikolai had graphically detailed countless attacks in his futile attempts to dissuade Alexi's unwavering request for **Restoration**, Alexi had never seen their violence unleashed. He was shocked and more than a little unnerved by Tatianya's transformation as she quickly went from fragile waif to seductive huntress. Nikolai caught Alexi's eye and gave a sad laugh. He now let Alexi see his own baser side as well, hoping for a change of heart.

"Come Alexi, Tatianya and I need to commit yet another string of atrocities. You will witness our commitment of murder after murder. I never wanted you to see that we are savages. But you need to know the hell you crave for your soul. Be especially careful of Tatianya, she is a fearsome hunter. Stay by my side as she descends far deeper into the chaos than I have ever done. I once saved Isaiah from her hunger. But I will not betray her if she decides to turn on you."

Alexi only nodded. He was fascinated by the changes in their countenances. Their eyes were wild and unfocused but clearly hungering for his essence, his soul. He knew it was only their deep-rooted love for him that was saving him from their hunger. As they made their way to the slums, Nikolai divulged that they chose to prey on those whose evil they could sense or beings so pitiful that taking them could be viewed as mercy. But he made it clear to Alexi that they were killers, murderers and there was no way to ever justify what they did, night after night.

Without a sound and not much warning, Tatianya silently approached a tall, well-dressed man that was having his way with a young prostitute. The girl was still a child and clearly did not belong on the streets, selling herself to these vermin. As Tatianya slipped up behind the man, she flung the girl out of his reach, motioning for her to flee. The girl was both grateful and afraid. Legends abounded in New Orleans regarding the resident vampires. The girl rightly suspected Tatianya intended on decimating her attacker. She did not linger.

As the man spun around to face the person who had interrupted his sexual release, he was surprised to see a petite innocent. He was still caught up in his sexual ecstasy and failed to see she would be his demise. As he attempted to place his hands on her, he caught sight of Nikolai whose jealous rage made him stagger. Tatianya lunged forward and latched onto the man's shoulders. With her eyes inches from his face, he became mesmerized with her beauty, her deceptively sweet breath. He let his guard down, much as Isaiah had done in the swamp years ago. She anticipated, craved this precise moment. She not only needed their essence, but she also needed to dominate them in every way. Her fragile-looking, sensuous mouth slowly descended to the man's neck. At first, she gently sucked, sending chills down his spine. When she felt she had made him mad for her, the fragile chin and full lips dissolved into a sneer and crazy laughter. With a force that shocked both her victim and Alexi, she imprisoned the man within her strong embrace. She ripped wide his beckoning neck, encircling the jagged wound with her luscious, murderous mouth, unleashing her intense scalding heat. The man screamed in agony as if nothing could be worse. He quickly saw how wrong he was as she placed her other hand over his chest. Heat blazed from this hand as well, melting his skin, his bones until nothing stood between her and her prize. Violently, she possessed and consumed his essence with abandon. She then cast aside the decimated body; eyes torn open with the fear of knowing there had been no escape. Still in predator mode, Tatianya stood victoriously over her kill.

Nikolai struggled to fight back his jealousy as he watched his angel entwine with her victim. He knew it was nothing but sustenance to her. But he couldn't help feeling enraged when male victims laid their hands on her. He knew it was irrational. He knew he was the cause of her needing to resort to murder to survive. He reminded himself if they had stayed in Russia, she would never have needed to touch another man. She would never have needed to feast on human blood. And she would have been a mother to his heir.

As Tatianya released her victim, she became aware of them both intently watching her. Alexi was clearly hypnotized by her animal-like prowess. She knew her style of hunting was much more aggressive than Nikolai's. It was odd to her that she needed to dominate her victims while Nikolai merely wanted their life force. She found it hard to meet Alexi's eyes but forced herself to do so. He looked visibly shaken but she did not see any reproach or disgust. He had tried to feel repulsed, but couldn't. She wished for his sake that he had.

"Alexi", she cooed with a voice as velvety as her beloved roses, her victim's blood and entrails staining her expensive dressing gown, "Did you enjoy my style of hunting? Is this what you desire to sentence yourself to, you stupid, foolish man. Perhaps I should claim your essence next."

She advanced towards him, brushing against his evening coat, marring its beauty with the blood from her latest kill.

Clear gray eyes stared back at her. Alexi stood his ground, barely glancing at the blood and gore soaking his garment. Quietly he smiled, "You have done nothing but heighten my fascination."

Tatianya had failed to alter Alexi's conviction to be **Restored.** She softened for a moment and stood on tiptoe to kiss his cheek. She smoothed away the blood that was tainting her lips and now his cheek, "Very well my dear precious mortal Alexi, I have done for you what I could. I will support your misguided descent into hell."

Nikolai diverted his eyes. He knew this was merely Tatianya's attempt to dissolve Alexi's conviction to be **Restored.** But the heat between his wife and friend was hard to endure. He picked up Tatianya's victim's lifeless body. With very little effort he cast it into a murky canal that led to the great river. Before morning, the body would be submerged beneath the muddy waters. The creatures of the canal would finish off the corpse, hiding any evidence of the carnage a duke's daughter had inflicted.

Alexi silently followed as Nikolai led Tatianya down another alley. It would now be his turn to hunt. As Nikolai selected his victim, the aristocratic finesse almost made Alexi laugh. He watched Nikolai approach his victim. As the young man turned to face Nikolai, he smiled. He elegantly slid his hand around the thin dirty wrist. With the slightest motion and smallest protest, Nikolai dominated first the neck and then the chest.

Nikolai was able to subdue and claim his victim's essence much quicker than Tatianya. His composure immediately returned. His eyes no longer contained the wildness of the hunt. He had no need or desire to dominate his kill. With a detached flick of his wrist, he hoisted the second body into the canal. A faint trail of blood briefly swirled with the current before evaporating into nothingness. Nikolai scanned Alexi's face for any signs of disgust. Again, Alexi found himself feeling only fascination. Nikolai sadly shook his head.

Alexi followed his friends, watching attack after attack until they were done reeking their unique brands of havoc. Silently, they made their way home. When Nikolai had Alexi safely inside their home and Tatianya was settled comfortably against his chest, he directed his gaze toward Alexi. Somberly he spoke, "Do you still want to be **Restored** after what you witnessed tonight? I will **Restore** you in this house, in the very room where I **Restored** my angel. But you don't have much time to decide. We cannot risk staying in the city much longer. Tomorrow we will visit our son's grave. We will grieve and then I will **Restore** you if you still crave this depravity."

Alexi was appalled by what he had witnessed but felt all the more compelled to join them. He tried to rationally feel disgusted. He knew he should take this last opportunity to run, to board the next ship bound for anywhere, but all he could think was that they would finally be equals and together forever. He was so lonely, even when he was with them. He hungered to join them in their nightly depravity, to understand everything that they instinctively knew. He knew it was madness, but reason was no longer ruling. He stood and faced Nikolai. Alexi's clear direct gaze made Nikolai's heart sink. He had known Alexi his whole life. He was the first friend he had ever had and Alexi had stood by him thru everything. He knew him well enough to read that expression. Alexi had made his decision five years ago to be **Restored**. He had never once wavered. Tonight had done nothing to diminish this resolve. Nikolai accepted this decision with mixed feelings. He was elated for himself, indulging a selfish desire to have Alexi with him forever. But he was conflicted that he would be the one to condemn Alexi's soul, to end his human existence. Nikolai nodded and embraced his friend. "Tomorrow night." was all he said as he allowed himself to study Alexi's aristocratic features. He wondered if he really could go thru with this second **Restoration**.

Chapter Twenty-Three:
Alexi and Nikolai II

Alexi had chosen to spend his final human day walking the streets of New Orleans, enjoying the mundane. He ignored Nikolai's pleas to stay by his side, hidden away from the resident vampire element. He basked in the sun, tilting his face to take full advantage of being kissed by this warmth. The impenetrable curtain of humidity that constantly shrouded the city slowed his movements, forcing him to savor each moment all the more. He indulged a last decadent supper. He walked by the river watching the setting sun glance off the ripples in the wake of a riverboat. He was saving up memories, savoring feelings, sensations. But he was ready. He'd been ready for five years. He searched the sky, knowing the heavens were already turning away from saving his soul. He didn't care.

True to his word, Alexi had attempted to find a life apart from Nikolai. He had stayed in San Francisco for weeks at a time, accepting social invitations, attempting to find another spark. But when he had finally given his heart to Olga, it had been forever. Alexi had given it the five years Nikolai had demanded. That time had come and gone. Tatianya knew Alexi still yearned for **Restoration**, maybe now more than ever. She knew Nikolai also wanted Alexi's **Restoration** but was filled with strife that his closest friend could very well end up despising him. Tatianya sensed something different. If Nikolai could just still his thoughts, quiet his fear of rejection, he would see it too. Alexi needed to belong somewhere, not just anywhere. And that somewhere was with Nikolai in every way. Since Olga's death and the deaths of his children, he had been adrift. Alexi lived with them but was not truly a part of their new way of life. Isaiah and Angeline had each other and now a baby on the way. Nikolai and Tatianya had each other again. She could see that if Nikolai **Restored** Alexi, he would know once more where he belonged. She had initially feared that by **Restoring** him, Alexi would mourn Olga for eternity. But he seemed to find comfort in her memory more often than not as the years wore on. Each year on the anniversary of the deaths, he would find himself in Russia, working his fingers into the soil which separated him from his Olga. He always came back renewed. He spoke little of this private time, but Tatianya knew as Alexi lay on Olga's grass-covered grave, she would come to him in dreams. It seemed that this was enough for him. At least for now.

Alexi was thankful that Nikolai had made him wait. It had given them all time to prepare. It had allowed time for them to become established in San Francisco, then Napa, and now also New Orleans. He was glad he'd been able to help smooth the way. He suspected many people knew Nikolai's and Tatianya's true nature, but as they were so gracious and charming, it was easy for most to find a way to look past the obvious.

As a human, Nikolai had always been able to win over anyone, including the irrational and ill-tempered duke. Alexi was always amazed that anyone who came in contact with Nikolai did not readily see what he had become. With Nikolai's deep pockets and deadly charm, he was able to easily move among any populace with very little need for calculation. If anyone did get too close to the truth and unwisely felt it their duty to expose them, Nikolai had no compunction about ridding himself of the latest nuisance at hand. These past five years had hardened him to all the death. It almost seemed to bore him at times.

Alexi hoped his **Restoration** would leave him more like Nikolai than Tatianya. She had always had peaks and valleys when it came to emotion. Her **Restoration** had only intensified this trait. Alexi knew he had always been more open with his emotions than Nikolai, except when it had come to Tatianya. There, Nikolai had worn his heart on his sleeve right from the start. Tonight, Alexi would be a vampire. He would soon see where his new path led. His soul screamed for this curse to descend upon his life, but this eagerness was tinged by one regret. Olga. He had never confided this to her on his yearly trips to Russia. Every night while lying on her grave, Alexi had wrestled with confessing his pact with Nikolai, but never did. He ultimately saw no reason. He did not want to sully his dreams of her. He knew it was insane to believe she came to him there in the cemetery. Except for physical intimacy, it was all so real. He needed to believe in this and chose not to look too closely. Human nature. He was no different than the people who chose to not look too closely at Nikolai.

As the shadows began to fall, Nikolai joined Alexi in the elegant but understated dining establishment overlooking the river. He sat opposite Alexi, watching him savor a brandy. He eyed the half-empty decanter of vodka Alexi was fingering, lost in his thoughts. A waiter silently approached. He looked at Nikolai with fear in his eyes but maintained his composure. Nikolai ordered a brandy and refreshed Alexi's. Nikolai smiled, "I still enjoy the aroma and the feel of the crystal in my hand. Tonight will be easier for you if you are a little drunk. Finish the vodka if you so desire. Enjoy this last brandy. How I wish I had known to savor my last! Drink up. Tatianya is waiting for us; she is anxious to get to the cemetery. You should be prepared that I expect some company in the cemetery. I am not anticipating any trouble but I need to be vigilant so stay close to me." Alexi nodded as he savored the last human sustenance he would ever enjoy.

They found Tatianya waiting on their mansion's sweeping veranda that was designed to catch the occasional breeze wafting in from the river. She was simply dressed but looked beautiful. Her hair fell about her shoulders. She was unadorned except for her wedding rings and the sorrow that tinged her gaze. In her hand were roses bound with a pale blue sash. She clutched them tightly, unaware of the thorns piercing her skin or the trickle of blood staining her elegant gown. Nikolai's heart caught in his throat. He wasn't sure he could do this.

Silently they made their way across town to the crumbling, long-forgotten cemetery where they had laid their son to rest. Demon after demon slowly fell into step behind them. Alexi became acutely aware that he was the only truly living being in this growing gathering. He could sense his essence exciting some of the lesser controlled participants of this odd mourning procession. He took comfort knowing this vulnerability would cease to exist tonight.

Nikolai had not anticipated such a large show of support if that is what it truly was. He drew Alexi in closer. Nikolai knew that he and Tatianya were unusual in that they had the strength to keep alive bonds from their previous lives. That they had been able to keep Isaiah and Angeline with them all these years without losing control was further proof of their power, their restraint, their grace. This funeral procession was an olive branch from the resident vampire population to symbolize that they denounced this infant's death. But more importantly, it symbolized their acknowledgment of Nikolai as a power they had chosen to accept and respect. He could have easily taken control of this murderous band, but he had made a life elsewhere. He would broker peace and form an alliance, even as he mourned his child.

Tatianya barely noticed the growing procession behind her. She just wanted to reach the crypt that cradled her son. As they neared the crypt, all but the three Russians hung back in reverence. Tatianya stepped forward as Nikolai and Alexi gave her a moment to carefully arrange her roses at the base of the crypt. She placed a bloodied hand on the cool stone. As she gently fingered the letters of her son's name, she thought she felt a warmth emanating from the crypt. She knew it was illogical, but Tatianya felt a strange connection as if her son was reaching out to her. With a flash of realization, she understood what Alexi experienced each time he returned to Olga's grave. Even though it was beyond difficult to stand in front of her infant son's grave, she felt a peace she had not known these past five years. Tatianya softly spoke to her son, willing herself to remember how it had felt to hold his tiny perfect but lifeless body. She bent and kissed his name. Again, she felt that warmth.

Nikolai came up behind her and tentatively encircled her waist. Try as he may, he could not bring himself to touch the moss-covered granite. The demons behind them strained to watch this private moment. The power, the quiet power, Nikolai had hungered after was again very much in evidence, further cementing his position in this community.

Nikolai acknowledged their respect and deference to him. He was now the one to be feared, his only weaknesses being his love for Tatianya and his still human friend Alexi. He did not want to rush Tatianya, but it was urgent that he **Restore** Alexi tonight. Nikolai gently squeezed her shoulders, it was time. As Tatianya said her final words to her son, promising to return, she bent to kiss his name. Again, she felt that warmth.

As the procession made its way down the lane and the crypt faded from sight, Torrin, the leader of the resident vampire coterie approached Nikolai. The two powerful demons broke from the procession that had stopped to observe their exchange. While in the depths of despair, having just turned from his son's grave, Nikolai succeeded in forging the agreement of his choosing. He wore Torrin down, his grief driving him to succeed. Torrin had chosen this moment to test Nikolai's true powers. Torrin felt certain that Nikolai had grown into a being that could summon this depth of strength while wrestling with overwhelming guilt and grief. But Torrin had been compelled to know for sure. He needed an ally, a strong ally. He too felt the growing evil just beyond the fringe of his comprehension. He prayed Nikolai would be up to this coming challenge.

One by one the vampires disappeared into the night as silently as they had appeared. When they reached their home, Alexi stopped at the foot of the steps leading up to the veranda. Alexi knew he would go in human but emerge something much different. Nikolai held Alexi by his shoulders, "This is your last chance to change your mind. Once the process has begun you will only have two choices, to complete the **Restoration** or die tonight in my arms. If you choose to accept this madness, I will rip wide your wrist, your neck, and then your chest. I warn you, the pain I will inflict will be beyond any you have ever imagined. Once I have dominated your essence you will need to bond with mine, **Sear** our union by melding with my wrist. I can guide but you alone must make the connection with your maker, with me. You alone must claim this destiny." Alexi met Nikolai's eyes and nodded. Tatianya led the way up the stairs. Nikolai and Alexi followed, arms around each other, much the way they did as carefree boys.

Alexi entered the chamber of his **Restoration**. He felt the peace that had eluded him for years. He smiled at Nikolai who shook his head at this disastrous decision. Nikolai motioned for Alexi to sit on the bed. Tatianya settled herself on the settee near the balcony. She winced remembering how her cruel assailant had entered thru these doors. She would stand watch and not allow anyone to interfere. She knew Torrin was close by, waiting, praying. She tried to **read** him, assure herself that his kindness had not been eroded by time and power. She knew she wasn't strong enough to reach into the recesses of his mind, but Torrin took pity and opened himself to her. She smiled knowing Torrin still retained a shred of decency. She wondered at his audacity to pray.

Nikolai had prepared himself for this moment while ascending the stairs. With a swiftness that sent Alexi reeling, Nikolai sunk the thorn he had been fingering deep into Alexi's wrist, splaying wide the scar from his **Searing**. He encircled Alexi's wrist and his warmth became a raging inferno. He assaulted Alexi's neck, then his chest, sapping him of his essence. As his life force was dominated by Nikolai, Alexi realized he was drowning, being pulled under by a power he could not fight, would not fight. It was much more painful than he had anticipated. He screamed out in terror but submitted fully to Nikolai's embrace. Even if he had wanted to free himself, it was too late. Nikolai was in full frenzy. Nothing would have stopped Nikolai from tearing into Alexi, robbing him of his essence, until the last ounce of his delicious humanity had been consumed.

When Nikolai had claimed Alexi's soul, devoured the last of his essence, he gently laid him down on the bed. Alexi's head was pounding as the last of his heartbeats feebly thundered away.

Nikolai looked down at his ghostly pale, dying friend, his neck, his chest both viciously torn wide open, devoid of any essence.

Alexi's mind was spinning out of control, but he forced himself to focus on his blood that had spilled from his jagged wounds. Silently Nikolai pulled back his sleeve and offered his wrist to Alexi. "You don't have much time Alexi. If you are committed to this folly, you must act quickly, or you will die. You can let go, Alexi. Join Olga. I will take you back to Russia, dig your grave myself. I will understand. It is your choice. I will always love you whatever you decide."

Alexi could feel his mortality slipping away. He knew he was losing his grasp on his human life. He wanted to complete his transformation but was losing strength more rapidly than he had expected. He groped for Nikolai's wrist and the blood caked thorn. Nikolai placed his wrist within Alexi's grasp. Alexi found the waiting wrist and sunk the thorn into Nikolai with a hunger that had been five years in the making. He melded their wrists together. He fought the urge to let go and encircled Nikolai's wrist. He felt his skin come alive, blazing with his own newly ignited inferno. As Nikolai's lifeforce flowed into him, he felt an awakening so acute, the thundering of the blood flowing back into his all but collapsed veins. This pain was far worse than anything he had ever endured, just endured. But he persevered, determined to see this thru until Nikolai finally broke free.

The two friends slumped against each other on the bed, equals once again. Tatianya gently stroked Alexi's cheek. He looked up at her with newly ravenous eyes. "Come, Alexi, you need to rob someone of their soul, and I need to finish retracing our steps." He nodded and stumbled to his feet, silently following her out into the night.

Alexi was grateful to see that he would hunt more in line with Nikolai's style. He found he had no desire to dominate his victims. His first few forays were clumsy. Nikolai stepped in to finish the kill, allowing Alexi to consume his victim's essence. His third attempt was more skillful. He had committed his first murder. He knew he should feel remorse but all he could think of was drowning in his next victim's beautifully pulsating essence. The need for more screamed from somewhere in his depths. Alexi was shocked at just how elusive satisfaction had become. Nikolai and Tatianya helped him sate himself, throwing corpse after corpse into the canals as they ventured toward the dilapidated mansion in the swamp.

Chapter Twenty-Four:
The Mansion in the Swamp

The three Russians made their way towards the decaying mansion, propelling themselves deeper into the dank murky waters and dense overhang. The past few days had been filled with sensory overload for all of them, especially Alexi. Seeing New Orleans for the first time, feeling the oppressive humidity, visiting Nikolai II's grave, and being surrounded by the resident vampires had been overwhelming. But the few hours since his **Restoration** had pushed Alexi to the edge of his breaking point. Nikolai had tried to explain this turmoil to him time and again. Alexi realized that Nikolai had done his best to describe this chaos, this personal devastation. It was painfully obvious now that nothing except firsthand experience could adequately convey the darkness that was descending over him, into him. He truly understood that his very being will now and forevermore be the epitome of evil.

Resolutely, Alexi willed himself to at least try to reinstate some calm into his shattered mind. Every sound, even the quietest whisper was like an explosion going off inside his head. He longed to block out everything and wait for the nightmare to end. But he knew it was just beginning. What had he done? Somehow, Alexi managed not to shout accusations at Nikolai who understood all too well the chaos and remorse of this very moment.

Nikolai kept searching Alexi's face for a sign that he had not lost his closest friend, his brother. He couldn't bear the thought of losing this most cherished confidant. Being with Alexi these past five years had kept a small part of him human. Nikolai was gripped by fear that he no longer had Alexi's kind and patient countenance to balance his own innate calculating ruthlessness. Nikolai felt a cold sweat run down his spine. He too wondered what they had done.

Try as he may, Alexi found he could not stop tearing into victim after victim. It was the only thing that would quiet the raging. So consumed by this hunger for murder, he found he could not still his mind enough to utter a single word. Nikolai knew of instances where a newly **Restored** vampire had cracked under the pressure. They had been **Restored** in the truest sense of the word, **Restored** to the most basic of instincts. Reduced to animal-like behavior, they spent their nights hunting without any thought to consequence, unable to speak or reason. Nikolai knew that if Alexi did not rise up out of this initial chaos, and soon, he would be lost forever. Tatianya silently gave thanks that Angeline and Isaiah were being spared this spectacle.

Several encampments of fugitives were scattered along the periphery of the swamp. Nikolai led Alexi there to lay waste to these scourges of humanity. He knew none would be missed. No whispers of their devastation would ever reach the city. Nikolai joined in the frenzy as well, nonchalantly killing a few as Alexi sought to sate his unrelenting appetite.

Night was fading into the soft glow of the morning sky. Nikolai knew they had to retreat into the darkness afforded by the dense overhang deep within the swamp. He needed to get Alexi to the mansion for the much-needed rest that would descend when he was finally sated. But before this sleep overtook, Nikolai would do everything within his power to aid Alexi's battle against the animal instincts that had obliterated his aristocratic upbringing and breeding.

"Alexi, we need to go. The sun's strength is no longer something to welcome." Nikolai needed all of his strength to pull Alexi from yet another victim. Nikolai stilled his mind and used his power to reach deep inside his newly **Restored** friend. As their eyes met, Alexi felt Nikolai reaching into his core, pulling him from the depths. Alexi's newly unleashed animal instincts wanted to lash out at Nikolai. The only thing Alexi cared about right at this very moment was the hunt. The abandon was intoxicating, giving in to any and all of his baser instincts. He had never experienced a surrender so seductive. He was finding the release these murders were providing alarmingly addictive. He had never felt so out of control and at the same time so free.

But Alexi still possessed a shred of dignity. He grabbed hold of the lifeline Nikolai was throwing him. He found he wanted to rise up out of this chaos. Alexi found himself choosing to relegate his animal instincts to the recesses of his being. Right then and there, he made the commitment not to leave Nikolai. He could see that even in his current state of devastation and turmoil, there was something in him that Nikolai needed. He would be the ever-loyal brother and rise up. He had always been at Nikolai's side. Human or demon, he realized this allegiance was more important to him than the need to crush and devour another's essence. He willed himself to be as human as possible, for Nikolai.

Alexi slumped against his brother. Nikolai caught Alexi as his last victim fell to the ground. Alexi had not been able to finish the man off. His eyes were wide with pain and fear. With Alexi in one arm, Nikolai deftly broke the man's neck with the other, putting him out of his misery. The eyes of the dead replaced the eyes of the knowing.

As Nikolai carried Alexi back to the mansion, he tried to get Alexi to speak. He needed to have him say at least one word before the catatonic state of the first sleep overtook. It would be much easier in the coming days if Alexi could manage to break thru and speak tonight. Nikolai kept talking, rousing Alexi as they made their way deeper and deeper into the swamp.

Tatianya stood on the wide veranda that ran the length of the second floor. She scanned the swamp as far as she could see. She felt them coming long before she saw them. She felt Nikolai's concern and fear. She ran down to meet them and saw Alexi crumpled in her husband's arms. They lay Alexi on one of the chaises that Nikolai and Isaiah had sat upon years ago, devising their plans to head to San Francisco.

Tatianya looked at Nikolai in confusion. She had not anticipated that Alexi would have such difficulty rising out of his chaos. He had been thru so much, and she had always viewed him as strong, a victor. She was at a loss. Nikolai knew the one word that would get thru to him. Nikolai bent over his friend and whispered in his ear. "Olga." Alexi's unfocused eyes snapped open. Nikolai looked at Tatianya who nodded, "Again." Nikolai cupped Alexi's face in his hands, their skin now the same scorching temperature. Nikolai said the name of Alexi's beloved again but louder. Each time, Nikolai could see Alexi was reaching deep within to release himself from the lower levels of degradation. In desperation, Nikolai began shouting Olga's name and sharply struck Alexi's face.

It took several long moments and more than one gut-wrenching slap to rouse Alexi from his depths. Nikolai had never struck Alexi in his life. It had killed him to do this. But as he saw response, he struck Alexi time and again. Sobbing, Nikolai readied himself again to slap Alexi and scream Olga's name. An anguished tear alighted on Alexi's cheek and his eyes focused. As Nikolai's hand came down to land yet another heart rendering blow, Alexi's hand came up swiftly, grabbing Nikolai by the wrist, stopping the assault. With a wan smile and focused direct clear eyes, Alexi whispered "Olga."

Nikolai fell to his knees, all but smothering Alexi. He sobbed uncontrollably as he made Alexi say Olga's name over and over again. Tatianya ached for her husband. She knew he was trying to save Alexi while reliving those months of loneliness her rejection had subjected him to as she had fought thru her own personal hell.

When Nikolai was satisfied that he had rescued Alexi from the depths, he gently laid Alexi on the chaise. He rested his forehead against Alexi's. He searched Alexi's face for any sign of rejection. There was none. He tenderly brushed Alexi's matted hair out of his face and kissed his cheek. The two friends had their first conversation in five years as equals. It was the manna that Alexi had craved. This is what he had envisioned during all those years of waiting. He found this connection with Nikolai to be worth the price of selling his soul. He knew he would murder again, that was now a fact of his existence. But it was this bond as equals that he had been searching for these past five years. He smiled, "Nikolai, I am finally home. We did the right thing."

As the first slumber overtook Alexi, Nikolai finally relaxed his grip on his friend. Tatianya knew Nikolai would not leave Alexi until he had awoken. Watching Nikolai rescue his friend, bringing him back from the brink of total depravity, Tatianya felt a new depth of love sweep over her. She wanted so badly to love her husband, reaffirm just how much he meant to her. But she knew this would have to wait. Tonight was all about Alexi. She silently came to Nikolai. He reached out, imprisoning her on the chaise beside him. Fully clothed she melted into him. She didn't want a single inch of him not feeling her love. Nikolai understood her actions. He was humbled knowing she was falling deeper in love with him. Long ago, he had stepped off into the abyss that was his love for her. There was no end to the depths of his love. As Nikolai felt a small ray of hope that Alexi would come thru his **Restoration** unscathed, he knew his love for Tatianya was now his only weakness. He tightened his embrace instinctively. He sighed and caressed the cascade of curls that was intertwining with the dark hair on his chest. She wound her fingers into his jacket just as she had done in her bed chambers years ago. She smiled up at him and he gently kissed her cheek. "Nikki" she whispered, nuzzling into his chest. Nikolai relaxed, closing his eyes. Relief flooded over him that he had been able to right his world one more time.

Chapter Twenty-Five: Alexi

As Alexi slept the sleep of the newly **Restored**, his dreams brought little rest. His mind was awash with a kaleidoscope of grisly images of the victims he had claimed last night. Their screams were a mantra that incessantly repeated, boring a scar into his now lost soul. His memory was etched with the horror in his victims' eyes. The terror he had instilled brought a crushing reality to his new life. His long-held beliefs in right and wrong no longer applied. Nikolai used to joke that Alexi was his conscience as he must have been born without one.

As Alexi began to rouse himself, he mumbled, "Who will guide me?" He knew Nikolai would be there for him, but he found himself suddenly in need of a safe harbor. His mind was screaming that he needed someone like Tatianya, a mate. For a brief essence drunk moment, he thought Tatianya could also be his beacon in the dark. He was appalled at the thought. He knew this was impossible. He would need to quell any thoughts regarding Tatianya. The last person he wanted to anger was Nikolai. They were brothers. He did not want Nikolai to take these irrational thoughts as a sign of betrayal. He was just so lost. He ached for Olga. He wondered if she knew what he had done. He always felt her close to him. Over the years he had begun to imagine her gentle hand running delicate fingers thru his hair, soothing away his worries. But where was she now? He was going to have to speak with Nikolai about how to handle this new and unwanted feeling of needing a mate by his side. He needed not to anger Nikolai in his newly **Restored** confusion. He didn't want Tatianya. He needed someone like Tatianya. What he really needed was his Olga.

Nikolai and Tatianya sat watchfully over Alexi as he began to stir. He had lain corpselike for most of the sleep. But he was now stirring, tossing fitfully as he fought to shake off the first sleep. Alexi began moaning what sounded like Tatianya. Nikolai was taken back. He had never sensed any attraction between Tatianya and Alexi. Nikolai turned his eyes to Tatianya to see if she had heard her name. He could see by the look on her face that she had. She looked as surprised as he.

Whatever this was, he knew it wasn't mutual, but he had to be sure. Nikolai reached deep into Tatianya's mind and she opened herself to his probing for the truth. She touched his cheek and sighed. No matter what she did, he would always worry he was losing her. It was his Achilles' heel.

As they interacted more and more with other vampires, she knew they saw the depths of his love for her. She hoped it would never be his downfall. She now prayed that Nikolai would not needlessly turn away from Alexi.

As Alexi was now almost fully awake, Tatianya got up to leave. Nikolai pulled her back to him and held her face in his hands, searching her eyes. "Why Nikki, why do you torture yourself so? This is Alexi. Has he ever given you a reason to doubt him? He is reeling from his ordeal. He is now coming to terms with all the killing he did last night. Do you not see the difference between his **Restoration** and ours? We had each other." She placed a finger over his lips as he began to speak. "And yes, I know I shut you out, but I never left. I wish you could believe that I will never do that again. You must know by now you are my one and only."

Nikolai relaxed his grip on Tatianya's face but continued looking miserable. She brushed his lips with hers. Her breath was sweet, intoxicating. Nikolai leaned in for a kiss, for assurance. With a glint in her eye, she slightly pulled away, sending him into a tailspin. His eyes became black with desire and doubt. His response sent a shiver down her spine. "Nikki" she whispered taking his lower lip into her inviting mouth. She gently bit down, sucking, coaxing a sweet surrender to her ecstasy.

Nikolai would never get enough of her. Even when tinged with the aroma of a fresh kill, he was always taken back to that first night in the gazebo. He knew she was right. He knew she could have left at any time. Any fool could see she would have very quickly been taken under another vampire's protection. He never failed to notice the lustful glances from men of all ages, human or demonic. But as Tatianya never seemed to notice, he let it go. He made no move for vengeance. He made sure she knew her freedom would always be hers for the asking. He had to know she had no doubts. But this was so very different. This was Alexi, his brother, a member of his household, someone with unrestricted access to his angel, someone he had invited to sleep under the same roof as Tatianya.

Alexi stirred enough to make Tatianya break away from Nikolai's imploring searching caresses, making his irrational mind fill with turmoil. Tatianya chided, bringing him out of his tailspin of jealousy. "Nikki, talk to him. He is your brother. He is my brother, it meant nothing."

Alexi realized he must have been talking out loud. They had heard him say Tatianya's name. His body ached. His head was pounding. The last thing he wanted to do was face a jealousy crazed Nikolai. He needed Nikolai's help. He hoped he hadn't lost his friend. He dreaded the coming accusations. He braced himself for the assault.

Alexi sat up and swung his legs over the chaise and faced Nikolai, demon to demon. It felt good to be equals. Nikolai sat quietly, dark eyes piercing deeply. Alexi met Nikolai's probing stare. He waited until Nikolai broke off his probing's trancelike hold. Nikolai was still on edge but seemed satisfied. Alexi took Nikolai's hand in his, "You have to believe me, I do not have thoughts about your Tatianya like that. I remember the dream. It was more of a nightmare. I was thinking that you had had Tatianya by your side during your **Restoration**. Who do I have? I was thinking I wished I had someone to be my compass, like Tatianya is for you. I don't want Tatianya, I never have and I never will. You must believe me. But I now feel the need to have someone by my side. What I really need is my Olga." Alexi dropped Nikolai's hand to cover his face. "If only there was a way."

Nikolai knew deep down that this was true. He had seen this in Alexi's depths. He was at a loss as to how to advise Alexi. Since Olga's death, no one had turned his head. It would be much harder to find a mate as a vampire. Nikolai didn't think he could **Restore** another. It simply was too devastating. But they would find a solution. He understood his friend's anguish. But he was uncomfortable knowing another man had dreamt of Tatianya.

Nikolai chose the path of kindness and understanding. This would not have been the case with just anyone. Alexi knew this and was grateful. Nikolai got up and stood at the railing of the second-floor veranda, looking out over the swamp. Night had fallen and they all needed fresh victims, especially Alexi. The second night was always the hardest. The newly **Restored** now knew what they were capable of inflicting. Even when taking the life of a murderer, it was small comfort. Nikolai finally spoke. There was no anger in his voice, "I have an uneasy truce with my own demons. They are different from yours. We will figure something out, you and me, together. We have always come thru for each other and now will be no different."

Tatianya sensed the two friends had come to an understanding. She slowly approached the pair, giving them time to finish their private conversation. She had chosen not to listen. As was her habit, she would stand on tiptoe and give Alexi a small peck on the cheek. She smiled sweetly up at him and bestowed the now familiar greeting. Both Alexi and Nikolai were well over six feet tall and towered over her. She loved the feeling their dominance brought to her. She loved feeling protected and possessed. Alexi was grateful to Tatianya that this small familiar habit would still be a part of his life. He desperately needed an anchor to shelter him from the storms that were now his life. Even though Tatianya couldn't be his anchor, he could accept her kindnesses. He would lean on her, just a little.

Nikolai fought not to react watching Tatianya kiss Alexi's cheek. It had never bothered him before. It shouldn't bother him now. He wouldn't let a small act of kindness to a friend in pain be refused. He once again chose to be the bigger man, but only because it was Alexi. Tatianya knew her kindness to Alexi had been hard for Nikolai to accept. She would well reward his restraint. Tatianya slowly turned to face her husband. She approached him with a look that made his knees buckle. She reminded Nikolai and Alexi of the duchess, seducing the duke before they had taken their leave as Nikolai had fought for Tatianya's hand. Alexi thought that if Nikolai ever wondered where Tatianya's heart lies, he was mad. Nikolai shot Alexi a love-drunk look and smiled. He had **read** Alexi's thoughts. Alexi smirked at Nikolai. They were boyhood friends once again.

Chapter Twenty-Six: Beginnings

Before leaving New Orleans for Napa, Nikolai met with Torrin one last time. Nikolai wanted to tell Torrin first, alone, that Alexi had been **Restored**. This meeting was a courtesy, a nod to mutual respect. Nikolai and Tatianya had sensed Torrin close by during Alexi's **Restoration**. Nikolai knew Torrin had felt the shift, it had been ugly.

Torrin had not only witnessed Alexi's **Restoration** but also the vile subsequent depravity. Nikolai was met with respect. Few vampires possessed the strength to **Restore** those closest to them. Nikolai had done this now not once but twice. Both vampires glossed over the extent to which Alexi had sunk that first night.

Nikolai also spoke with Torrin about Alexi's longing for a mate. He told him about the fate of Alexi's family and his love for Olga. Nikolai requested Torrin allow one of their newly **Restored** females to accompany them back to Napa. Torrin stroked his chin as he pondered this request. He knew Nikolai to be a complicated contradiction. He was able to nonchalantly kill at will and yet concern himself with his friend's happiness. Torrin was very tempted to have one of his own join this growing powerful dynasty in the west. But ultimately, he declined much to Nikolai's disappointment. Torrin had witnessed Alexi's **Restoration** and knew it had been beyond difficult. Torrin felt he was still too unstable. Nikolai argued that a mate was just what

Alexi needed, but in the end, he relented leaving the door open that someday Alexi could possibly find a mate from this family.

Tatianya was now anxious to get back to Angeline. She wanted to be there for the birth. She wanted to ensure nothing would happen to this baby. Her maternal instincts craved holding this baby in her arms. They all knew Angeline carried a son. Tatianya knew this was the start of passing the torch from Isaiah to his successors. She felt strongly that this child should know them right from the start, nurturing a natural desire to follow in his father's footsteps. They would instill the wisdom and bondage of the **Searing** but that was years away. Right now, her only concern was for this baby to be happy, healthy, and to grow to love her, Nikolai and Alexi as much as his parents, maybe even more.

Tatianya was grateful Angeline's time had not come while they were away. She spent all her time with Angeline, waiting on her hand and foot. It broke Nikolai's heart as he knew what this baby meant to her. He would have given anything to give her another child. He had hoped initially that somehow there would be another child for them, another chance for him to do things right. It was not to be. Tatianya never spoke of it as it would do no good. She had no desire to hurt Nikolai with the harsh truth that he had cost them their only chance for a child. She knew he suffered enough at his own hands. He was a master of many things. Punishing himself was one of the things he did best.

Alexi was gaining more control and composure every day. Once he had left New Orleans behind, he had blossomed in their gently rolling vineyard. Nikolai kept a watchful eye on Alexi and probed his mind often. No trace of longing for Tatianya was ever detected. His devotion to Olga only got stronger with each passing day. Nikolai knew that an unknown female from the family in New Orleans would not have been able to reach him. But Nikolai was glad he had tried. He hoped someday someone would catch Alexi's eye as he now had a need for something more than a memory. New Orleans had been very overwhelming for Alexi on so many levels. Being in the vineyard, working with the vines and the soil was good medicine for him. He found refuge and solace working side by side with Isaiah. As much as he loved Nikolai, he simply found it easier sometimes to be with Isaiah. Both men were far less complicated than Nikolai. They would sometimes toil for hours in the star-filled moonlit nights, uttering not a single word. Nikolai had no desire to commune with nature. Business dealings and playing high-stakes games for economic victory were what made his soul soar. He was very content to leave the day-to-day nurturing of the vineyard to Isaiah and Alexi. He was pleased that the wines they were crafting were gaining more and more acclaim. Alexi and Isaiah saw the wines as a victory in their own right. Nikolai saw the wines as merely another asset to parlay into bigger monetary gains.

Alexi planned his first trip back to Russia as a vampire soon after returning to Napa. Nikolai had wondered if he would still want to make this pilgrimage, but Alexi saw no reason to stop. It had always brought him so much peace. He hoped it would continue to salve his now condemned ravaged soul. He needed Olga to know he had been **Restored**. He felt the need to confess so strongly. He wondered at his urgency.

Angeline's time came while Alexi was away. Her pregnancy had been hard for Alexi to witness and he was glad for the chance to escape. He had no fears of wanting to feast on the defenseless infant. His sadness came from remembering how he had been so careless with Olga. Watching Isaiah hover and Tatianya fawn made his own long-buried guilt resurface. He needed to walk on Russian soil and dig his fingers deep into the earth that surrounded his wife. As Alexi lay night after night in the cemetery, he could see Olga's ghost shimmer in the moonlight. She would lie next to him, just out of reach. As they lay there side by side in the evening dew, he could swear that a warmth now emanated from the soil. With his newfound strength, he dug deeper into the soil. He tried in vain to feel this warmth emanate from the graves of his children, but their soil remained cool to his touch. He confessed to Olga that he had finally succeeded in convincing Nikolai to **Restore** him. He hoped she wasn't angry. He swore he felt her ghostly hand caressing his now blazing cheek. There was no reproach in her eyes. He felt she was imploring him to somehow rescue her. He assumed he was mad. He knew he wasn't drunk. He had had his last brandy in New Orleans weeks ago. He did not understand why, but it appeared his **Restoration** had pleased Olga. It was as if his **Restoration** was bringing them closer. He sensed an urgency in her ghost for him to do something. He was at a loss as to what that was. Alexi had no way of knowing that his ultimate destiny, his influence on their growing dynasty in Napa, would have its beginnings in this cold Russian grave.

Chapter Twenty-Seven: The Alliance Lives On

Nikolai wanted to cement the legacy of his alliance in the vineyard, right from the very first wine-scented breath. Nikolai knew Tatianya would want to be present for the birth. If the child was born after daybreak this would not be possible. Nikolai arranged for Angeline to give birth in their caves. Isaiah had wanted to protest but Angeline quickly hushed his efforts. She knew it would be of no use. When it came to Tatianya, her fearsome husband would give her anything he could. The cost to those standing in the way of her happiness was of no consequence to him. Angeline knew Nikolai could not give Tatianya the one thing she wanted most of all. It drove him to do what he could to make her happy and soothe his guilt. She did not want to anger Nikolai. She knew this would be hard for them and had a nagging fear that they would kill her child. Nikolai was getting more powerful as the years went by. She knew the punishments he exacted on those who crossed him were getting more vicious. While he was very generous and treated both her and Isaiah with respect, this all came at a price.

Angeline had no wish to alter the balance that had afforded her a life far better than any she had ever imagined.

The baby was born during the strongest part of the sun and Tatianya was grateful to Nikolai for his foresight. The baby was a healthy boy Angeline named Joshua. The baby was lively and had immediately taken to Angeline's breast. As he slept after suckling, Angeline held her breath and handed her precious baby to Tatianya. She could see Tatianya was aching to hold this child. Angeline knew she had to eventually let her hold the child and decided not to delay. The room was filled with the smell of fresh blood from the birth. The child smelled of new life. Angeline's essence had burrowed into every nook and cranny of the cave, released as she gifted the world with her son. If Nikolai or Tatianya were to lose control, it would be now.

As it turned out, Angeline had nothing to fear. They too had worried about their reaction and had taken victim after victim with a vengeance born out of the sadness that they had failed to conceive a second time. They vowed to guard this child and treat him as their own. Joshua would be with them all the days he walked the earth. Isaiah had accepted Nikolai's terms in exchange for his protection. None of Isaiah's descendants would ever leave the vineyard. It was the foundation of the alliance.

Tatianya took tiny Joshua in her arms, gently cradling him to her breast. The top of his head was covered in dark coarse hair. His skin was smooth and his breath smelled of mother's milk. She nuzzled the tiny face as large brown eyes fixated on her. She hoped her touch didn't repel him with its intensity. She had done her best to dim the blazing heat her skin contained. She placed a tendril of her hair in his tiny fist. She wanted him to recognize her feel and smell almost as much as he would come to recognize his mother's. She had no desire to hurt him or devour his essence. But she did desire to possess him. This tiny beginning in his first hour of life secured the foundation for his devotion to her, Nikolai, and Alexi. It would make his destiny easier to accept, indeed embrace. His path was already laid out for his entire life and he was barely an hour old. Joshua had taken his place in the alliance.

Angeline watched in relief as Joshua wound Tatianya around his tiny chubby brown finger. For all her killing, for all the misery she had become capable of unleashing, she was still at her core innocent to the point of fragility. At that moment, as Tatianya's eyes met Angeline's, glistening with tears of joy and sorrow remembering her own son, Angeline knew Isaiah's decision to accept this bondage had been the right choice, not only for them but their descendants as well. She knew she would have nothing to fear from Nikolai as long as Tatianya was enchanted with her child. She would do a mother's best to foster this devotion.

Joshua's eyes shone with an understanding, a knowledge, well beyond his tender, precious few moments of life. He reached out to Tatianya, brushing away her tear, taking this tear into his mouth, possessing her love, her essence. It seemed he needed to devour her. From the moment of conception, Joshua's tiny soul had already belonged to Nikolai, his mother's **Searing** unknowingly passing on the bondage. He had known from the start of Nikolai's benevolence as well as the malevolence. But he had craved this delicate creature's love and innocence. He was now at peace with his lot in life. He hoped the best was yet to come. But just like Nikolai, Alexi, Isaiah, and Torrin, he couldn't help but feel that evil. He too knew the call of New Orleans, the swamp and the crumbling mansion mired in the filth. He knew all about the baby in the graveyard. Thru the knowledge the **Searing** had passed onto him, he knew a storm, more of a hurricane, was gathering in the distance. He knew they would have to one day face this evil to finally be free. Tiny Joshua knew their life in Napa was far from secure.